The Dimension Stone

Book One of
The Dimension Wars

Andrew Laird Charles

ISBN 978-1-0670378-0-2

Email: andrew@thedimensionwars.com

About the author

The name Andrew Laird Charles honours my grandparents, Henry Laird Taylor and Charles Gilbertson. I'm certain they'd be pleased to be remembered in this way.

I was born in Palmerston North, New Zealand, and after living in Sydney, Australia, and London, England, I now call Wellington, New Zealand, home.

This novel has been eight years in the making and is finally complete—a fact that will likely surprise many of my family and friends who've heard me share these ideas over the years. I'm equally sure it will astonish my former high school English teachers!

This book is the first book of four in The Dimension Wars trilogy. (three books plus a prequel) It draws inspiration from my love of trivia and the incredible trips I have taken to Angkor Wat, Cairo, and Alexandria.

Email: andrew@thedimensionwars.com

Find me at www.thedimensionwars.com
or www.andrewlairdcharles.com

Acknowledgments

I extend my deepest gratitude to my beta readers and the friends and family who supported me throughout this eight-year journey of bringing this novel to life.

A special thanks to Evan Little for helping me with the last-minute edits. After reading the book so often, it was great to have a new perspective.

Special thanks to my amazing niece, Bridgette Taylor, for her beautiful design of the front cover.

I want to express my heartfelt thanks to my late parents, Arthur and Glenys, who always believed in me and knew I could accomplish this.

Finally, a heartfelt thank you to Brendan Malley. Your diligent reading, rereading, and reading again, plus invaluable feedback, were essential. Without your insights, this book might have required another eight years to complete.

PART ONE

Chapter One

"It seems to get brighter every time I look at it," said Captain Will Chambers as he peered at the object filling the front viewscreen of the spacecraft *Stardust*.

He turned to the shuttle's co-pilot seated next to him: Major Jessica Turner. Originally from the historic city of Williamsburg, Virginia, the thirty-six-year-old was known for her exceptional skills and keen intelligence. Jessica's focus was intense as she monitored the control panel, her blue eyes sharp and attentive.

"Does it seem brighter to you?" he queried, attempting to gauge her perception.

Jessica had a background as impressive as her focus. Before joining the space program, she had excelled in flight school and served in the army, where she gained significant combat experience. This experience had sharpened her resilience and tactical acumen, making her a formidable force in any mission. Despite the occasional misconception that her achievements were due to her appearance, Jessica knew her success was earned through sheer determination and tenacity. With a wry smile, she sometimes acknowledged that while her looks might have caught some initial attention, it was her commitment and skill that had truly paved her path in life.

"It also seems to darken in shade the closer we get to it," she replied, turning to her commanding officer, noting once again how lightly his fifty-something years sat on him, aided by his full head of brownish hair.

Will had charted an illustrious career from the Air Force to the burgeoning Space Force. With years of experience, his leadership style was distinctively different. Rather than dictating terms or relying solely on rank and tradition, he believed in fostering an environment of collaboration and mutual respect, a trait that set him apart from his contemporaries.

Although he wasn't the first pick for the critical mission at hand — most of the top-tier candidates had their sights and commitments set on the Martian expeditions — no one doubted his capabilities. His vast knowledge, combined with his collaborative approach, made him the ideal candidate to spearhead the team, even if by serendipity.

The object in question was a rock, roughly the size of two football fields, designated as Cometoid 687G. Discovered four years prior, it had been on a direct trajectory towards Earth from the Asteroid Belt. Initially, it seemed like a typical asteroid, but scientists at NASA had discerned an anomaly: its mass was disproportionately large for its size. And as if that wasn't puzzling enough, it had begun glowing a peculiar shade of orange nine months ago.

Governments around the world faced a grim realization: the cometoid had at least a 45% chance of striking Earth. Although its unusual characteristics suggested it wouldn't destroy the planet, officials decided to repurpose the backup spacecraft from the Mars manned mission to investigate Comet 687. As this mission only required five astronauts and not any Martian settlers, they managed to launch three months ahead of the original Mars mission schedule.

Their mission was twofold: investigate the cometoid and attempt to divert its path using *Stardust* as a gravity tractor. If that failed, they had four nuclear weapons on board as a last resort. Now, after six arduous months in space, they were positioned between Mars and the Asteroid Belt, and the crew were eager for some action. About 24 hours ago, they had reached their destination, positioning themselves just over five kilometres behind Cometoid 687G and matching its speed as it hurtled towards the Sun—and hopefully not Earth.

"How long until we launch the first probe?" asked Will.

"According to Jim, it should be ready as soon as Richard finishes the programming. Jim's rockets are ready, but the AI is causing some problems," Jessica said. She was referring to two of the other three members of the *Stardust* crew: Jim Washington and Richard Coberg.

Jim was not just a name; he was a legend in the world of space mechanics. His innate talent for machinery was nothing short of prodigious. The heart of the *Stardust*, its engines, bore testimony to his unparalleled skills. With little to no external assistance, Jim had innovatively upgraded them, redirecting their course from Mars to this new, more ambitious journey. It wasn't just his handiwork that stood out, but the years of experience and intuition he poured into every gear and every bolt.

Having devoted nearly his entire professional life to NASA, Jim was more than just an employee. He was a part of its legacy. And when it came to space rocks, Jim was the undisputed master. Every shard of meteorite, every curious rock formation that landed on Earth, had at some point passed under Jim's discerning eyes. As the primary consultant on meteorite discoveries, he had been the deciding voice on many an occasion, classifying, understanding, and sometimes even debunking findings.

Even at 60, age was but a number for Jim. His silver hair and the occasional creak in his joints were the only concessions to his years. The wealth of knowledge he carried, the assurance in his voice, and the twinkle in his eyes when faced with a challenge made him an irreplaceable asset to the mission. For the crew, Jim was more than just a colleague; he was their anchor, a reassuring presence that bolstered their confidence, reminding them that with him on board, they were in the safest hands possible.

Standing in stark juxtaposition to the crew was the enigmatic AI savant, Richard Coberg. Whispered nicknames like "King Dick" swirled around him, a cheeky nod to both his attitude and his distant connections to the British Royal Family. Born into the drizzly landscapes of England, Richard's youth was a mosaic of different schools, each leaving a faint imprint on his formative years, but none capturing his true passion.

However, life has its own way of charting courses, and for Richard, it was the moment he encountered the intricate world of robotics. It was like the missing piece of a puzzle, and everything suddenly clicked into place. With the vast resources of his blue-blooded lineage at his fingertips, he plunged headfirst into the world of aviation, emerging as an adept helicopter pilot.

Later, his course took him to the Euro Space Robotics Program, a testament to his passion and newly discovered purpose. Though Richard was svelte with a somewhat pallid complexion, it was his unique facial expressions that some found grating. It was a face one might not easily forget, and not always for the most flattering reasons.

But biases aside, this was a mission that called for unity and expertise from every corner of the globe. Richard's dual mastery in both robotics and aviation made him indispensable. His association with the European Space Agency further sealed his spot, ensuring a balanced representation of global talents in this monumental endeavour.

"Why not see if Sela can assist him?" Will pondered aloud, casting his thoughts toward the effervescent Sela Chea, a vital cog in the *Stardust*'s crew wheel. Originating from Cambodia, Sela had a zest for life that was infectious, a young dynamo whose spirit echoed the lively streets and historical tapestry of her homeland.

It was near Siem Reap, amidst the ominous presence of undetonated landmines, that had Jim first crossed paths with Sela. A new but formidable presence in the field of archaeology, Sela was swiftly gaining recognition as one of Cambodia's foremost experts in unearthing ancient temples engulfed by the relentless jungle. Driven by a passion for preservation and innovation, she dedicated herself to devising an automated system designed to defuse the perilous landmines that littered the excavation sites, a move that promised to revolutionise the safety protocols of temple exploration.

Jim, possessing an exceptional talent for spotting emerging geniuses in their formative stages, was immediately struck by Sela's inventive spirit and her bold endeavours. Seeing in her the spark of unparalleled potential, he committed himself to mentor her. With his extensive knowledge and discerning guidance, he meticulously sculpted her innate abilities, sharpening her skills and enhancing her innovative techniques. Under his adept tutelage, Sela's raw talent was crafted into a refined brilliance, solidifying her status as a budding expert in both the archaeological and engineering fields.

"Good idea," Jessica said, picking up the microphone. "Sela, can you report to the lab and assist with the AI?"

"Already on it," came the quick reply, brimming with assurance. "I'm confident that with the three of us working together, we'll have it sorted out in no time."

The trio found themselves hard at work within the heart of their advanced spaceship. Its design, while reminiscent of the historical Space Shuttle program, had clearly evolved. Stretching to an impressive 80 metres the spacecraft dwarfed its predecessors. Dominating the flight deck were three expansive windows. Through the marvels of cutting-edge technology, these were not mere windows: at the touch of a button, they could transform into panoramic screens, providing the crew with a seamless 360-degree view of the cosmos. This was a feature the team had come to rely on, especially during intricate navigational sequences.

Just below the flight deck was the middle deck, which seamlessly merged functionality with comfort. It housed a state-of-the-art laboratory stocked with mission-specific equipment ready to decipher the mysteries of deep space. Adjacent to the lab, there was a dedicated gym. The importance of this facility couldn't be overstated. The crew engaged in daily workouts here, an essential regimen to counteract the muscle atrophy that threatened astronauts during extended space journeys.

Further into the spaceship, one would encounter the Launch Bay. This area was a testament to humanity's ambition. It harboured advanced robotic equipment, originally conceived for the ambitious Mars expeditions. These robots, combined with the intricate assembly tools stored alongside them, were designed to construct habitat modules on the Martian surface. These modules weren't mere concepts; they had been physically sent to Mars via two preceding unmanned missions. The foresight of these prior missions had proved invaluable. The crew, ever resourceful, had ingeniously repurposed one of the balloon rockets from this Martian gear to aid in their current endeavours.

"The problem is with the landing program," Richard explained. "These Martian rockets were designed to parachute their payload onto the planet, but that approach won't work here. We need the rocket to strike the object directly. I've tried disabling all the sensors, but there are so many backups that they just reprogram themselves."

"How about disabling the entire AI module?" suggested Sela.

"That wouldn't work," replied Richard. "We still need some braking to ensure the probe doesn't get completely destroyed upon impact."

"So, what we need," mused Jim, "is for the AI to believe it's executing a safe landing. It should fire the braking thrusters, but a few seconds too late. That way, the probe penetrates the surface but isn't entirely disintegrated."

"Yes, that's the essence of it," replied Richard.

Jim gazed up, his wrinkled, ruddy face reflecting deep concentration. Sela exchanged a knowing glance with Richard. They had both seen this expression many times, usually preceding either a stroke of genius or an unconventional idea.

Returning his attention to the group, Jim recounted, "In the early days of space cooperation, a lander was sent to Mars. It crashed due to a mix-up between Europeans and Americans over measurement units: feet and inches versus the metric system."

"How does that help us?" asked Sela.

"From then on," Jim continued, "all computer programs adopted the metric system, but it was mostly a configurable setting."

"So, you're suggesting we set the rocket system to feet and inches, while the AI continues operating in metric?" Richard asked, his voice filled with excitement. "That means the AI would think it's three metres from the surface when it's actually only three feet away."

"Exactly," said Jim. "Let's inform the bridge. Launch Bay to Captain, come in, Will."

"Jessica speaking. Jim, Will is preoccupied right now," came the response.

"Alright, well, we believe we've found a solution. We need to reprogram this rocket and move it to the Launch Bay. It should take us about thirty minutes."

"Understood. You have permission to proceed," Jessica instructed.

Turning off the microphone, Jim muttered, "As if I need your permission." He then turned to Sela and asked, "Do you want to program in my brilliant idea?"

"Robotics is my area," Richard murmured, avoiding eye contact with Jim.

Jim met his gaze with a "Don't mess with me" stare. Sensing the tension, Richard quickly added, "But it's always a good idea to spread the load. I'll check on the sensors and make sure everything's functioning properly."

"Good idea," said Jim, softening slightly as he stood up to allow Richard to move to a different part of the lab.

Thirty minutes later, the three of them were easily manoeuvring the 800kg rocket in the spaceship's Zero G environment towards the launch bay. They then loaded it into one of the launching tubes.

Jim radioed up to the flight deck. "Will, Jessica, we are ready to launch."

"Go ahead," replied Will.

"Do you want to do the honours?" Jim asked, looking at Sela.

"Sure," said Sela, beginning the countdown. "5... 4... 3... 2... 1... launch." She pressed the launch button, and a whooshing sound erupted from the tube, signalling the departure of the probe.

"We have three minutes until it reaches the surface," announced Sela. "Plenty of time to get back up to the flight deck."

With that, the three astronauts left the launch bay, making their way in Zero G through the lab area and onto the flight deck so they could follow the probe's progress on the main viewscreen.

Jim, Sela, and Richard entered the flight deck, gazing at the bright orange object occupying most of the screen. "It seems to be even brighter than before," said Sela.

"Yeah, we just had that conversation," said Jessica.

"Have we come up with a name yet?" inquired Richard.

"No, not yet. And before you start on again, we are not calling it 'Borange'," interrupted Will, hoped to immediately halt the seemingly endless discussion that had been ongoing for the last six months about how naming it "Borange" would mean there was now a rhyme for "Orange".

"Mission Control said we had the right to name it, and '687G' is so boring," whined Richard.

"Stop arguing, you two," interrupted Jessica. "The probe is only 45 seconds away."

The team watched as the probe got closer and closer to the mysterious cometoid. Just before it slammed into the object, the braking rockets engaged, and the probe wedged into the surface of the object that may or may not be called "Borange".

"Perfect," said Will. "Well done, team."

A minute later, data began transmitting from the probe to the onboard computers. Several minutes after that, the crew gathered around the main computer console as the analysis of the vaporised samples came in.

"So far, it seems reasonably normal: about 40% silicon, 20% iron, and about 5% sulphur," said Jim.

Richard, leaning against a console, let out a sigh tinged with disappointment. "So, we came all this way just to look at something we could have found on Earth?" His words, a mix of wonder and disillusionment, hung in the air, mirroring the thoughts of many in the room.

"What about the other 35%?" inquired Will.

"The analysis is ongoing; we should have the complete data shortly," Jim stated, patience evident in his voice as the anticipation in the room intensified.

Moments later, a chime signalled the end of the computer's deep analysis, drawing all eyes to the screen as the final results materialised. Jim, his brows furrowed in perplexity, stepped forward. "That makes little sense," he voiced out loud, a clear reflection of his confusion and disbelief. The rest of the crew, united by a shared fascination, leaned in closer, their gazes locked on the revealing data.

Jim continued looking over the results, broke the silence with a measured tone, filled with a blend of scientific curiosity and evident surprise. "35% of the sample comprises an unknown element—one that, according to our current understanding, shouldn't exist in a stable form," he explained, his words underscoring the gravity and mystery of their discovery.

"164 protons? Seriously?" exclaimed Sela. "That makes this one of the theoretical magic-numbered elements," she added.

"Magic-numbered?" inquired Will. "Please explain for the rest of us who weren't chemistry majors."

"Well," began Jim, pausing to choose his words carefully, "in the simplest terms, an element is made up of atoms, and all atoms of a particular element have the same number of protons in their nucleus. This number of protons is what we call the atomic number. Now, elements are the building blocks of matter and can't be broken down into simpler substances through chemical reactions.

"Here's where it gets interesting—magic numbers in chemistry refer to the number of protons or neutrons in an atom's nucleus that create highly stable configurations. Think of them as 'sweet spots' where, because of how the particles are arranged, the atoms are extra stable compared to others. Common examples include elements like helium, with two protons, or oxygen, with eight. These numbers are not random; they correspond to the filled shells of protons or neutrons in the nucleus, making the atoms less reactive and more inert.

"Additionally, theoretical physics predicts more magic numbers beyond those we observe in common elements. One such theoretical element is Unbihexium, which would have 126 protons, a number predicted to form an extremely stable nucleus due to its filled proton shells. But what's extraordinary here," Jim added with emphasis, "is that the element we're discussing has 164 protons! This is beyond anything we've previously detected or even theorised in stable forms, potentially making it a superheavy element with properties we can only begin to imagine."

"Great chemistry lesson, Doc," exclaimed Richard, "but what does it all mean?"

"It means," Jim continued, "that some force beyond our knowledge is interacting with the strong nuclear force of each atom, keeping this compound from exploding. The energy released from a chunk of this stuff would wipe out a city block."

"Wow, that's impressive," said Richard.

"Should we name it Boranganium?" joked Sela.

"Not you as well!" exclaimed Will. Turning around, he said, "Jim, send the findings to Earth, and we'll see what the boffins back there make of it."

"Understood, Captain Will," Jim said with a playful smirk, emphasising the title a bit more than necessary. He gave a mock salute, his eyes twinkling with mischief. Sela stifled a laugh, exchanging a knowing glance with Jim.

The pair left the flight deck, the clink of their magnetic shoes echoing as they made their way to the laboratory. Within its confines, an array of equipment and machinery blinked and hummed, standing by for their commands. They wasted no time, meticulously analysing the wealth of data retrieved from the probe.

After ensuring the data was securely packaged and encrypted, they initiated a transmission back to Earth. Both were acutely aware of the vast distance separating them from home. The signals they sent would travel across the void, taking approximately thirty minutes before they even reached their destination. Receiving a response would require a similarly lengthy wait.

As they anticipated the long gap in communication, Sela and Jim delved deeper into their own analysis. The data was dense, a rich tapestry of information that held the potential to unlock new scientific horizons.

Time seemed to blur as they engaged in a methodical back-and-forth with their colleagues on Earth, each communication refining their understanding and shaping the direction of their research. However, when the responses finally arrived, Jim found himself increasingly frustrated.

This isn't right," Jim muttered, shaking his head as he reviewed the latest set of recommendations. "Their approach is too conservative. We're missing something crucial here."

Sela looked up from her own work, concern etched on her face. "What do you suggest, Jim?"

"We need a fresh perspective," Jim said, his voice firm. "Get Professor Fiona Morrison to have a look at this data. Her expertise in quantum anomalies is exactly what we need. I don't trust these initial interpretations."

As Sela moved to initiate another transmission, Jim's thoughts drifted momentarily. *Working with Sela... it's seamless*, he thought. *She doesn't just follow; she challenges and complements my thinking. It's like a well-oiled machine—the way she can immediately grasp where I'm headed and take the next step without missing a beat.*

During their intense discussion, other members of the crew, including Will and Richard, stopped by the lab, offering their help. They could sense the tension and the critical nature of the work at hand. However, finding Jim and Sela so deeply engrossed in their task, they quickly realised that their intervention might disrupt the duo's concentrated flow.

Will leaned in, whispering, "Need anything from us?"

Jim glanced up, his focus momentarily broken. "Thanks, Will, but we've got it covered for now. I've got an old colleague of mine, Fiona Morrison, looking into it; she is an expert in all kinds of space rocks, and we're waiting on her insights."

Nodding understandingly, Will and Richard retreated, allowing Jim and Sela to continue their meticulous work without interruption.

Sela placed a reassuring hand on Jim's shoulder. "We'll get through this, Jim. The Professor will see what we aren't seeing, and together we'll figure it out."

Minutes turned into hours as they continued to analyse the data, refining their hypotheses and preparing for the next steps. The lab's hum seemed to sync with their thoughts, a constant reminder of the stakes. Finally, after what felt like an eternity, a new transmission arrived. Sela quickly accessed the message, her eyes scanning the text. "It's from Professor Morrison," she said, a note of relief in her voice.

Jim hurried over, reading over her shoulder. Fiona's insights were sharp and precise, highlighting several overlooked aspects of the data. Her suggestions opened up new avenues of exploration, confirming Jim's suspicions and providing a clear path forward.

"She's got it," Jim said, a smile breaking through his earlier frustration. "This changes everything."

Equipped with Professor Morrison's analysis and a comprehensive plan informed by their rigorous work, they returned to the flight deck, ready to brief Will and chart their next steps. The mission's success depended on their collective expertise, and they were now more prepared than ever to face the challenges ahead.

Jim began the briefing with a sense of profound revelation. "So, after all these hours of analysis," he started, "it appears we've discovered a superheavy element within the cometoid. Under conventional physics, such an element shouldn't exist for any appreciable length of time."

"It's incredible!" exclaimed Sela, her voice filled with excitement. "This could redefine our understanding of the universe. And we're not talking about just a trace amount; 35% of the cometoid is composed of this element. It's like finding a new cornerstone of cosmic structure!"

Jessica looked pensive. "Could this be the reason why the cometoid is glowing that peculiar shade of orange? Could it be related to this mysterious element?"

Jim nodded. "It's highly likely. The presence of such an element might interact with other components and produce this luminous effect. But the implications of this discovery are enormous. If we can harness this element, it could change energy production, medicine, and countless other fields on Earth."

Will stood at the back of the flight deck, his gaze sweeping over the crew as Jim and Sela shared their groundbreaking findings. The gravity of the moment wasn't lost on him, but alongside the scientific excitement, there was a deep sense of satisfaction about the team itself.

Six months ago, we were virtually strangers, thrown together by fate and necessity, Will thought to himself. *Jim, I knew—and trusted—from past missions. His brilliance was a given. Jessica was a name I'd heard, her reputation stellar, which is why I requested her for this mission. But Sela? She was an unknown, a wildcard that came as a package deal with Jim.*

His mind then drifted to Richard. *Richard... I hadn't wanted him. His inclusion felt more like a bureaucratic checkbox than a tactical decision. But over these months, he's proven himself more than just a reluctant necessity. He's grown into his role, shown grit, and surprisingly, he's meshed well with the rest of us.*

Look at us now, Will mused as he listened to the excited chatter, *from cautious collaborators to a cohesive unit, each of us indispensable. We've faced challenges that would have fractured a less resilient group, yet here we are, more than just functioning—thriving.*

A small smile played on his lips as he realised just how proud he was of what they had become. *We were thrown together by circumstance, but we've built something that feels a lot like family. And whatever comes next, I know we're ready to face it— together.*

He then took a deep breath, absorbing everything he had heard. "We need to ensure the safety of this mission and gather as much data as possible. What do they suggest we do?"

"Fiona believes that the next step is to modify the laser to shoot an X-ray beam at 'Borange'," explained Jim.

"What will that do?" asked Jessica, choosing to overlook that the object now seemed to have acquired a permanent name.

"She thinks, and I agree, that it will give us more information on the unknown element," said Jim.

"Will it explode?" inquired Richard.

"We don't think so. We both agree that a concentrated X-ray pulse of around 20W will excite the electrons but leave the protons untouched. So, we should get some interesting data on how stable this element is, rather than if we were to fire a gamma ray at it, which would excite the protons," Jim explained.

"OK," said Will, "if the brightest minds think that's the way forward, and if you're certain it won't detonate, let's proceed."

Jim replied, "Shouldn't detonate."

Will looked hesitant for a moment. "You say 'shouldn't'. That's not exactly reassuring. This entire mission has been about venturing into the unknown, but we can't risk the safety of the crew."

Jim nodded. "I understand your concerns, Captain. But considering the potential benefits of understanding this new element, I believe the risk is worth it."

Richard seemed sceptical. "But we have no clue how to extract this element, let alone harness its energy. We're making a lot of assumptions here."

Sela chimed in, "That's true, but every significant scientific discovery began with an observation and a series of assumptions. We have to start somewhere."

After a moment of silence, Will finally spoke. "Alright, let's do it. But I want every possible safety measure in place. And if there's even a hint of something going wrong, we abort immediately."

Jim nodded in agreement. "Understood, Captain. We'll start preparations right away, but we'll have to get a bit closer."

"How close?" Will asked.

"Within 100 metres," Jim replied.

"OK," Will responded. "Jessica, take us just inside 100 metres of our rock here."

"Aye, Captain," replied Jessica.

The next few hours were a flurry of activity as the crew modified the laser equipment and set up the necessary instruments to capture and analyse the data from the X-ray beam. With everyone in position and all safety measures in place, Jim initiated the X-ray beam, targeting Borange.

The team watched with bated breath as the beam hit the object. Instead of the expected flare or visible change, Borange simply absorbed the X-rays, radiating them back out in a series of beautiful and mesmerising patterns.

Richard let out a low whistle. "That's... unexpected."

Jim stared at the readings on his console. "The patterns... They seem to be conveying some sort of information. It's like the X-rays triggered a response from Borange."

"Charge the X-ray up to half power, 32W," said Jim.

"32W charged and ready," said Sela, firing the beam.

This time as the beam hit the surface of Borange, the glow intensified, spreading until it became unbearable to look at. Where the X-ray struck the surface, a dark area, darker than the deepest black, began to form, quickly swallowing the blinding orange light. It appeared as if a massive hole was being created in space.

The shape expanded, evolving into an archway that grew larger and larger, eventually becoming at least three times as large as *Stardust*.

"Turn it off," shouted Will.

Chapter Two

Jim quickly hit the prominent red off-switch, but as soon as he did, they found themselves trapped within the confines of the mysterious archway. The darkness momentarily gave way to the spectacle that lay ahead. An imposing door stood in front of them, with intricate patterns and a cryptic symbol deeply engraved on its surface, radiating an ancient aura.

For a moment, all was still. Then, the immense door began to shift. A low rumble echoed through the archway as the door creaked open, revealing a vast darkness beyond. It felt as though an invisible force gripped the *Stardust*, pulling the ship effortlessly into the cavernous space.

The vastness that lay before them was truly staggering. They were in an enormous corridor, its structure made of an alien material that shimmered and pulsed with energy. It dwarfed the *Stardust*, with its width easily ten times that of the ship. Stretching out in both directions, it seemed to have no end, its purpose and origin a mystery.

As the door they had just passed through began to close, the crew looked back. A colossal five-headed snake, sculpted or grown atop the door, appeared to come to life. Each head, with glistening scales and gleaming eyes, hissed threateningly at the *Stardust*, marking the entrance to this otherworldly corridor.

The closing door released a pulsating energy that, when combined with the orange luminescence that had initially ensnared them, propelled the *Stardust* forward at an astonishing velocity. The walls of the corridor became a blur as they raced ahead.

"What on Earth... or rather, where on Earth are we?" Richard exclaimed, his voice reflecting a mix of amazement and apprehension.

"We're not on Earth," Jim replied, his face pale. "And those symbols... they're unlike any script or language I've ever seen."

Jessica's hands gripped the controls tightly. "I can't slow us down. Something's propelling us forward."

Taking a deep breath, Will instructed, "Stay calm, everyone. We need to think logically. Jim, any ideas on what might have caused this reaction?"

Jim stared at the mesmerizing symbols on the doors each paired with another of the five-headed snakes. "The X-ray might have activated some dormant mechanism within Borange. The energy from it created a portal or gateway of sorts. But where it leads... I have no idea."

"Could this be another dimension? Maybe even a different universe?" Sela's voice echoed with wonder and a hint of fear.

Jessica, gripping the controls with pale knuckles, said, "That might explain the physics being all haywire. The *Stardust* is moving without any propulsion. And for the life of me, I can't seem to control its trajectory."

As they were drawn deeper into the alien corridor, the surroundings began to change subtly. The pulsating walls, initially a uniform, gleaming metal, now showed patterns that seemed to flow and move like liquid. These patterns occasionally coalesced into forms that resembled written characters or symbols, hinting at some form of communication or perhaps a story being told.

Richard, who had been quiet, pointed out, "Look at those formations on the walls. They're changing—almost like they're reacting to our presence."

"It's as if the entire corridor is alive, observing us, maybe even studying us," Sela added, her eyes wide with both curiosity and a trace of fear.

The crew's conversation fell to a hush as they absorbed the surreal experience. The silence was broken only by the occasional adjustments of the ship's machinery, straining against the invisible force that guided them. With each passing moment, the sense of advancing towards something unknown grew stronger.

Suddenly, the corridor seemed to expand, opening into a larger, cavern-like space. The patterns on the walls grew more intricate and complex, joining at what appeared to be a central point in the distance.

"The designs are converging up ahead. Whatever's there, it seems important," Jim noted, his voice low, almost reverent.

As they approached, a colossal blue structure began to take shape in the distance. It wasn't just any statue; it was alive, moving with grace. With two of its four arms, the statue was intricately carving a symbol on one of the doors—a symbol eerily similar to the one that had led them into this peculiar corridor.

The anticipation built as the *Stardust* approached. The massive blue figure slowly turned its head, revealing a pair of deep, ancient eyes that seemed to contain galaxies within them. As their ship neared, a slow, knowing smile crept onto its face, and with a majestic gesture, it swung open the door it was etching.

Sela's voice was full of awe and trepidation. "Holy Vishnu!"

Before they could brace themselves, the *Stardust* was drawn out of the corridor with an overwhelming force, passing through the newly opened door. The speed was disorienting, but as quickly as it had started, the movement ceased.

And then, silence.

Everything was plunged into darkness. The only sound was the blaring of the ship's sirens, a stark reminder that they were now in uncharted territory.

"Is everyone all right?" shouted Will.

"Yes," came a chorus of replies. "But what on earth just happened?" exclaimed Richard. "It's like we entered a fantasy video game with all those snakes and things."

"Where the hell are we?" asked Will, looking at the black viewscreen.

"The viewscreen is down," said Jessica.

"I'm working on it," Jim replied, moving to the control unit.

Jessica continued, "I've checked with the computer, and it seems we're in the exact same place as we were before that door opened."

Jim fiddled with the viewscreen controls for a few minutes. "Something seems different," he observed.

"What do you mean?" asked Sela.

"Hang on a moment," Jim replied. The viewscreen sprang to life.

As the crew looked out, they all came to the realization that Borange had vanished.

"What the hell is going on?" Jessica exclaimed. "And what did we just see?"

"Before we get into all that," said Will, "let's see how the ship is doing. Check all essential systems and report back."

The crew busied themselves, each attending to their allocated systems, trying to process what they had just witnessed.

After about twenty minutes, they returned with their reports:

"Propulsion looks good."

"Life support is functioning."

"Nothing wrong with the hull."

"The bloody radio must have fried. We haven't received a ping from Earth for over an hour now," said Jim, frustrated.

"Well, keep trying," replied Will. "And Sela, see if you can help. The rest of you try to find where Borange has gone. Look through the sensor logs and see what they recorded."

Sometime later, everyone regrouped, awaiting an update from Jim and Sela.

"According to our space charts, we are in exactly the same place we were before we got sucked into that door. The radio seems fine, but we're getting no signal from Earth, and our tracking signal to Earth isn't getting any bounce back," Sela explained. The tracking signal was a device that continuously pinged between Earth and the *Stardust*, determining their exact location.

"OK, what did the sensor logs tell us?" asked Will.

"Well," Jessica began, "the video log shows the X-ray hitting Borange, then that bright glow appeared, and afterwards, they just recorded black until shortly after we arrived here."

"What about the door?" asked Jim.

"And the snakes?" added Richard.

"The multi-headed snakes," corrected Sela.

"And that... whatever-it-was at the end of the corridor," said Will.

"Nothing shows on the logs except black and silence," replied Jessica. "But we all saw it, didn't we?"

"Yes!" everyone chimed almost in unison.

Will glanced around, his gaze settling on each crew member, a question lingering in the air. "Can anyone make sense of what we just witnessed? And Sela," he added, directing his attention to her, "you exclaimed 'Holy Vishnu'. What was that about?"

Sela paused for a moment, collecting her thoughts. "Well," she began, her voice tinged with both excitement and nostalgia, "there might be a cultural connection. I grew up in Siem Reap, where Angkor Wat stands. Despite being famous for its Buddhist origins, many don't realise that the complex also boasts numerous Hindu temples dating back to the 1300s."

She clicked a few keys on her terminal and projected an image onto the screen, showcasing intricate carvings and reliefs. "See this?" She pointed to a snake-like figure. "It strongly resembles the Nāgas, or serpents frequently depicted in Hindu lore, especially in these ancient temples. They're considered sacred and are often associated with water, creation, and sometimes destruction."

She scrolled through the images, stopping at a grand statue. "Now, this," she said, her voice dropping a note, "reminds me of what we saw at the end of that corridor. It bears an uncanny resemblance to Vishnu, one of the principal deities in Hinduism, often known as the Preserver. He ensures the cosmic order."

She met Will's eyes. "Given what we're dealing with, the similarities between our observation and these ancient representations could be more than mere coincidence. Perhaps there's a deeper connection we've yet to uncover."

"So, you're suggesting that by flooding Borange with X-rays, we somehow got sucked into the world of Hindu gods?" Will asked incredulously.

"I don't know," exclaimed Sela, defensively. "But it looked like many of the things my parents and grandparents talked about."

"But," Richard interjected, "how is that even possible? Mythology and space travel? It doesn't add up."

Jim, who had been lost in thought, said, "What if our understanding of mythology is wrong? What if those myths are memories of some ancient interaction between our ancestors and beings from other times or dimensions?"

Jim sounded a little exasperated as he continued. "We have no record of what we appear to have seen. We may have hallucinated the whole episode as a result of the energetic interaction with Borange. All we know for sure is it is nowhere to be seen and we seemed to have lost contact with Earth."

"What do you suggest?" asked Will.

"Investigate our surroundings and see if we can find some facts," replied Jim bluntly, "then plan accordingly. Let's not rush down the God rabbit hole too quickly. I've had more mind-bending experiences on recreational drugs back in the day."

Will looked askance at Jim, trying to reconcile his current self with his youthful druggie avatar with little success and then, after a pause, issued orders. "OK, let's examine the comms issue with Earth; look for any sign of the asteroid in near space, and let's check out the rest of the belt for anything out of the ordinary. We can't just sit here in the middle of nowhere for long. Report back on progress in four hours."

A couple of hours later, Will nursed a cup of coffee as he sauntered over to where Jessica was interacting with the main viewscreen.

"How's it going?" he enquired.

She looked up briefly and replied, "Interesting."

"How so?" he continued, as he stepped up to look over her shoulder.

"Well," she began, "I have been scanning our locale for any residual signs of Borange, with no result so far."

"But?" anticipated Will.

"But," she said, "I have found some anomalies of a different nature."

Will stopped in some surprise. "Such as?"

"Well, we should be the only ship out here at present, but I'm picking up a couple of objects within about 250,000 kilometres, which don't appear to be moving in regular orbits as an asteroid would. I'm checking now on some apparent vector changes just in the last hour."

"What's your diagnosis?"

"It has to be some sort of spacecraft to manoeuvre like that. I'll need another couple of hours to be sure of what I'm seeing."

"Multiple spacecraft?" mused Will. "Out here?" He raised an arm to swallow the last of his coffee. "Keep me posted," he ordered quietly as he turned away.

In the lab, Sela, Jim, and Richard were becoming increasingly frustrated with the comms situation.

"It makes no sense," Richard moaned for the umpteenth time. "I can't find a damn thing wrong with our comms, apart from the fact I can't communicate with Earth!"

"Let's examine the situation from first principles," suggested Jim.

"Such as?" sneered Richard.

"Well, I've gone over our equipment thoroughly, as have you and Sela, and I can find no malfunction. Everything appears to be working fine."

"I just said that!" cried Richard, thoroughly frustrated.

"I know, but we can all agree that there doesn't appear to be any technical problem."

"OK, we can all agree that," said Sela quickly, to stave off another Richard explosion.

"OK then, if our equipment is working fine, the logical conclusion is that the equipment at the other end isn't working fine," said Jim.

"Do you mean it's broken at Earth's end?" asked Sela, with a puzzled frown.

"Not exactly," replied Jim. "If they'd had a technical problem, surely they would have fixed it by now."

"So, what are you saying?" demanded Richard, still cranky.

Jim adopted a patient air. "Well, I'm minded of the old saying of Sherlock Holmes – when you've eliminated the impossible, whatever remains, however improbable, must be the truth."

"And what remains?" asked Richard, genuinely puzzled now.

"What remains, my dear Watson," he said, smiling as he said the name, "is that there is no equipment remaining on Earth for us to talk to, or if there is, it's not manned."

Richard balked at the idea. "But that's crazy. Do you think they all went on holiday or something? Even if they did, we'd still have the automatic ping."

"Good point," said Jim agreeably, clearly enjoying Richard's discomfort. "No ping, so that means not missing people but missing equipment. Somehow, it's all gone."

"That's just crap!" exploded Richard and he stormed off to the galley.

Sela looked concerned for him, but stayed with Jim, staring at his face to see if she could discern some aspect of a joke, but no.

Later that evening, the team convened to discuss their findings. Will started the session with a simple "OK, what have we got? Let's discuss comms first. Sela, what's the story?"

Sela looked frustrated as she admitted that there was no story. "We have no comms. We can't even ping Earth. They aren't pinging us, and we get no response to any hails. The equipment looks like it's working fine, but – I can't even pick up loose fragments of transmissions. It's as if the Earth doesn't use radio anymore."

Jim joined in the discussion by agreeing with Sela's findings with an additional, "That's the only conclusion I can come to – strange as it may seem."

Richard snorted derisively but said nothing.

"OK. Thanks, guys," concluded Will. "Now let's hear from Jessica."

"Well, I have the sort of opposite story. I should have found nothing but the odd rock in local space; instead, I have found a couple of definite somethings!" she began excitedly.

Richard looked like he was going to interject inappropriately but was quieted by a look from Will. "Let's have the details, please."

"Well, with the help of the computer, I began analysing the local area for any objects with relative movement to us. It takes a while to obtain candidates, as they have to be analysed in a sort of time-lapse against position method, and then obtain further data on each one's relative movement to us to identify a distance, relative speed, and vector, then with the help of some Newtonian mechanics, its mass. This identified eight large-ish objects within about 250,000 kilometres, but as we're in the Asteroid Belt, a few decent rocks were to be expected.

"However, as the computer continued to track each of them, it detected an anomalous movement in one of them."

"How do you mean – anomalous?" interjected Richard, now curious.

"Quite simple," said Jessica briskly. "It changed its orbital vector suddenly and intercepted another of the objects in less than a minute."

"Intercepted?" exclaimed Richard excitedly. "It's a spaceship!"

"It would seem so," agreed Jessica with a grin. "However, I need to add that the object it intercepted so quickly was at least 25,000 kilometres from it at the time of the course change!"

The whole team started talking at once until interrupted by a loud "Quiet!" from Will. "Let's hear the rest of it before we get too excited. Jess?" He waved an arm for her to continue.

"Well, the computer was tracking the object at the time of the vector change. As far as it's concerned, the object disappeared at one point, then reappeared less than a second later very near the second object."

Jim had that look on his face as he announced quietly to the room, "Oh my god, asteroid miners – with a warp drive."

"Quite possibly," agreed Jessica. "Only, the Earth never had any of either."

The meeting descended into a back-and-forth about what those ships represented and what was wrong on Earth. Will let it run on a little to relieve the tension, then called the meeting back to order.

"OK, next steps. There isn't much more we can do about the comms. I suggest that you explore whether there's anything coming from these miners, or whatever they are. Jess will give you the coordinates."

"Next, we need to keep these ships, if that's what they are, under 24-hour observation. I want to know everything there is to know about them by this time tomorrow."

"Captain," interjected Richard, "if we can see them, they can probably see us."

"True," agreed Will, "but they may not be looking as hard as we were. Either way, there's not much we can do to prevent them, so the sooner we understand what they are and what they are doing, the better." Various nods came from around the table. "OK, dismissed," said Will, and the team went back to their stations, a little subdued by the implications.

Later that evening, Sela and Richard had taken a break in the lab section for some dinner and were chatting amicably as the others continued with the investigation of the "miners."

"Can you tell me a bit more about Vishnu?" Richard asked, a hint of fascination in his voice. "I can't get that image out of my head—the one with the blue skin and four arms."

"Well," Sela started, trying to recall her religious study lessons, "Vishnu is part of this big trio in Hinduism—the Trimurti. There's Brahma, who's like the cosmic creator, and then Shiva, the destroyer... and Vishnu, the preserver. He's sort of the middle guy, keeping things balanced." She chuckled. "It's all a bit hazy, but the four arms deal? I think they represent his reach in all directions of the universe, handling everything at once."

"So, he preserves," Richard observed thoughtfully. "What else is he known for?"

"Something about stepping in when things get out of hand," Sela said with a shrug. "Like a cosmic troubleshooter. He shows up in various forms to fix what's broken in the world. Honestly, it's been ages since I went through any of this with my parents."

Richard smiled, picking up on her uncertainty. "Sounds like a handy bloke to have around. But these forms—avatars, right? They're just mythological, or could there be more to it?"

"I always figured they were just good stories," Sela admitted, her voice tinged with nostalgia. "But seeing that corridor, I'm questioning what 'just stories' really means. Maybe these myths are more like echoes of truths we can't fully grasp."

"It's all pretty wild," Richard mused. "The roots of these beliefs might be tangled up in real events our ancestors couldn't explain any other way. And now, maybe we're on the verge of something just as unexplainable."

Sela laughed, easing the weight of their conversation. "Or maybe we've just been in space too long, starting to see things!"

Their laughter mingled, a brief respite from the enormity of their situation. Just then, Richard, seizing the moment, placed his hand over hers with a slight smirk. Looking deeply into her eyes, he replied, perhaps too smoothly, "We're all in this together. It will be alright."

However, their light moment was abruptly interrupted as Jessica breezed into the lab area, dressed in gym clothes and evidently ready for a workout on the exercycle.

"Hey, you two, any breakthroughs with dinner or just breaking bread?" Jessica teased, waving a hand at their scattered meal.

Sela quickly withdrew her hand from under Richard's as he remarked, "Much as usual—boringly healthy. Ah well, time to get back to our miner friends." He stood up from the table. Sela rose, too, and they headed back to the flight deck.

"See you later," said Jessica cheerfully as she switched on the bike.

Chapter Three

The next morning found Jessica beavering away at the main console as Will joined her. "Any news?" he asked.

"Some," she began. "I've been analysing the recording of the ship trace when it did that vector change to intercept that asteroid, with interesting results."

"Do tell."

"Well, it seemed to accelerate to an incredible speed almost instantly and stopped in much the same way, which makes sense only if it's a 'warp' drive, as Richard called it."

"What speed did it reach?" asked Will.

"Well, as best I can measure," said Jessica with a deadpan expression, "about three-quarters of the speed of light."

Will just looked at her. "All the while starting and stopping on a dime?" he asked.

"Fraid so," agreed Jessica.

"What's it doing now?" he asked.

"Nothing that I can see from here. I assume if they are miners... they're mining," she said with an impish smile.

"OK, maybe that will occupy them for a while. Can you plot a course to intercept them?"

"Already done," she replied.

"How long?"

"Nearly two days at full power. I'm afraid we don't have that clever drive of theirs."

"OK, get the ship on that course," ordered Will, "before they decide to warp away again. This may be our only chance to find out what's happened to us."

"Aye aye, Captain. I'll advise the crew and get us underway shortly," she said sliding into the pilot's chair.

"Jim, I'm about to fire up the engines. Are we ready?"

"As ready as we can be," came the reply.

"Engines online firing in 3, 2, 1... engage," she said as the *Stardust* engines burst into life.

Two days later the mining ship loomed large on the viewscreens as they slowly approached it. The whole crew was gathered to watch the mining ship's image grow before them. It was much bigger than their ship. An unusual shape with a long core cylinder with what appeared to be giant shipping containers attached at each quadrant – three sets of them, culminating in a large engine tube that was X-shaped with five engines – one in the centre and one on each arm of the X. Smaller, lateral tubes were also visible in the gaps between each set of containers. Attached to the "front" was a long tube-like affair, almost like an old pea-shooter sticking out, and on the end was some sort of large complex structure, roughly wheel-like.

"Are we sure that's the front?" asked Sela.

"Must be," Jim grunted. "That drive tube has to be at the rear."

"Why do they have that if they have a warp engine?" asked Sela.

"Manoeuvring," observed Jim. "Imagine trying to park that thing if you could only use a warp drive," he added with a grin.

Jessica, concentrating fiercely on her approach and making frequent adjustments, muttered a sarcastic, "Trying to concentrate here," to the rest of her crewmates, and silence ensued.

A few minutes later she released the controls, with a satisfied "There we are", the miners' ship looming large not 20 metres away, and the larger, roughly potato-shaped asteroid immediately behind it.

Jessica pointed excitedly at the upper end of the ship on the side facing them. "That looks like a manual airlock." She zoomed the view for the others and the airlock dominated the screen.

"Much like ours," observed Jim.

"Form follows function," chirped Sela.

"I wonder," said Richard, "could they be aliens? No human ship operates this far out."

"Not unless they use the same alphabet as we do," replied Will.

"What do you mean?" continued Richard.

"See on the carriage there," he said, pointing at the viewscreen.

The crew looked, and there, clearly written, was the code AQX2456J.

"It must be, as I first thought, a mining train in space," said Jim. "If you took the ore trains they use in Australia and multiplied the size by ten, this is about what it would look like."

"And stuck it in space," added Richard.

"Yes," continued Jim. "I think we can be reasonably sure now that it is taking pieces of rock from out here, probably mostly from the asteroid belt, and transporting them to Earth for extraction."

"So, you think this is an unmanned ship then?" asked Jessica. "Like a Von Neumann machine?"

"A what?" Richard interjected.

"A scientist in the '50s proposed the idea of building self-replicating robots that could strip-mine asteroids. After fully mining an asteroid, they'd move on to the next one, creating as many robots as they needed. The mined ore would then be shipped back to Earth using giant space trains."

"Quite possibly," said Will thoughtfully.

"OK," said Will after a moment, "only one way to find out. Richard, suit up. The two of us will investigate."

"Aye aye, Captain," said Richard gleefully.

Jim objected and said, "But I need to see that drive."

"We don't know what sort of reception we're going to get, Jim, and I need you here until I know it's safe. You'll be able to see what we see anyway, so please be patient."

Jim looked like he wanted to say more, but subsided.

Thirty minutes later, they were fully suited and making final checks of their gear by their airlock. Jessica came through on their headphones with "Cameras fine. Sound OK?"

"Yes," the two replied together.

"Good luck," replied Jessica as they moved into the airlock, sealed the door and began decompression. While they were suiting up, Jessica had rotated the ship so that their airlock faced the mining airlock. Now, as they opened the outer door, the other airlock loomed large before them.

Will floated out and pushed gently off the hull towards the mining ship. As he drifted across, he made a slight correction with his suit's lateral thruster and gently connected with the other airlock, where he grabbed a handhold next to the opening wheel. "Clear," he announced, and Richard performed the same manoeuvre.

They both waited a few moments to see if there was any reaction from the mining ship, and then Will began to slowly turn the wheel with one hand. After a slow minute, Will felt the vibration of the lock fully releasing and leant on the wheel. The airlock door swung slowly inwards and a slight burst of their thrusters sent them both inside.

While Will closed and sealed the airlock, Richard checked out the controls on one wall. "Much the same as ours," he announced. "This switch activates the compression cycle."

"Let's do it," said Will, and Richard obliged. A hiss of gas filled the chamber, bouncing them gently, and finally it ceased and a green light flashed on the control panel. In the new quiet, Will reached for the inner lock and began to turn the wheel. Once again, a final click released the inner lock and Will pushed the door open slowly.

The opening door revealed a low-lit corridor that ended in what looked like another airlock door ten metres away. "Nobody to greet us," stated Will for his listening audience. "Surely the airlock activity would have raised an alert of some sort."

"Maybe they're waiting on the other side of that door," observed Richard cheerfully.

"Let's go see," said Will. He began opening the door, commenting as he did, "This looks like a safety door for the airlock." The click and release occurred as before, and he pushed it open slowly.

This time, the corridor extended for at least thirty metres, with a clear intersecting passage less than ten metres ahead. It was deserted. In the background, the hum of active machinery resonated from afar, marked by a steady, rhythmic thrum. Will and Richard activated the magnetic locks on their boots to ensure they remained grounded and didn't drift through the corridor.

"Maybe everyone's asleep," muttered Richard, which Will ignored as he progressed slowly up the corridor. As he reached the intersection, he peeped around to his left and then turned into the side corridor. Richard followed close behind and saw that this corridor was wider and stretched a good 50 metres in front of them to a large double door with a number of intersections along the way.

"Might need to leave a breadcrumb trail," joked Richard into the nervous silence.

"Let's see what's beyond that door," said Will, and moved determinedly towards it.

As they passed the intersections, glances revealed that there were doors along each, but not in any regular pattern. Reaching the end doors, it had a simple handle that Will used to open it. Behind the door was similar to their own flight deck in many ways. Consoles, big screens, the odd blinking light.

No people.

"Looks like the control room," announced Will for the others. "Haven't seen any sign of people yet."

"Can we get out of these suits?" asked Richard.

Will checked the atmospheric and temperature readings on his suit arm panel. "Looks standard," he confirmed. "Go ahead."

They removed the suits and made a closer examination of the control panel. One screen was showing what looked like a close-up of the asteroid being steadily hit by what seemed like the end of a jackhammer. Dislodged material was being sucked past the camera viewpoint somehow.

"Clever mechanism," observed Will.

"Like a vacuum cleaner for asteroids," joked Richard.

"Quite," agreed Will. He turned his gaze to part of the panel, where lit-up in bright red lettering was displayed the message AUTOMATIC OPERATIONS, adjoining an unlit message reading MANUAL OPERATIONS with a large switch underneath, currently pointing at the lit-up section.

Richard examined this excitedly. "Looks like it is currently operating independently, in some sort of robot mode. That's why no one's around, maybe."

Will nodded in agreement. "Does that mean we can 'borrow' the ship, I wonder," he said quietly, almost to himself.

"Why not – although I'll need time to familiarise myself with its flight controls," agreed Richard with his usual confidence. "I'll need access to whatever its equivalent of a 'help' feature before I go anywhere near that warp drive of theirs, though," he added with unusual caution.

Will went to his spacesuit to update the others on what they had found while Richard immersed himself in investigating the controls. It was decided that Jim and Sela would join them to assist in Richard's education, while Jessica was reluctantly left minding *Stardust*.

Some hours later, Jim clapped Richard on the back and turned to the other two. "I think we have it sussed."

"Excellent," responded Will happily. "Let me position one of the suits so Jess can follow, and then tell us what you've discovered." So doing, he gave his suit the prime seat in front of the boys at the console.

"First of all," said Jim, "it's quite safe to go to manual operations." As he said that, he leaned over and flicked the switch before Will could react. The MANUAL OPERATIONS message was now lit up. At the same time, the thrumming background noise slowly subsided, followed by various clanks of machinery withdrawing back into the ship. They all looked relieved when quiet finally settled over them.

"Ahhh," said Sela into the silence. "That had been starting to get on my nerves."

"How about their warp drive?" asked Will anxiously. "Can you use it?"

"I'm pretty sure I can," answered Richard with his typical confidence. "It's actually quite simple, fortunately. It's just such a genius concept." He tapped at the console and another screen showed a representation of the ship. "First you need to deploy the space-time bubble maker here at the front."

"Is that what it's called?" asked Jessica, through the suit.

"No, they call it the Alcubierre device, after the guy who dreamed up the original concept in the '90s. I'm just calling it by what it does – it makes a space-time bubble around the ship and creates a major 'expansion' of our bubble of space-time behind us while contracting space in front. The ship is then accelerated as part of that space expansion, and we ride it a bit like a surfboard riding the waves to shore. When we switch it off, we are instantly back at our original speed. No acceleration or deceleration sensation."

"How long would it take it to get to Earth?" Jessica asked.

Richard paused dramatically, then replied, "Well, if we use it cautiously – maybe an hour."

Through the impressed silence that followed his assertion, Will asked, "What about the Stardust?"

Jim fielded that one with an assurance, "I've been studying the ship schematics, and we can easily float *Stardust* into one of the empty containers. They are similar in concept to the old shipping containers, just much bigger."

Jessica piped in with, "Won't *Stardust* get banged around when the drive comes on?"

"Nope," said Jim confidently. "It will be inside the warp bubble, and within the bubble, the mining ship will be at rest, as will *Stardust*."

"OK!" enthused Will. "Let's make preparations for a fast trip home!"

After some hours, the crew had safely transferred the *Stardust* into an empty container and managed to utilise the equivalent of webbing structures within the container to secure *Stardust* from any minor manoeuvring the mining ship might do. Jessica decided to stay on board the ship "just to be on hand if there's a problem in flight" – evidently not a total believer in Jim's explanation.

The rest were together in the control room of the mining ship as Richard began a slow disengagement from the asteroid, and then slowly turned the ship until it was pointing towards Earth. "Never done this before in space," he observed happily.

"What's that?" asked Will.

"I pointed at where we want to go. Typically, you've got to head towards where it's going to be in a few months, not just where it is now. This is fun!"

"Engage when ready," ordered Will.

"Aye aye, cap'n," cried Richard happily, and with a tap on the touchscreen, he initiated the deployment sequence.

After a moment, they could hear machinery activating within the ship. The console displayed the central wheel feature protruding from the front, slowly unfolding and extending like a huge parasol wider than the entire ship. A green light appeared on the console, and Richard proceeded to input further commands.

The group tensed in anticipation, but nothing obvious happened, not even a sensation of movement. After 30 seconds or so, Sela asked, "Are we moving?"

"We are indeed," cried Richard joyously. "According to this, we're at 0.7 of the speed of light." After a pause, he commented, "Check out the Earth; it's already a bit brighter."

The others could now detect the steady change in their destination.

"This is amazing," said Will. "With a drive like this, we could reach the stars!"

Jim observed drily, "I'll settle for Earth right now."

The journey remained uneventful, but still transfixed the crew, realising what they were doing. After about 40 minutes, the Earth had grown into a beautiful blue ball. Richard manipulated the controls, and the Earth suddenly stopped growing.

"All stop," announced Richard, a little giddy on the thrill of what he'd just done. "All ashore for Earth, Moon and Satellites!"

Will clapped him on the back. "Well done!"

Richard was uncharacteristically modest as he demurred with, "Hey – it was basically just point and click!"

The rest of the crew busied themselves retrieving the *Stardust* while Richard manned the mining ship. Before long, it was back, alongside the mining ship, with airlocks facing each other.

While waiting, Richard donned his spacesuit in preparation for rejoining the *Stardust*.

"OK, Richard," came Jessica's voice from his helmet. "Ready to leave when you are. Get your gear on and float over."

"Way ahead of you," replied Richard. He took a last look around the flight deck and leaned over the controls to flick the main switch from MANUAL to AUTOMATIC, muttering, "Don't want to leave you hanging here, buddy," then finished donning his space suit and headed for the airlock.

He was just approaching the airlock when Jessica exclaimed in his ear, "Richard! The ship is starting to rotate about its long axis. What are you doing?"

"Oh crap! – I switched it back to automatic – it's set to return to base. I'll go back and put it back on manual."

"No!" ordered Will. "Get out NOW!"

"I'm coming," muttered Richard as he spun the airlock wheel and finally pulled it open. He leapt in and pulled it shut behind him as fast as he could, re-spinning the wheel until there was a reassuring click and the airlock controls lit up.

As his heart raced, he engaged the airlock cycle. "Cycling now," he said as calmly as he could.

"The ship has nearly repositioned itself," cried Jessica. "We're already firing laterally to make sure we're out of range of that bubble. When you get out, fire half your suit thrust reserves straight out from the ship. Maximum acceleration. We'll pick you up."

"You'd better," muttered Richard, as the cycle finished and he yanked the wheel around until it clicked. He pulled the door inwards, stepped through by grabbing the external handhold, pulled the door shut, and gave a quick spin to the wheel.

Stardust was already nearly invisible in the distance as it retreated. "Hurry, Richard!" Jessica called, and he quickly typed on his arm controls for the required thrust and hit the GO button. "On my way," he stated, in professional calm that belied his adrenaline burst.

With what felt like a decent kick in his lower back, he erupted from the ship. His right arm flailed outwards in reaction, and he quickly pulled it back into standard "flight" mode for the jetpack to be at his centre of gravity. He realised that had induced a slight clockwise spin, and with the thruster still going, he was curving into a path parallel to the mining ship, about to clip the edge of the still-deployed parasol.

"Richard, watch out!" came the cry through his helmet. Thinking fast, he quickly extended his left arm until his clockwise spin stopped and began to spin back; he immediately brought his left arm back to the "rest" position, and the jetpack curved him away from the mining ship, so he missed the parasol by about ten metres. He breathed out in relief, not realising he had held his breath with the tension. He immediately stopped the thrust once he was travelling mostly away from the ship rather than continuing to draw complicated curves in the sky.

"Newton's laws are a pain," he observed drily for the benefit of the crew. He still had some residual spin, but without the thruster firing, it merely gave him a 360-degree view every minute or so, and he watched the shrinking mining ship with interest each time it came into view. Between one rotation and the next, it vanished.

"Phew, glad that's done," said Richard.

"Agreed," said Jessica. "We're locked onto your transponder and will come and collect you. I've seen drunks do steadier jet-pack manoeuvres," she joked, "so it will take a few minutes."

"Trust me," Richard said, "I feel stone-cold sober after that little jaunt!"

A short time later, after Richard was successfully rescued, the crew assembled on the flight deck to take stock of their situation.

Jessica, gazing out of the observatory window, took a deep breath. "It's uncanny. The continents, the oceans, and even the weather patterns. Everything resembles Earth." Her voice was hopeful but tinged with caution.

Richard, ever the sceptic, raised an eyebrow as he fiddled with some instruments. "It's an almost perfect replica, if not Earth itself," he mused. "But there's something that's been bugging me." He directed their attention to the lunar spectacle unfolding outside.

The others followed his gaze, squinting against the gleaming radiance of the Moon, which now dominated their view as the vessel adjusted its trajectory. It wasn't just the presence of the satellite that was mesmerising; it was the anomalies that it displayed.

Jim, leaning forward with his chin resting on his hands, remarked, "I've seen that glow before. It's artificial, like when you're flying over a sprawling metropolis at night. But that's impossible... isn't it?"

Sela, who had been quiet for a while, whispered in awe, "The dark side of the Moon shouldn't be this luminous. Not without significant human intervention. Are we looking at colonies? Mining operations? Maybe even entire cities?"

Will adjusted the zoom on their high-resolution telescope, bringing the Moon's details into sharper focus. The magnified view revealed structures, moving vehicles, and even what looked like large bio-domes.

"It's as if humanity has not just visited but thrived there," said Richard, his voice barely above a whisper.

The crew was abuzz with speculation. Had they returned to an alternate Earth, one where lunar colonisation was more advanced? Or had they been gone from their Earth much longer than they realised, and in their absence, humanity had made leaps in lunar exploration and habitation?

Chapter Four

"Do we land on Earth or try for the Moon colony?" asked Jessica. "That two-day side trip to the mining ship means we now don't have enough fuel for both."

"Our best shot is Earth," said Will decisively. "At least we can breathe there. Fire up the radio, Jim, and see if we can get something now we're this close."

"Ever the optimist," muttered Jim as he focused the radio dish on Earth and directed the sound to the shuttle's speakers.

"This is the *USS Stardust* calling NASA Control, come in NASA Control," he announced to the microphone.

After a few moments, he repeated, "This is the *USS Stardust* calling NASA Control, come in NASA Control."

After his tenth repetition, Jim stopped with a sigh and said, "Still nothing. Everything checks out OK, but there's no one home."

The central chamber was suddenly filled with the raspy static of an incoming transmission. The team, already tense from recent events, stood still, eyes darting toward the ship's communication console.

A gruff voice edged with a mix of annoyance and scepticism boomed through the speakers. "*USS Stardust*, is that some kind of joke? If you're one of Maury's boys trying to pull a fast one, your Pa's gonna hear about this. This frequency is reserved strictly for Military Reserve traffic, not for pranks."

Jim quickly dashed back to the radio console, pushing a few buttons before speaking urgently into the mic. "This isn't a prank. This is the *USS Stardust*. We're a civilian vessel currently stranded in orbit around Earth. We're having... technical difficulties."

A moment of silence followed before the voice on the other end spat out, dripping with disbelief, "Civilian vessel? In orbit? Do you take me for a fool? No one's used this archaic radio wave frequency in space for ages. Modern communications all shifted to subspace frequencies."

Jessica, from the other side of the room, whispered to Richard, "Subspace frequencies? We must have been out of the loop longer than we thought."

Jim took a deep breath, trying to sound as convincing as possible. "Listen, our subspace comm is down. We had no choice but to rig this old frequency up, hoping someone— anyone would pick it up. We need assistance."

The voice on the other end seemed to pause, contemplating. There was a slight softening when he replied, "Good, let's say I believe you for a second. If you really are who you say you are, there's going to be a lot of explaining to do. And if you're playing games... well, it won't end well for you."

Jim looked around at his team, his expression serious but hopeful. "We understand. Just... thank you for responding. We really need help."

The gruff voice gave a small chuckle. "Alright, *Stardust*. Hold tight. Let's see what we can figure out."

After a small delay, he continued. "Well, I suppose I can patch you through to Bismarck Space Park in Australia. We don't talk to the European bases much from here, but I know someone at Bismarck."

"What about Andrews Air Force Base in California? We've landed there before," said Jim.

"Andrews Air Force Base? What are you talking about? There is no spaceport there, and we don't have much to do with those Empire lovers."

Jim looked at the others questioningly, but they all appeared as bewildered as he was.

"Keep going," said Will. "Ask him where he is."

"Sorry, sir," continued Jim, "where are you talking to us from?"

"Oh, I've completely forgotten my manners," came the swift reply. "My name's Doug Kraver, hailing from the Sovereign Nation of Florida."

"Sovereign Nation... of Florida?" echoed the other crew members in astonishment.

Before the confusion could unsettle Jim, Will intervened, "Our fuel situation is dire. We need a landing strip approximately two miles long. Our current trajectory won't get us to Australia."

Doug's voice paused. "There's an abandoned drag strip about 40 miles from Fort Lauderdale. It's not exactly commercial runway material, but it might just work. I could contact the local authorities to facilitate your landing."

Jim's eyes widened in alarm. "Absolutely not. Our mission is classified. But if you could meet us there, we'll explain everything."

Doug was clearly intrigued. "This sounds highly irregular. I thought you were a civilian mission," he remarked.

"Civilianish," replied Jim. "Please, can you help us?"

"What the hell," Doug replied. "Life's short. I've had dealings with the owner of that strip, and he owes me a few favours. Besides, the opportunity to see a spaceship made by those backward loonies from the US up close. That's not something you pass up."

True to his word, within a span of a few minutes, Doug relayed the coordinates, and the crew swiftly adjusted their course, ready for the unexpected touchdown.

"What do you think will be waiting for us?" asked Jessica.

"I have no idea," said Will. "I can't think of what is going on or what has happened to us. We'll have to wing it, I guess. Jim, keep talking to Doug," he added. "We need to find out as much as possible about where we are."

Thirty minutes later, the *Stardust* made its final approach to a long, four-lane straight road: the drag strip Doug had mentioned. No activity could be observed from their distance. As they got closer, they noticed the place seemed completely abandoned. There was a large hangar-type building on one side, with a tractor-like vehicle in front of it and an odd-looking truck with a large red cross painted on the roof parked beside the road.

"Final approach," announced Will, and after a pause, "Touchdown in 3... 2...1..." As they rolled to a stop, he continued, "We have landed, folks, wherever we are."

Will stepped away and opened the main hatch. Turning to Jim, he said, "I think it's best if you go first, Jim, since you're the one he's been talking to."

Walking toward the *Stardust* was a well-built man, about 1.9 metres tall, with grey, almost white, hair. He stopped underneath the hatch and shouted, "Hi, I'm Doug Karver. Pleased to meet you."

"Hi!" Jim shouted back. "Any idea how we can get out of here? We're all a bit gravity-sick from being in space for six months, so we can't really climb down the emergency ladder."

"Hang on!" shouted Doug. "I'll be back!" He walked over to the hangar-like building and climbed into what looked like a tractor with a front-end loader. However, it was much larger, and instead of a bucket, had a wooden tray that had probably been used as a viewing platform for mounting a camera during the drag races.

Doug started the tractor, and silently it moved towards them.

"Must be electrically powered," mused Jim to Will, who was now standing next to him. Both men held tightly to the hatch; although they had used the gym facilities extensively on *Stardust* over the past few months, the impact of Earth's gravity was affecting them.

As the tractor reached the *Stardust*, Doug lifted the tray until it was level with the hatch. Jim and Will then stepped onto it. Jessica appeared next, but Will told her to stay put until they saw what kind of welcome awaited them.

"Good idea," said Jessica. "Be careful," she added.

Doug lowered the platform to the ground, dismounted the tractor, and went around to greet Will and Jim.

"Hello again," Doug greeted with a curious tilt of his head, staring at the spaceship before him. "But I have to ask: what the hell are you flying?"

"That's our spaceship, the *Stardust*," Will replied, extending his hand. "I'm its Captain, Will Chambers."

"It looks like something out of a museum," Doug remarked, shaking Will's hand. "Typical US junk. I'm amazed it can even fly."

"It not only flies," Jim interjected proudly, "but it has taken us beyond Mars."

"I didn't mean to offend," Doug quickly added, "but it's been over fifty years since I've seen a ship like that one. So, where did you say you're from?"

Will locked eyes with Doug, his voice mixed with nostalgia and confusion. "I grew up in what we call the United States of America, but from what we are learning, it seems to be a different time or reality from yours."

"Different time, you say?" Doug exclaimed, checking the date on his device. "It's April 8, 2035 here."

"That's today's date for us, too," Jim confirmed.

"So, you're not time travellers then. What's an alternate reality like then?" Doug asked, his intrigue tinged with a hint of scepticism.

Will's eyes softened as memories flooded back. "I remember the Fourth of July celebrations in Washington, D.C., the fireworks over the Lincoln Memorial. The U.S. has always been united."

Jim, sensing the building tension, added a note of nostalgia. "And San Francisco, with its iconic Golden Gate Bridge and that chilly summer fog. That's where I dreamt of space. Not to mention New York City, a truly international city that never sleeps, bustling with energy day and night."

Doug's scepticism seemed to deepen. "The Golden Gate Bridge? That name's been lost to history here, replaced with 'Western Archway' decades ago." He sighed heavily. "And New

York City is nothing like the cultural melting pot you describe. Your United States sounds almost like a dream. Here, it fragmented into regional alliances after the 1930 economic collapse. That explains why your technology seems so... antiquated. And this Andrews Airbase you were trying to reach has never existed here."

Doug paused, pondering their claims. "Tell me, how did you get here?"

Will started, his voice filled with wonder and confusion. "It's bizarre. We were analysing a comet, hit it with an X-ray beam, and then we found ourselves in this corridor in space with strange creatures. Suddenly, we were here."

Doug listened, his brow furrowed in thought. "Dimension travellers," he echoed slowly as if testing the words. "Your story, if true, would redefine reality itself. But such claims... they need substantial proof."

The group fell into a contemplative silence, grappling with the magnitude of their situation.

Doug finally broke the silence. "Let's explore this cautiously. Your ship, your experiences—they don't align with our world. But I need evidence, solid proof that what you're saying is possible."

Jim nodded eagerly. "We'll gather what we can. Differences in history, technology, maybe even physics."

Doug's acceptance was cautious, tempered by a need for empirical evidence. "We start with what you know. Let's compare notes on our worlds. If there's truth to your story, we'll uncover it. But first," he added, pulling out a small box from his pocket, "take these space supplement pills. They'll help you adjust quickly to the gravity and build up your bone density. How many of you are there?"

"Five," said Will.

"Good," said Doug. Turning to Jim, he asked, "As the engineer on board, do you think you can drive this tractor while I go fetch the medicine?"

"I'm sure I can drive anything," said Jim.

"Excellent," Doug replied. "You get the rest of your crew, and I'll meet you back in the hangar. It's too hot out here to hang around."

"Sounds like a plan," said Will. "We will get on it."

As Doug walked off to his truck, Jim moved the tractor back to the hatch, raising Will so he could summon the others. He quickly filled them in on what they had learned.

"Can we trust him?" asked Jessica.

"We really have no choice but to trust him," said Will. "Jim seems to trust him, and we really have no other options available." He shrugged. "We are stuck here and need all the help we can get. He seems fascinated by our story, so I think we have struck it lucky."

Shortly after, the crew had all assembled in the hangar, waiting for Doug to return with his truck. Jessica turned to Will and said, "That flag on the roof is the old flag of the Spanish Empire."

"Yes, the saw-toothed Cross of Burgundy," said Will. He looked at her and winked. "I've studied too," he said, acknowledging her astonished look.

Doug walked in with a bottle of capsules and handed them to Will, saying, "Here, take two each and another two in four hours or so."

"Allow me to present my team," began Will, motioning to the group behind him. "Major Jessica Turner stands as one of our finest pilots."

Jessica stepped forward, extending her hand with a warm yet professional smile. "We deeply appreciate your aid. We were caught in quite the predicament."

Doug nodded, his expression still a mixture of caution and curiosity. "You're welcome," he replied.

Will continued, pointing to Jim, "You already know Jim and beside him is Flight Engineer Sela Chea."

As Sela approached Doug, her friendly demeanour was evident in her bright eyes and grin. Doug returned the gesture, shaking her hand firmly. "A pleasure, indeed."

Will's introduction flowed seamlessly. "Lastly, meet Richard Coburg, our resident Technology Specialist."

But Doug's reaction shattered the calm like glass under a hammer. In a split second, his hand darted to his belt, producing a sleek device that bore a striking resemblance to a *Star Trek* phaser gun. He aimed it directly at Richard, his arm steady despite the tremor in his voice. "What game are you playing at? I knew your story was too fantastic to be true! Why is the Empire's Director of Intelligence on board your ship?"

The air thickened with tension, Richard, his eyebrow arching, looked more perplexed than alarmed. "Director of Intelligence? Me? I think you're sorely mistaken."

Will stepped forward, his hands raised in a calming gesture as he tried to diffuse the mounting tension. "Doug, this might be a result of the alternate dimension dynamics. In our world, Richard is our AI expert. Here, he seems to be entangled in something much more complicated. It's entirely possible that each of us has an alternate version in this universe."

Doug's grip on the weapon slightly loosened, but his eyes remained narrow slits of suspicion. "Alright, make your case then. Prove that you're not a spy for the Empire."

With a solemnity that drew a quiet from the room, Richard responded, "I swear by His Majesty King William the Fifth that I have never been, nor will ever be, part of any Intelligence Service."

"His Majesty?" Doug's confusion deepened, his weapon lowering just an inch as he grappled with Richard's words. "You mean Her Majesty Victoria the Third?"

Will, sensing an opportunity, quickly added, "See, Doug? The histories and leaderships we know are different. It wouldn't make sense for Richard to serve an empire that doesn't exist in his reality."

Richard quickly added, "Where we are from, the head of the British Empire is King William V, son of King Charles III, grandson of Queen Elizabeth II, who was the daughter of King George VI, granddaughter of King George V, great-granddaughter of King Edward VII, and great-great-granddaughter of Queen Victoria."

"Wait a moment," said Doug, his weapon now pointing harmlessly at the floor as he tried to process the conflicting information. "I'm no expert on Empire Monarchy, so hang on a minute."

Doug tapped the watch-like device on his arm and said, "Alyssa, are you listening?"

A six-inch hologram of a young woman, all in blue, appeared above the watch.

"She looks just like Cortana from *Halo X*," said Jessica quietly to Will.

"You played *Halo*?" whispered back Will.

"My brothers did when we were kids. She was the AI assistant who helped you through the game," she added.

"Alyssa," continued Doug, "Did you hear his list of the Empire Monarchy?"

"Yes, Doug," said the hologram. "The list is different until Queen Victoria; her eldest child Victoria became Queen rather than her son Edward."

"Maybe that's when the timelines split," Jim mused aloud, his voice tinged with a mix of fascination and unease.

"Timelines split?" Jessica and Sela exclaimed simultaneously; their expressions turned from confusion to alarm. The atmosphere in the hangar grew tense, with the weight of their situation settling like a heavy cloak around them.

"Yes," Will interjected, his face drawn with the gravity of their discovery. "It appears we are on an Earth whose history diverged significantly from our own. It now seems clear it happened sometime during the Victorian era." He paused, letting the implications sink in. The crew exchanged uneasy glances, the reality of their predicament dawning on them.

Doug nodded to the hologram. "Thank you, Alyssa." As her image faded away, a sombre silence enveloped the group.

Trying to lighten the atmosphere, Doug turned to Richard and attempted a joke. "Alright, I admit you do look a bit different from the Director... less rat-faced," he said with a forced chuckle, which did little to ease the tension.

He holstered his gun and switched to a more practical tone. "We need to conceal your ship so it remains unseen by unfriendly eyes. Can it be moved, or does it require towing?"

Jim, looking over at the ship with a protective gaze, replied, "I'm sure your tractor can handle it. It should fit in here just fine."

"Good, then I'll hitch her up, and we can move your museum piece inside," Doug declared, trying to project confidence as he prepared to tow the ship.

"*Stardust*," the crew corrected almost in unison, their voices blending—a mix of pride and a poignant reminder of their connection to their own reality.

"*Stardust*," Doug echoed as he began the task of attaching the tractor to the ship. He worked methodically, the metal clinks echoing in the quiet.

As the crew followed Doug through the dimly lit hangar, the air was thick with contemplation until Jessica broke the silence, her voice tinged with a mix of anxiety and determination.

"This is unsettling. I mean, with everything we saw in space, this was our most logical guess, wasn't it? Stepping into an alternate reality?" she mused, trying to find some grounding in their extraordinary situation.

Jim nodded, his eyes reflecting a mix of resolve and wonder. "True. We've encountered phenomena that defy explanation— that corridor and the things in it. Yet, confronting a changed history on Earth itself feels as surreal as any cosmic anomaly we've faced."

Sela chimed in, her tone laced with both awe and a hint of fear. "It puts everything into perspective, doesn't it? Our explorations, our theories about the universe—they didn't prepare us for this. It's one thing to theorise about alternate realities; it's another to visit one."

Will, leading the group with a steady presence, acknowledged their thoughts with a nod. "Exactly. That's why we need to be methodical about this. Just as we navigated our way here, we must navigate this altered history with caution and curiosity. Our experiences out there, they weren't just tests of survival—they were lessons in adapting to the unknown."

Doug, overhearing part of their conversation as he secured the tractor, turned back to them briefly. "Sounds like you folks are used to tackling the impossible. Let's get you to a safe place where you can regroup and figure this out. My home's just the spot for that."

Reassured by his pragmatic approach, the crew piled into his truck. It was a tight fit, but they all managed to squeeze in, the engine, humming softly as they left the hangar behind. Inside the truck, the conversation dipped into a more strategic discussion.

Jim, looking out the window at the passing landscape, shared his thoughts. "Our stint in space taught us to expect the unexpected. We apply the same principles here—observe, learn, adapt."

Will leaned forward, his voice infused with a leader's resolve. "First order of business is to establish what's known and what's different in this world. We'll draw parallels, find discrepancies, and use them to navigate."

Sela pulled out a small notebook and began to write some notes. "Let's approach this like we did with our missions—systematic, thorough. We're charting the unknown, just on our home turf this time. Think of it as navigating a new sector of space, but the variables are historical events, not asteroids."

Jessica managed a half-smile. "Undercover historians in an alternate Victorian timeline—it's like a new expedition. And if there's something we're good at, it's charting the unknown."

Silence enveloped the truck as Doug drove them onto the main road. Each crew member, lost in their own thoughts, grappled with the reality of their situation and the uncertainties of what lay ahead.

PART TWO

Chapter Five

Over the next few days, the crew busied themselves with learning as much as they could about the new world and how they got there. Joining them was Doug's wife, Savina, an attractive fifty-something Latina with long black hair. Savina was among the many Cubans who had settled in Florida as part of the special Florida-Cuba relationship. She was also an experienced psychologist who ran her own clinic in nearby Fort Lauderdale.

Jessica and Savina had an instant connection from the moment they met. Savina spent most of the time showing her the new technology that was common in this world but often completely unfathomable to the travellers. Savina was also able to answer the burning question that had occupied the minds of all the stranded astronauts.

"Why do you think Doug is taking such a risk in helping us?" Jessica asked Savina. "And what makes him hate both the Empire and the US Government so much?"

"Well, we all hate the Empire," said Savina. "That's an easy one, but for his hatred of the US, you must understand Doug's family history. As he has told you, his surname is Kraver, and his family is originally from Henderson, Kentucky. They were the owners of Peerless Distilling, one of the premium whiskey makers in the whole country back in the 1930s. Prohibition basically drove them to bankruptcy, and the whole family was ruined after a particularly nasty faction of abolitionists drove them out of

Kentucky. They bounced around, completely broke, until settling here in Florida."

"Drove who to bankruptcy?" said Jim as he walked into the kitchen.

"Doug's family. They were the founders of Peerless Distillery," replied Jessica.

"I've heard of them," said Jim. "They make a nice drop, and I've been to the factory in Louisville a few times."

"So, in your reality, Peerless is still going?" said Savina. "You should tell Doug." She continued, "It will make him very happy because he has tried a couple of times to restart the family business. In fact, that's how we met, when he tried to set up a distillery in Cuba."

"Oh, what happened?" replied Jessica.

"While I was finishing my psychology degree, I worked part-time at the Havana Club office, where they produced rum. It was there that Doug introduced a proposal to add a bourbon distillery to their operations. We immediately hit it off and spent the next three months working together. Unfortunately, the proposal fell through, and Doug returned to Florida. A year later, I joined him here."

"Do you go back home very often?" Jessica asked. "Cuba, in our world, has a very different history," she added.

"You must tell me about it sometime," said Savina.

"I will, but I'm not sure you'll like it," said Jessica solemnly.

Savina and Jessica then joined the rest of the team in Doug's man cave, which had been turned into a "war room" to plan their next moves.

"Well, guys," said Will, "we have all been hard at work sorting out when or where we are and what we can do about it. Let's start with a history lesson and what is different here compared to home."

"Yes, well," said Richard, rifling through a stack of notes, "it's all very fascinating."

"I'm sure," said Will. "You're not going to read that entire stack of paper, are you?"

"Can we just have the summary?" said Jessica.

"Even just the executive summary," said Will sarcastically.

"Ah, umm, OK," said Richard. "Are you sure? It's all really fascinating. Especially the bits about me."

Everyone groaned simultaneously.

"Get on with it," said Will.

"OK, well, we established before that the timeline changed during Queen Victoria's time, with her eldest daughter being placed in the line of succession rather than her eldest son, Prince Edward."

"Yes," said Doug. "Her daughter became Victoria II and reigned for about 10 years."

"Correct!" said Richard. "Because in this timeline, Parliament ratified Prince Albert's dying wish that his eldest and favourite child would become Queen. And as Prince Edward didn't really ever want to be King, he accepted the idea willingly. So rather than becoming King, he ended up buying most of the Canary Islands and becoming a cross between our Hugh Hefner and Richard Branson."

"Good for him," said Jessica. "But how does that explain the breakup of the USA? It's not meant to happen under the Constitution; the Civil War settled that!"

"Yes," said Sela, "when I did my citizenship exam, one of the topics was on how the 10th Amendment and a Supreme Court decision involving Texas stopped states from leaving the Union."

"Patience – I'm getting to that," said Richard. "Let me tell you of the ironic twist of the changes so far. I recall a favourite quiz night question in our timeline was: 'Who would have been King of Great Britain during WWI if Princess Victoria had become Queen Victoria II?'"

"Who cares!" interjected Jessica, not wishing to indulge Richard's segue.

"The answer is," began Richard loudly, "her son Wilhelm, who instead of being Kaiser of Germany in our timeline, became King of England in this reality." He looked around smugly. "Thus, various tensions leading up to WWI never happened, mainly due to the fact that Otto von Bismarck remained advisor to the German King and was firmly against the expansionist policy that triggered our WWI. There's a lot more about the impact on various treaties, but that's the major European impact – no WWI!!"

"There was a smaller war around the time of WWI that did occur, but it was essentially between Europe and the Ottoman Empire. It was over in a few months rather than the four years in our timeline. Britain, France, and Germany then halted the Russian Revolution, which had been attempted in 1919 but failed in our reality due to exhaustion from WWI. This prevented the rise of both Stalin and Hitler. Hitler, as far as I can discern, remained an artist and eventually became a historical fiction author."

"Fine, No WWI. Can we get to what happened to the States now, please?" said Jessica.

"One last important point in Europe," said Richard. "No WWI allowed a lot of critical science to continue uninterrupted, with sustained cooperation between German scientists and those in Great Britain. A pivotal event was when the nuclear scientist Ernest Rutherford postulated a neutral particle in the nucleus in 1915, not 1919 as he did in our time. Another British scientist, John Chadwick, joined Hans Geiger in Germany in 1914. In our timeline, he was interned for the duration of the war and discovered the actual neutron much later – in 1932. However, in this timeline, without the war and with the collaboration with Geiger, and inspired by Rutherford, they discovered the neutron in 1917. The neutron was the gateway to atomic power. With essentially unlimited funding, they built a vast team, resulting in this timeline having nuclear power since the late 1920s. This revolutionised their industries and explains why they are technologically much more advanced than us."

"Now can we talk about the US?" demanded Jessica.

"Certainly," replied Richard, with a saccharine smile. "The first major divergence from our timeline was the Spanish-American War in 1898. America won in both timelines and occupied Cuba. They also purchased Puerto Rico, Guam, and the Philippines from Spain as part of the settlement. In our timeline, they allowed Cuba to form a republic around 1902, with a few conditions, like the leasing of Guantanamo Bay, and left them to their own devices. In this timeline, they retained Cuba, similar to what they did with Puerto Rico, and Cubans became citizens in 1917, just as they did in Puerto Rico. By 1921, Cuba was effectively absorbed into the state of Florida."

"No surprise," joked Jim with an ironic grin. "Most of Cuba moved to Florida in our timeline anyway."

Richard paused for a moment, letting the weight of his previous revelations settle on the group before continuing, "The next significant deviation in our timelines pertains to the economic ramifications of a world without WWI. In the history we know, the US capitalised significantly from its involvement in WWI. It led to a massive industrial boom, transforming the nation into a production powerhouse."

He took a sip of water and continued, "However, in this alternate timeline, without the war acting as a catalyst, the acceleration in industrial and economic growth remained much more tempered. Think of it as a consistent, yet modest, upward curve." Leaning forward for emphasis, he added, "The ripple effects of this moderate growth are manifold. The economic roller-coaster that our world experienced due to rapid expansion was absent here. We witnessed a nine-year bull market, followed by the infamous Wall Street crash and the devastating Great Depression. But in this version of history, those monumental economic events simply... never transpired. Their financial landscape remained relatively stable, devoid of such dramatic peaks and troughs."

"What did they have?" asked Jim.

"Well, they still had Prohibition as the 18th Amendment. They were super-isolationist—much more so," said Richard thoughtfully. "In this reality, the various religious groups and upright coalitions that had initially passed Prohibition increased their influence, especially in the eastern states."

"What happened then?" Jessica inquired quietly.

"By the time the European powers started demonstrating nuclear energy in the late 1920s, these groups identified a common enemy in this devil's power that no one seemed to understand, expanding their political base accordingly. Prohibition became associated with anti-nuclear sentiment, putting an incredible strain on the Union. Most of the western states, led by California, with Florida's support, resisted. By 1930, a second civil war seemed imminent."

"Jeez, so what happened?" inquired Will.

"The British Empire, under King William VII, along with their European allies, showcased the newly developed neutron bomb. They then advised that they would supply these to the more agreeable group in California if the primary USA didn't allow a peaceful secession. All Britain wanted was uninterrupted trade. After a few demonstrations of what these new weapons could do, the religious US folded like deckchairs," Richard joked, "at the threat of fire and brimstone!"

He continued, "Having forged a fragile, separate alliance with the Empire apart from the Western States, Florida now sits isolated in the east—dependent on the Empire but politically separated from it."

"Wow!" exclaimed Jessica. "Nukes scared everyone senseless in the '50s and '60s in our time. Imagine the reaction in 1930!"

"Exactly," said Richard, looking smug. "...and Britain saved the day," he declared solemnly.

A few groans attempted to pierce his smug smile, to no avail.

"Wow, that's quite a story," commented Jim.

"What about the rest of the world?" Will asked.

"European countries have largely maintained their pre-World War borders, now powered extensively by affordable nuclear energy. As Great Britain and Germany championed the cause for nations to govern themselves, most non-European territories— such as Algeria, Libya, Australia, and Canada—opted to remain colonies. These regions benefited significantly from advancements in space technology, which diminished their drive for independence. By the early 1960s, most European nations had formed an alliance akin to our European Union, now globally recognised as 'The Empire'."

"Does it have an evil Emperor and some lightsabre-wielding secret police?" asked Jim.

"No, it's not *Star Wars*," Richard joked, "but let me continue. China and Japan have fought a few times, but both have backed down when the Empire gets involved."

"So, can any of this help us get back to our reality?" Will asked, his voice tinged with urgency.

"I have the semblance of a plan coming together, but it's dangerous and not very likely to succeed," Richard admitted, rubbing his temples.

"You could all stay here," Doug suggested, looking around at the group.

"What about Richard?" Jessica interjected. "We all saw the effect he had on you. I don't think the rest of the country would be as easy to convince."

"Good point," Doug acknowledged with a nod. "Okay, what's your plan then?"

"Well," Richard began, glancing at Jim, "I've been discussing it with Jim, so perhaps he should explain the science behind it."

"Thanks to Savina's clinic, we have access to what is known in the industry as a Dream Catcher machine," Jim explained to the group. His tone was serious, reflecting the importance of the tool they were about to use. "If each of us hooks up to it and focuses intensely on our entire life experiences before we reached the corridor, Savina can pool our memories, and we might get a clearer understanding of what we encountered," he continued. "The machine works like a therapy device—it's more effective if it understands you fully before trying to recover specific lost memories.

"Each of us will have to go through this process several times, so it will take a few days," Jim added, noting the gravity of their task.

"Unfortunately, the machine cannot be moved, so we will have to go to my clinic," Savina chimed in, her voice calm but firm.

"Isn't that a risk, especially for Richard?" Jessica asked, her brow furrowed in concern as she considered their high-profile companion's safety.

"I believe we can disguise him enough so he won't be recognised, but we will have to be careful," Savina reassured her, understanding the stakes involved.

"Good idea," agreed Will, his tone resolute. "Sounds like a plan."

Early the next day, Will and Jessica gathered around the Dream Catcher in Savina's clinic, its soft hum filling the room with a sense of anticipation. Will glanced at Jessica, noting her expression mixed with curiosity and slight apprehension.

"Ready for this?" he asked gently, his voice low to match the quiet of the morning.

Jessica nodded, her eyes steady on the machine. "As ready as I'll ever be," she replied, her tone reflecting a mix of determination and the nerves that naturally came with revisiting deep memories.

Will offered a supportive smile. "Okay, I'll go first," he declared, stepping towards the machine with a resolve that seemed to solidify with each step. He settled into the device, taking a deep breath as he prepared to confront his past.

Jessica watched him for a moment, her own resolve strengthening. "Then it's my turn," she murmured, more to herself than to Will, mentally preparing to follow his lead into the depths of her own history.

The apparatus hummed softly, its gentle light enveloping Will as he delved deep into the tapestry of his past. He first revisited his childhood, a collage of fleeting images from various military bases. Each relocation brought new challenges—new schools, new faces, and the perpetual feeling of being an outsider. These early experiences ingrained in him resilience and adaptability, becoming his core strengths. His parents, consistent figures amid constant change, instilled in him strategic thinking and the value of optimism.

As Will grew taller, he remained lanky into his late teens; he became a target for bullies. This changed when he discovered boxing and martial arts. The Dream Catcher vividly reconstructed a defining moment in a school playground where Will, cornered by bullies, used his newfound skills to assert himself. His efficient, controlled response not only defused the situation but also instilled in him a confidence that extended beyond physical confrontations.

The narrative then shifted to Will's early days at the military academy, where he faced a different kind of challenge—a heated argument among his peers. With calm authority, Will stepped in, using his inclusive manner to guide the discussion toward a constructive resolution. This ability to negotiate and maintain harmony became a hallmark of his leadership, earning him respect among his peers and superiors.

Amid these recollections of growth and leadership, the machine also unveiled the more personal sacrifices of Will's career. It conjured memories of fleeting romantic relationships, each doomed by his deep commitment to the military. There was Sarah, a fellow cadet whose dreams diverged from Will's unwavering path; their mutual respect was evident as they parted ways under the stars. Later, there was Ana, a local teacher at a foreign base, whose warmth momentarily pierced Will's disciplined exterior. Yet again, duty called, and their brief romance flickered out.

Suddenly, an image of a beautiful black-haired girl appeared, startling Will and overwhelming him with grief. The machine, detecting his emotional spike, automatically retracted, allowing him space to process. Stricken, Will softly uttered, "Susan," his voice thick with sorrow.

After what felt like mere moments to Will, the machine's hum quieted, signalling the end of his session. He slowly opened his eyes, disoriented by the sudden return to reality and the poignant memory of his Susan.

"Who was she?" asked Savina, her voice filled with concern. "I haven't seen a reaction like that for a long time."

"My sister Susan," he replied, sadness in his voice. "She died."

"I'm so sorry to do that to you; those memories were buried deep."

"How long was I in there?" Will asked, his voice carrying a hint of disbelief.

"Just over two hours," Savina replied from her position at the control panel.

"Wow, it didn't feel that long," Will said, rubbing his temples as the weight of the memories lingered in his mind.

He stepped out of the machine, making room for Jessica, who had been observing quietly from the other room. She gave him a reassuring nod, her face set with determination as she prepared for her own journey through the past.

"Ready, Jessica?" Savina asked, checking the settings on the device.

"Yes, let's do this," Jessica responded, taking a deep breath before settling into the seat Will had just vacated.

Will moved aside, offering a supportive smile as Savina initiated the session. He knew all too well the emotional rollercoaster Jessica was about to experience.

Jessica settled into the Dream Catcher, her mind instantly whisked back to the spirited cheers and vibrant energy of her high school days in Williamsburg. At the centre of it all, she wasn't just a cheerleader but a leader who commanded the crowd with her charisma and meticulous choreography. Her popularity stemmed not just from her presence on the field; it was rooted in her ability to connect with people, motivating and inspiring her team and peers alike.

As the machine hummed, her transition from high school to university unfolded. Her brief stint at university was uninspiring and too conformist for her taste. The predictability of academic life didn't satisfy her thirst for challenge and real-world impact, prompting a pivotal decision that would redefine her path: joining the military.

Her father's influence subtly wove through her career choice. Known for his tactical genius in the courtroom, he had always inspired Jessica with his strategic battles. Though she chose a different battlefield, the lessons in strategy and critical thinking were not lost on her.

Jessica's memories smoothly transitioned from the high school stadiums to the starkly different landscapes of her military intelligence career. She recalled her first deployment, where the skills she had honed as a cheerleader—leadership, public speaking, and quick decision-making—played unexpected roles. During a night raid in a volatile region, her ability to rapidly assess situations and coordinate with diverse teams proved critical. Her commands were clear and confident, reminiscent of calling plays on the field but with much higher stakes.

Her personal life echoed the themes of her youth. Popular and engaging, Jessica found herself in a whirlwind of relationships, each as intense and fleeting as her assignments. There was Michael, a fellow operative with whom she shared a deep, albeit short-lived, connection. They met during a high-risk mission and found comfort in each other's understanding of the sacrifices their jobs entailed. Like her high school romances, these relationships were passionate but always secondary to her overriding commitment to her career.

As the last echoes of her past adventures faded, the hum of the machine subsided, and the light around Jessica dimmed. She slowly opened her eyes, adjusting to the ambient lighting of Savina's clinic. The weight of her memories still pressed heavily upon her, a mix of exhilaration and exhaustion clear in her posture.

"How long was that?" Jessica asked, her voice carrying a mix of curiosity and a slight sense of disorientation.

"Almost three hours," Savina replied, checking the machine's readouts.

"Really? It felt like both a lifetime and just a moment," Jessica remarked, a reflective smile touching her lips as she unstrapped herself from the machine.

She stood, stretching slightly, then glanced at Savina with a decisive nod. "Let's head back to the house. I have a lot to share; I hope these initial reflections will help us greatly in the next phase," Jessica said, understanding the importance of these foundational memories.

Together, they left the room, finding Will waiting outside. He offered her a knowing look, one that spoke of shared experiences and mutual understanding.

The three then drove back to Doug and Savina's house, where Jim, Richard, and Sela were discussing their upcoming sessions.

"As Jess and I have just completed our initial sessions, tomorrow, Jim and Sela will go next. We've started to lay the groundwork with some intriguing insights," Will briefed the group, his tone a mixture of anticipation and the seriousness of their ongoing mission.

"Richard's session is scheduled for Sunday," Savina added softly but clearly. "It's quieter then, which should minimise the risk of him being recognised. Given the circumstances, we need to maintain a low profile for him."

Jim nodded, ready to delve into the layers of his own past, while Sela looked around at the others, gathering her resolve.

"Tomorrow then," Jim said with a firm nod, setting the stage for their upcoming introspections.

Early the next day, Jim and Sela found themselves in Savina's office, staring at the Dream Catcher. It stood imposingly, yet the morning light casting through the blinds softened its edges, making it seem less daunting.

"Who's going first?" Savina asked, her voice calm, her hand resting lightly on the machine as if to reassure them of its benign purpose.

"I will," Sela declared with a mixture of determination and a hint of nervousness. "Let's just get this over with," she added, her voice betraying the bravado she projected.

"Imagine it's just a time machine, Sela. You get to be the hero of your own sci-fi movie without any of the scary alien invasions," Jim joked, winking to punctuate his humour.

Sela laughed softly, the edges of her nervousness smoothing out. "I'll take time travel over alien invasions any day. Just make sure you pull me back if I start drifting into the Jurassic period, okay?"

"Deal," Jim chuckled. "But honestly, from what Will and Jess were saying it's going to be more like a deep dive into your own personal documentary. You might even find it pretty enlightening."

"Or terrifying. I'm not sure I want to remember everything," Sela added, her tone playful yet tinged with genuine apprehension.

Jim placed a reassuring hand on her shoulder. "You're braver than you think."

Encouraged by Jim's words and the lighter atmosphere, Sela took a deep breath and nodded, feeling a bit more fortified for the journey ahead. "Alright, let's do this. It's time to see what the past has in store for me."

As she settled into the machine, it hummed to life, guiding her through the corridors of her memories. The journey began in her childhood home near Siem Reap, Cambodia—a place infused with history and spirituality, where her family's deep Hindu beliefs framed her early life experiences. The device painted vivid scenes of rituals and prayers, reflecting the profound spiritual atmosphere that enveloped her youth.

However, the narrative didn't shy away from her tumultuous teenage years, when she found herself drawn to a bad crowd. The Dream Catcher delicately navigated these memories, showcasing a period marked by rebellion and the allure of danger. This chapter of her life highlighted her internal conflict, caught between the thrill of defiance and the foundational values she was raised with.

As the session explored deeper, it revealed her crisis of faith—a significant turning point where she began questioning the beliefs she had grown up with. This spiritual upheaval marked a significant shift, leading her away from Hinduism and toward a more scientific understanding of the world.

Her journey from a rebellious teen to a respected expert in archaeology and engineering was vividly brought to life. The Dream Catcher emphasised her innovative efforts to develop an automated system to safely remove land mines from excavation sites, blending her passion for preservation with her commitment to protecting life. This innovation led to the most significant moment of her career when this breakthrough caught the attention of Jim, who had a keen eye for spotting emerging talents in their formative stages. After reading about her success, he travelled to see her work in action, impressed by the practical application of her technology in such high-stakes conditions. Witnessing her system successfully disarming a series of landmines, Jim saw the immense potential not only for archaeological safety but for broader applications. Recognising her talent and innovation, he offered his mentorship on the spot, eager to help her refine her techniques and broaden her impact.

As the last echoes of Sela's past faded, the hum of the device gradually quieted, signalling the end of her session. Slowly, Sela unstrapped herself and cautiously stepped out of the machine, her movements measured and a bit unsteady. The depth of the memories she had revisited left her visibly emotionally drained, a faint trace of past conflicts and revelations lingering in her eyes.

Jim, who had been waiting nearby, watched her emerge with a mix of concern and admiration. Knowing she might need a lighter moment after such an intense journey, he quipped with a gentle smile, "Welcome back, time traveller. Did you bring us any souvenirs from the past?"

Sela managed a tired smile, appreciating Jim's effort to ease the moment, yet the weight of her recollections still pressing upon her. "Just a few old memories, nothing worth putting on display," she responded softly, her voice carrying a mix of exhaustion and relief.

Jim nodded understandingly, offering a supportive arm to steady her as they walked away from the machine. "Well, if you ever decide to open a museum, you know who to call for the grand tour," he added, trying to keep the mood light as he got ready for his turn.

As Jim settled into the Dream Catcher, the humming began, drawing him back through the corridors of time to his childhood. He was a prodigy, often isolated from his peers and misunderstood by adults. The machine vividly recreated his solitary days, filled with complex equations and science projects that captivated his young mind but also widened the gap between him and other children.

A poignant memory surfaced of a science fair where his advanced project—a detailed model of a solar system with mechanically rotating planets—was admired by adults but alienated him from his peers. This moment underscored the dual nature of his gifts, bringing both recognition and a sense of profound solitude.

The session explored how these experiences shaped his meticulous nature and relentless pursuit of knowledge, as well as his deep-seated need to control his environment, traits that later defined his approach to exploration and crisis management. It showed him navigating unexpected system failures during test flights with calm, methodical problem-solving, highlighting his leadership capabilities.

As the memories continued to unfold, the machine highlighted a transformative phase in Jim's life—his relationship with his niece. After never marrying and dedicating his life to science, Jim found a different kind of fulfilment in his role as an uncle. The Dream Catcher displayed tender scenes of Jim teaching his niece about the stars and the mechanics of flight. Their bond was evident as they launched model rockets in the park and explored planetariums together. These interactions not only enriched Jim's personal life but also softened his approach, making him more empathetic and supportive as a mentor to young scientists and engineers.

Realizing the value of communication and collaboration, influenced by his nurturing relationship with his niece, Jim became a dedicated mentor, ensuring that the young minds under his guidance felt understood and valued—something he longed for in his own youth.

As the memories began to fade and the session concluded, Jim opened his eyes slowly. The wealth of experiences laid bare by the Dream Catcher—from his early years of isolation to his significant contributions to space exploration and the joyous moments with his niece—left him both emotionally drained and profoundly invigorated. Reflecting on the near-forgotten isolation of his childhood, Jim felt a renewed appreciation for the journey he had undertaken. The stark solitude that once defined his early years had been transformed into a life rich with connection and mentorship. His past, filled with challenges and triumphs, reaffirmed his deep-seated commitment to pushing the boundaries of human knowledge and ensuring a supportive environment for the next generation of scientists. This contrast between his solitary beginnings and his current role as a mentor and family anchor emphasised how far he had come, not just professionally but personally, making him cherish his present relationships even more.

As the device powered down, Jim unstrapped and stepped out, his mind still reeling from the intensity of the memories that had surged forth. Sela, waiting quietly outside with Savina, watched him emerge with a mix of concern and admiration.

Sensing the need for a gentle transition back to reality, Savina guided them to the car for the drive home. The journey was quiet, each lost in their own thoughts, but the shared experience of the Dream Catcher hung in the air.

Once they arrived at the house, Jim and Sela walked slowly towards the entrance, the distance from the car to the door offering a moment to start bridging their individual experiences with words.

"That was more intense than I expected," Jim finally broke the silence, his voice reflecting the profound impact of his session.

Sela nodded, understanding exactly what he meant. "It really takes you through the depths," she agreed, her tone equally affected by her own journey through the past.

As they reached the door, Jim turned to Sela with an appreciative look. "I'm glad we can talk about this. It's not easy revisiting some of those moments alone," he said, his voice conveying the value he found in sharing this experience.

"Absolutely, Jim. It's reassuring to know we're in this together," Sela responded warmly.

Without another word, they reached out and hugged each other—a little tighter than usual, a little longer than expected. It was a hug that communicated more than words could; it spoke of shared vulnerability, mutual respect, and a strengthened bond from having navigated the depths of their pasts together.

With a mutual nod of understanding, they entered the house, ready to rejoin the rest of the crew. The session had been intense, but it had also reaffirmed their commitment to supporting each other through the challenges of their mission.

As Jim and Sela entered the house, Will, Jessica, and Richard were waiting in the main living area, their expressions a mixture of anticipation and concern. Jessica was the first to break the silence, her voice tinged with curiosity, "How was it?"

"Intense," they both replied in unison, a slight smile touching their lips despite the weight of their experiences.

All eyes then turned to Richard, who was scheduled to be the next one to undergo a Dream Catcher session. Noticing the apprehensive look on his face, Jim clapped him on the shoulder reassuringly. "Your turn next, Richard. Good luck," he said with a knowing grin. "Prepare to remember some things you hoped you'd forgotten."

Richard nodded, a determined look settling over his features. "Thanks, I think I'll need that luck," he responded, trying to inject a bit of humour into his nerves.

As the laughter and light conversation continued in the living room, Doug and Savina stepped away into the quiet of the adjoining study. The door closed softly behind them, muting the sounds of camaraderie, and the room became a stark contrast of tense silence against the warmth outside.

Savina turned to Doug, her expression serious, the lines of responsibility etched deeply on her face. "You were right to trust them," she began, her voice low but firm. "They are definitely not from our reality, and they all seem to be good people."

Doug nodded, his gaze lingering on the books lined up neatly on the shelf, but his mind was elsewhere. "I thought so, but let's keep our options open until Richard has been through the machine," he replied thoughtfully. "It still could be an elaborate Empire plot. I told you about what happened in California. The Empire has long memories."

Savina considered this, her brows furrowing slightly. "But why would the Director be involved? We're not that important, no matter what you did in California."

"Exactly," Doug replied, the hint of a troubled past flickering across his features. "That's why I want to believe them. Richard's resemblance to the Director is uncanny. If the Director is steering this, it's either a deeper game, or they truly are who they say they are."

"Agreed," she said after a pause. "We'll proceed with caution. Richard's session might tell us more about their intentions and their origins."

Doug's expression softened momentarily, revealing a hint of the internal struggle he faced. "I so want to believe them," he confessed quietly, the sincerity in his voice unmistakable. "But we must be sure."

"Exactly," Savina responded, understanding the complexity of Doug's feelings. "Until then, we continue to observe and act as normal. It's important we don't tip our hand too early."

As they left the study to rejoin the others, their faces were schooled into expressions of neutral friendliness, hiding the weight of their private conversation and the gravity of the decisions that lay ahead.

The next morning, as Savina and a heavily disguised Richard headed off to the clinic for his Dream Catcher session, Will and Jessica quietly observed the subtle shift in the atmosphere back at the house. While there was a mild sense of caution, it was clear that Doug and Savina were hopeful, perhaps even eager to trust them fully.

Over their breakfast, Will and Jessica exchanged thoughtful glances. "They're being cautious, but it's clear they want to believe us," Jessica noted, her voice low but confident.

"Yeah," Will agreed, looking towards where Doug had been standing moments earlier. "It's like they're just double-checking, making sure everything lines up correctly. It's understandable."

As they discussed their situation, they realised their authenticity was under scrutiny, albeit subtly. This wasn't about doubt so much as it was about confirmation, a final step in fully integrating them into their lives.

"They're looking for consistency in our stories," Will added as they cleared the breakfast table. "As long as we remain honest and straightforward, I think we'll pass whatever test this is."

"Exactly," Jessica responded, her spirits lifted slightly by the realisation. "They're on our side, and they're hoping we're on theirs. Let's not give them any reason to think otherwise."

As they prepared for the day, joining the others with a sense of renewed purpose, Will and Jessica felt a quiet confidence. They understood the necessity of the scrutiny but also appreciated that it was rooted in a desire to trust, not to exclude. Ready to confirm their stories and solidify their roles within the team, they looked forward to the positive resolution they believed was imminent.

In Savina's clinic, the Dream Catcher whirred to life. Richard was instantly transported back to the formative yet challenging years of his youth in England. Wrapped in the cool drizzle and grey skies, his school days unfolded before him, revealing a youth marked not only by intellectual curiosity but also by a certain aloofness that others often misinterpreted as arrogance.

Each scene vividly portrayed his struggles with social interactions. He was often misunderstood by his peers, who found his demeanour off-putting—a combination of awkwardness and an unintentional air of superiority. Richard watched his younger self navigate the school corridors, always slightly apart from the groups of laughing students, his attempts at joining in usually faltering amidst their perception of his arrogance.

The machine also brought back memories of the numerous royal functions he was obligated to attend, thanks to his family's connections to the British Royal Family. Here, too, his awkwardness and perceived arrogance made these events challenging. He remembered standing amidst the opulence and formality, feeling both privileged and painfully out of place. While others mingled effortlessly, young Richard found himself more interested in the mechanical workings of the venue—the antique clocks, the hidden service elevators—than in making conversation.

Amidst these social struggles, another memory surfaced: his involvement in acting, specifically Shakespeare. Richard's passion for the Bard's works led him to participate in school plays, where his insistence on perfection often made him unpopular among his peers. He remembered the frustration of rehearsals, where his demanding nature and relentless pursuit of excellence often clashed with the more casual attitudes of his fellow actors. His vision for the perfect performance, while admirable, only further isolated him, casting him as the difficult and overbearing director in their eyes.

However, the session didn't just focus on his social struggles. It also highlighted the pivotal moment when he discovered robotics. This was where Richard truly shone, his passion and innate skill for technology providing a refuge from the isolation he felt elsewhere. The machine recreated the spark of joy in his eyes as he assembled his first robot, a moment when he felt truly in control and valued—a stark contrast to the awkward interactions in his daily school life.

As the narrative progressed, Richard's journey into aviation began to take centre stage. The Dream Catcher vividly reconstructed his training as a helicopter pilot, each session in the cockpit captured with thrilling detail. Flying became his second passion, a skill that not only complemented his technical prowess but also offered him a literal escape from the world below. He remembered the exhilaration of solo flights, the rotor blades cutting through the air, the landscape sprawling endlessly beneath him. This skill set was not just a personal achievement but also a crucial asset in his later work in aerospace and robotics, where understanding the machinery and its navigation in three-dimensional space was invaluable.

The machine also touched upon his brief romantic escapades in places like Tenerife and Ibiza, where his title and perceived status attracted fleeting relationships. However, these encounters never developed into anything substantial, leading Richard to the realisation that they were more attracted to his title than to him. This understanding eventually led him to stop pursuing such relationships, as they added little value to his life.

The narrative then shifted to his later achievements, showing how the once awkward and misunderstood youth transformed into a respected figure in the world of robotics and aviation. While he remained somewhat misunderstood, his significant contributions to the Euro Space Robotics Program earned him a grudging acceptance. Each project he led was a testament to his innovation and determination, pushing the boundaries of what was possible.

As the session drew to a close, Richard felt a complex mix of emotions. The memories, both challenging and triumphant, had painted a full picture of how his early experiences had shaped him. He stepped out of the machine, slightly disoriented but with a renewed understanding of his past, seeing his journey not just as one of privilege but as one marked by the pursuit of excellence and a deep passion for his work.

As his eyes adjusted to the room, he saw Savina standing nearby, a warm smile on her face.

"Well, you're definitely not the Head of Empire Intelligence," she said, relief evident in her tone.

Richard managed a tired smile in return. "I suppose that's good news."

"It is," Savina replied, her eyes reflecting the weight of the confirmation. "It means we can trust you. Let's get back to the others."

Chapter Six

After they had returned to the house, Doug called a meeting with the entire crew. The atmosphere was noticeably focused as they gathered, each member sensing the importance of this meeting for their future interactions and the mission itself.

Doug stood at the head of the room, his expression serious yet relieved. "It all checks out. You are who you say you are, even you, Richard," he announced, his voice steady and clear.

"Was there any doubt?" Will asked, his tone light but with a hint of tension underlying his words.

"We have to be careful," Doug responded, meeting Will's gaze with a frankness that spoke of his responsibilities. "I'm sure you would have done the same in our position."

"Yes, I would," Will conceded, nodding in understanding. The mutual recognition of their respective duties—Will to his crew and Doug to his wife—brought a moment of silent agreement between them. Each understood the weight of the other's commitments, fostering a crucial shared respect as they navigated their intertwined fates on this complex mission.

Stepping forward, Doug extended his hand to Will. It was more than just a formal gesture; it symbolised trust being affirmed. Will grasped his hand firmly, and the two men shared a handshake that cemented the bond they had tentatively built over the last two weeks. As their hands clasped, the last fractions of doubt dissolved, replaced by a mutual respect and a renewed commitment to work together.

"Let's move forward, then," Doug said as they released their handshake, his voice carrying a new warmth.

"With no doubts," Will agreed, his response echoing the sentiment of the entire crew.

Savina addressed the group with a calm, steady voice. "Now that the machine knows you all, it can fully integrate your experiences in the dimension corridor and what you saw, even if you don't register it in your memories," she explained. "It's time to head back to the clinic. We will do it in the same order as before."

Over the next few days, Will, Jessica, Jim, Sela, and Richard were each hooked up to the Dream Catcher again. This time, the machine searched deep into their most recent and elusive memories—their experiences in the mysterious corridor.

Will felt a surge of mixed emotions as forgotten details surfaced. His mind vividly replayed the corridor's immense structure, lined with doors bearing cryptic symbols. Each door seemed to pulsate with an energy that drew the *Stardust* forward, the alien markings shimmering like whispers from the past.

Jessica struggled more; the machine dredged up fears and doubts she had buried, making her sessions emotionally draining. The menacing hiss of the five-headed snakes atop each door echoed in her mind, their eyes seeming to follow her every move within the memory, intensifying her fear. Yet, as the session progressed, her military training kicked in, allowing her to suppress the rising panic. She mentally recited drills and focused on controlled breathing, techniques she had learned to manage stress in high-stakes environments. This discipline helped her navigate through the terrifying memories with a semblance of calm, anchoring her in the face of overwhelming fear.

Jim approached his session analytically, but even he couldn't hide his awe at the vivid recall the machine provoked. He meticulously noted the unique patterns on each door, theorising about their possible meanings and origins, intrigued by the advanced alien technology that seemed both familiar and utterly foreign.

Sela's experience was the most profound. As the Dream Catcher activated, she was instantly submerged in the surreal memory of the corridor. The massive blue figure, which she recognised as reminiscent of Lord Vishnu, was intricately carving symbols on a door. The sight was overwhelming, filling her with a deep spiritual awe. "Holy Vishnu!" she exclaimed within her recalled memory, the connection to her heritage making the experience both majestic and terrifying. The symbols on the doors, now clearly visible, seemed to tell stories of universes beyond her comprehension, each marking a gateway to unknown realms.

Richard was particularly drawn to the five-headed snakes that adorned each door. In his session, he focused intensely on their glistening scales and gleaming eyes. Each head seemed alive, almost sentient, as they hissed in a rhythm that felt like a warning or perhaps a greeting. Richard's fascination mixed with a primal fear, as he pondered the symbolism and power these creatures represented in this alien corridor.

A few days later, they all gathered back in the "War Room". "I've compiled a video combining what we all saw, and it's quite interesting," Jim announced.

"Interesting to you," Sela interjected, her tone laced with unease. "It was a nightmare experience for me."

"And me," Jessica added, her expression troubled.

"Anyway," Jim continued, trying to steer the conversation back to their goal, "from analysing our collective memories from when we switched on the main laser, it's apparent that the X-rays are hitting what I call Element X."

"Element X?" Jessica interrupted, raising an eyebrow.

"I haven't named it yet," Jim said with a slight grin, "and it's better than Borangnium. By hitting it with X-rays, it seems we opened a door into that strange corridor we travelled through."

"Yeah, if I hadn't seen your memories," Doug chimed in, half-joking, "and met all of you, I would've thought it was some B-grade science fiction plot."

"Well, I think if we hit a piece of Borange with another dose of X-rays, we might be able to get home," Jim proposed. "What I'm unsure of is the amount we'd need, though I estimate less than a hundred grams would be enough."

"Is that all?" exclaimed Will. "Why don't we just turn off the sun while we're at it? How can we possibly get to the cometoid? We have no means of returning to space, and even if we did, how could we locate it again?"

"That's not exactly true," Richard interjected, "which brings me to my plan."

"Go on," Will prompted.

"Well, you remember that train thing that brought us back to Earth?" said Richard.

"How could we forget?" replied Sela.

"We call them Space Rockers," Doug explained.

"Yeah, it might be better if you told everyone what they do," suggested Richard.

"Sure," Doug responded. "The Space Rockers are automatic asteroid miners. They head out into the solar system, search for minerals, grab them, and bring them back for analysis."

"Analysis?" inquired Jim.

"Yes," Doug continued. "They remain in orbit in those large carriages your ship travelled in and are later sent down near Alexandria, Egypt, via the Space Elevator built there 40 years ago."

"Space Elevator?" Will interrupted. "I've heard of the concept, but you actually have one? I thought they had to be at the equator."

Doug explained further, "It did have to be built at the equator. Initially, it was constructed in Somalia, then moved by ship through the Red Sea and Suez Mega Complex to near Alexandria."

"Why not leave it where it was built?" asked Will.

Doug answered, "The Empire has a stronghold on Northern Africa but isn't as influential around the Congo. Plus, anything brought down can easily be stored in the desert or shipped through the Suez Canal or the Mediterranean via the port of Casablanca, straight to the Empire Cities in Europe and beyond."

"What exactly is a Space Elevator?" Sela asked.

"It's essentially a massive looped rope made of diamond nanotubes. It begins on Earth and extends over 40,000km to the Queen Charlotte Space Station," Doug detailed.

"That's a ton of diamond," commented Sela.

"It came from one of the Space Rocker runs," Doug continued. "A massive chunk of rock, which was almost completely diamond and of too low a quality for jewellery, revolutionised numerous industries from planetary drilling to building this Space Elevator.

"My guess," Doug surmised, "is that your asteroid was intercepted somewhere between Jupiter and Saturn before the sun's rays struck it. I'm sure we would have heard of an orange-glowing rock heading toward Earth by now. I believe it's been broken up into smaller pieces and brought to Earth, and is stored somewhere in the Egyptian desert at a site called Amonn."

"But wouldn't it be glowing if stored in the desert?" Will wondered.

"No," Doug explained. "All minerals brought to Earth are sealed immediately upon mining and remain so until a thorough bioscan is performed. This process started due to a harmful alien virus that spread across the globe in the '80s. Given the influx of materials, a quarantine station near the Libyan border, Amonn, was established. There's a backlog of about a decade, so I'm confident your rock remains sealed and untouched."

"So, all we need to do," Will began, "is reach Amonn and locate our asteroid."

"That's the gist," Doug said.

"And how do we manage that? It sounds impossible," said Will.

Richard chimed in, "This is the clever part. In this reality, my brother-in-law, Chris Mountbatten, oversees the whole process. And I am the Director of Empire Intelligence."

"You're planning to impersonate the Director of Empire Intelligence? To your own brother-in-law?" Will asked sceptically.

"Yes, that's right," Richard affirmed. "Based on what I've found, he met me only once, during his wedding to my sister."

"Do you even have a sister?" Will asked.

"I'm an only child," Richard admitted.

"That explains a lot," Jessica remarked.

"Okay," said Will. "So we get to the Amonn Quarantine Station, find our asteroid, then what?"

"According to Jim's calculations," Richard explained, "we only need about 100 grams of Borange to create a portal large enough for all of us."

"And how do we return home?" asked Sela.

Richard explained his strategy. "I've analysed the Dream Catcher data and the normal readings from our journey through the corridor. As we entered, there was a symbol above our reality's door. My theory is we find the corresponding door and enter it. This should lead us home."

"What about the potential dangers, like snakes or stray gods?" Will inquired.

"We'll handle them as they come. They didn't seem overly interested in us previously, so I hope it remains that way," Richard replied.

"Well, in terms of plans, I've heard worse," said Will, and smiled. "But what do you think our real chances are?"

"About 25%," Richard admitted, "but think of the advancements we could introduce to Earth if successful, like diamond nanotube technology or a dimension stone."

"The Dimension Stone, I like that," said Sela.

"Better than 'Borange', for sure," laughed Jim.

"There's an issue, though," Richard declared. "Our X-ray laser is too large to transport to Egypt, and even if we managed, we couldn't power it."

"Why not borrow a portable X-ray from a hospital?" Jessica suggested.

"That's not feasible," said Doug. "We haven't used X-ray machines for over 30 years due to the invention of the Neuon

Imager. But parts of the US still use them, as they don't allow the fusion reactors required for imagers."

"What do you propose?" asked Will.

Doug replied, "A small team of Will and Jessica can accompany me to New York City. Savina and I have contacts there, and we should be able to secure a portable X-ray machine. It's essential we move quickly but also cautiously."

"That's a good plan," said Will. "Meanwhile, the rest of us can research the Amonn Station, and Richard can investigate his counterpart. But we need to discuss safety measures as well, given the nature of what we're dealing with."

Jim nodded, picking up on Will's concern. "Absolutely. Remember, thanks to Savina's clinic, we have a bit of an ace up our sleeve. She's integrated a fail-safe mechanism into the Dream Catcher. If any of us are captured, we can trigger it to suppress these memories, making them inaccessible to our captors."

This reassurance seemed to settle some of the tension in the room. "That's a vital safeguard," Richard added, clearly relieved by the additional security measure.

"Sounds good," Jim concluded. "Let's get to work. We have to stay sharp if this is going to succeed."

PART THREE

Chapter Seven

The countryside sped by as Will, Jessica, and Doug travelled from Fort Lauderdale to the US border near Jacksonville on a high-speed train.

"How long again?" Jessica asked Doug, watching the landscape zoom past.

"At 200 mph, just another 20 minutes to the border," Doug replied.

"Then another train to New York?" she continued.

"Yes, but a slower one. It'll take about 14 hours to cover the 930 miles," Doug explained.

"And crossing the border should be smooth?" Jessica persisted.

"Relax, Jess," Will interjected. "It'll be fine."

She glared at Will, but Doug reassured her, "The IDs we've given you are top-notch. You'll both be okay."

She gave Doug a pointed look before returning to the view. Jacksonville's altered skyline was barely recognisable.

"I had an aunt here," mused Will. "It's so different now."

"I wonder about New York," Jessica pondered. "Did they ever build the Twin Towers or the Comcast building?"

"Twin Towers?" Doug echoed; his brow furrowed in genuine confusion. "I can't say I'm familiar with them. Here, the Empire State Building reigns supreme in New York's skyline. Much like how Washington DC's building regulations revolve around the

Washington Monument, New York has its own restriction: No structure is allowed to surpass the height of the Empire State Building."

Will, absorbing this information, mused aloud, "It feels as if architectural and urban development came to a standstill sometime in the early 20th century in this world."

Doug nodded thoughtfully. "You've hit the nail on the head. Their leadership tends to look to the past more than the future. They hate anything that they didn't invent themselves."

"Haters are always gonna hate," Will said with a smirk.

Jessica, catching onto the jest, playfully added, "Might as well shake it off."

Doug threw his head back in laughter, thoroughly enjoying the camaraderie. "I have to say, that's a refreshing way to see things! Haters will always be there, but it's how we deal with them that counts."

As the train slowed, Will reminded them, "Stay calm. We'll be fine."

"Fine, famous last words," Jessica muttered sarcastically.

The three travellers gathered their luggage and stepped off the train, joining the long queue of people waiting to cross into the US. Ahead of them, stretching as far as the eye could see, was a thirty-foot wall reminiscent of China's Great Wall. Intermittent breaks in the wall marked where people queued. Soldiers manned gun posts atop the wall, keeping a watchful eye on all travellers.

"Wow, that's some wall," said Will.

"Yeah," Doug replied, "and we even got them to pay for it."

"Why is it here?" asked Jessica.

Doug explained, "When Florida and the Western States seceded, the government in Washington became paranoid. They thought we'd encourage more states to leave, so up went these walls. The ones near the Western borders are almost twice this height."

"Madness," observed Jessica.

"You're not wrong," Doug agreed.

They inched closer to the front of the queue, where a visibly bored border guard was briskly checking documents. When their turn came, the guard barely glanced at their papers and waved them through, "Welcome to the US."

"That was easy," Jessica remarked as they approached the train station.

****

Meanwhile, back in Florida, Richard and Sela were digging into the Director of the Secret Intelligence Service's background.

"How's it going?" Jim inquired, entering the room.

"He seems a nasty piece of work," said Sela.

"Yeah! I'm a right wanker," Richard joked.

"We already knew that," chuckled Jim.

Richard sighed, his expression a blend of disbelief and dread as he scanned the holo-screens. "In this reality, I'm even worse," he murmured, his voice laden with resignation. "I make competitors vanish or resign in disgrace. According to these holo-screens, I'm unbelievably arrogant."

He paused, his gaze fixating on a particularly chilling detail. "And my favourite method of intimidation? A dentist's chair. It seems this version of me has turned it into a tool for torture.

"Sela, standing beside him, glanced at the screen and then back at Richard, her expression a blend of concern and curiosity. "Do you think you can pull this off? Impersonating him?"

Richard met her gaze, his uncertainty clear. "I'm not sure I can pull off impersonating this version of myself. It's one thing to assume someone's identity, quite another to embody their cruelty."

Richard continued, "In this world, I go by Prince Richard. Admittedly, his connections to the royal family are closer than mine, but he whimsically adopted the title 'Prince' during his youth, wielding it with a mix of disdain and entitlement. It wasn't until Queen Victoria officially recognised it upon his appointment as Director that the title became an official part of his identity."

As he spoke, the gravity of what he needed to mimic weighed heavily on him. To convincingly portray this harsher, more ruthless version of himself, he would have to tap into a part of his psyche he had never willingly explored. The memories of his time in boarding school surfaced—days filled with isolation, mockery, and outright bullying. Each instance where he had felt powerless or humiliated became a thread in the fabric of this cruel persona he needed to weave.

With a resolute nod, he turned back to the holo-screens, his mind working rapidly to formulate a plan. Drawing on those painful memories, he began to construct a façade of arrogance and ruthlessness, channelling the darker emotions he had long suppressed.

"It's unsettling," he admitted to Sela, "to use these memories this way. But perhaps understanding the pain can help me portray him more convincingly."

Sela placed a reassuring hand on his shoulder, offering silent support as Richard prepared to navigate the dangerous waters of his alternate self's brutal reputation.

Jim, sensing the weight of the moment but recognising the urgency of their situation, chimed in. "You have to," he urged. "We can't stay here indefinitely. The longer we wait, the more dangerous it becomes for all of us."

Recognising the need to bolster Richard's confidence, Sela added in a comforting tone, "With the holo-screens, you can learn to emulate him. It's just a role, Richard. Think of it as stepping into a character—use the screens as your script."

Richard nodded, taking a deep breath as he internalised their words. The task was daunting, but the encouragement from his teammates fortified his resolve. He turned back to the holo-screens, ready to study his harsher counterpart's mannerisms and tactics.

The holo-screens were a revolutionary way of watching TV. Characters projected in perfect 3D, viewable from any angle. Currently, they were watching Richard's counterpart give a press conference about the conflict in German Africa.

"See? Stand next to him. Mimic his posture and speech," Sela suggested.

"I don't think I can replicate that sneer," Richard said, a hint of frustration in his voice.

"Practice makes perfect," Jim advised as he left the room and joined Savina in the kitchen.

A short time later, Savina and Jim were discussing the differences between their respective Cubas. After some time, Savina realised Jim's attention was fixed on a 24-hour news feed.

Jim, alarmed by the unfolding news story, said, "I need to gather everyone."

In the holoroom, Richard's frustration was evident as he grappled with the controls. "This isn't working," he said sharply, his voice marked by irritation.

"Don't worry," Sela reassured him, her voice calm and supportive. She moved closer, her presence comforting.

Their eyes met, and a moment of connection formed between them. They gradually leaned in, drawn together by a mutual attraction that was deepening beyond mere physical interest. However, just as their lips were about to meet, Richard hesitated and pulled back.

"Sela, I need to be honest with you," he began earnestly, his gaze fixed on hers. "My time in the Dream Catcher showed me things about myself that I'm not proud of. I've been shallow in the past, and I don't want to just rush into something with you. This time, I think this is real," he added, his voice softening, conveying the depth of his newfound feelings.

Sela listened, her expression one of understanding and appreciation for his candour. "Thank you for sharing that, Richard," she responded warmly. "Let's take things slowly and see where they go."

Grateful for her response, Richard nodded. "I'd like that," he affirmed, feeling a weight lift as he acknowledged his sincere emotions.

Just then, Jim burst into the common area, urgency in every step. Oblivious to the moment he had just interrupted between Sela and Richard, he looked at them with intense focus. "You both need to see this, now," he insisted, gesturing toward the kitchen.

Reluctantly breaking from their task, Richard and Sela exchanged a brief, puzzled glance before setting aside their role-playing and following Jim.

As they entered, Savina resumed a news clip that had been paused on the large screen. The footage showed a young woman being forcibly led away by police at a crowded border checkpoint. Despite the chaos around her, her voice rang out, clear and defiant, shouting for women's rights.

"In our version of the US, women must declare their virginity to qualify for free college education," Savina explained, her voice laced with disapproval as she glanced over at the newcomers.

Jim's attention snapped to the screen, his eyes widening in shock. "That's Josie, my niece!" he exclaimed, pointing at the young woman.

Sela moved closer to the screen, her expression turning serious. "This Josie?" she asked, pausing the footage on the young woman's determined face.

"Yes, but not exactly," Jim said quickly, his mind racing to reconcile the image with his reality. "She looks just like my Josie—same fierce look, same curly hair. But my niece is a biology student, not a protester. She's never faced such draconian measures."

"It's shocking," Savina said, turning to face them all. "Here, this Josie is quite well-known for her activism. It's brave, considering the circumstances."

"Jim stepped closer to Savina; concern etched on his face. "Where are they taking her?" he asked urgently. "What will happen to her?"

Savina leaned against the counter, her arms folded, her expression grim. "Florida has an intricate legal arrangement with the US government. Due to certain agreements and loopholes, prisoners—especially political detainees from border protests—often end up transferred to Florida facilities. It's a way to move high-profile detainees away from the public eye."

Jim's eyes searched Savina's face. "Is there any way we can help her? Get her out of there?"

She sighed softly. "It won't be easy. The facilities are heavily guarded, and the legal systems are convoluted. But perhaps with the right connections and a solid plan, there might be a chance.".

Savina moved toward the computer. "I'll see what I can find out," she promised, starting to type rapidly.

Watching the frozen image of Josie on the screen, Jim's determination solidified. "We need to help her."

"But there's only three of us," Sela pointed out, sceptical of their odds against a whole government.

"Four," Savina corrected firmly, meeting Jim's determined gaze.

Richard added with confidence, "And one of us is the Director of Empire Intelligence. We'll find a way."

Grateful for the support, Jim asked Savina, "Would your Cuban contacts help?"

"Absolutely," she affirmed. "We have a vast network. They'll be crucial. We all share your niece's commitment to fighting these extreme human rights violations. Let me see what I can do." She glanced at Richard, a stern look in her eyes. "You keep practising. You need to be perfect if we're going to pull this off."

Chapter Eight

"Back in the US, Jim, Jessica, and Doug were on the Silver Comet, heading to New York.

As their journey took them through Charlotte and subsequently Raleigh, Jessica gazed out at the familiar landmarks that seemed tinged with an uncanny alteration. "These cities," she mused, "I've spent so much time in both. The familiarity is there, yet there's an undercurrent that makes them feel alien in this world."

Will nodded, his gaze darting to a propaganda billboard they just passed. "There are strong echoes of our old Soviet Union here," he remarked. "But there's a twist. The slogans— they push the 'work hard' ethos but paired with an appeal to 'trust in God.' It's an intriguing mix."

Jessica, seeking some clarity, turned her attention to Doug. "There's a noticeable sense of paranoia in the air. What shaped this world's psychology?"

Doug took a deep breath, considering his words carefully. "From my understanding, our world took a divergent path from yours when Jerusalem was designated as an international city. The US never agreed with having to share Jerusalem with the Muslims from the Arab Federation."

Jessica's brows furrowed in confusion. "An international Jerusalem? What became of Israel in this reality?"

Doug looked slightly puzzled. "Israel? I'm unfamiliar with that term. Jerusalem was historically a significant part of Palestine. Following the dissolution of the Ottoman Empire, it was agreed that both Jerusalem and the Vatican would be international territories. They fell under the jurisdiction of the League of Nations, with Berlin and London overseeing their administration. The surrounding territories remained within the scope of the British Empire."

Will leaned in, intrigued and somewhat disturbed by this alternate history lesson. "In the reality we come from," he began, "Jerusalem's status is quite different. The Vatican indeed became an independent city-state. However, after World War II and the horrors the Nazis inflicted on the Jews during the 1940s, the Jewish people were granted their ancestral homeland, Israel, with Jerusalem as its heart."

"World War II?" exclaimed Doug. "And that's after you had a first world war? It all sounds terrible. Maybe the Empire was the best thing that happened in our world."

"You might be right," Will concurred. "World Wars I and II killed over sixty million people."

"That's barbaric," Doug stated.

"And then," Will continued, "after World War II, we spent the next 50 years building bigger and faster nuclear missiles and aiming them at each other."

"We've had a bit of that here," Doug admitted, "but the threat of the Empire's Space Cannons typically deterred most."

During their long journey, they began chatting with the couple across the carriage, who introduced themselves as Brandon and Marie, Australian missionaries travelling to Washington DC for a Catholic Talkfest. They hoped to get commitment from the US Church and government for an expansion of their mission in Ammon, Egypt.

Hearing the word "Ammon" immediately piqued the travellers' interest.

"Why would you establish a mission there?" asked Jessica.

"It's an odd story," said Marie. "Twenty years ago, the tomb of Alexander the Great was discovered just outside of Ammon near the Libyan and Egyptian border."

"Yes, I remember," Doug chimed in. "It caused quite a stir."

Marie continued, "Interestingly when they opened it, his body wasn't there. This absence has fuelled all sorts of wild speculation and led to the emergence of several unconventional religions. Some now believe Alexander was not just the son of Zeus but that he ascended to immortality and still influences the world. These groups are spreading their, let's say, unique views worldwide. The Catholic Church wants a presence at the oasis to counter some of these more distorted beliefs.

"What chance do you think you have of persuading the US to support this?" Doug asked.

"Not much," Brandon admitted, "but we're obligated to try."

As the train travelled further north, more passengers boarded. A young couple, accompanied by a man who appeared to be the woman's brother, sat across from the trio.

Conversation flowed until one of the men mentioned he was from Virginia.

"Virginia!" Jessica exclaimed. "That's where I'm from!"

"Oh, which part?" he inquired politely.

"Williamsburg," Jessica declared, "Go Griffins!"

The man's demeanour changed instantly. "What did you say?"

Jessica caught Doug's urgent gestures out of the corner of her eye but replied, "Williamsburg."

"So you're one of those Empire-loving pricks who still use that name," the man spat, fury evident. "I'm disgusted to share this carriage with you. Hey, everyone! This woman claims she's from Williamsburg!"

The entire carriage turned their attention to them.

"Now look," Doug interjected, standing up. "She didn't mean anything."

"It hasn't been called Williamsburg since that despicable King William bombed Atlanta in 1948," the man seethed. "Call it Patriotville, like the rest of us."

As the tension escalated, Will confronted the man. "Just calm down, buddy. She meant no harm."

"Don't call me 'buddy'," the man growled, shoving Will.

"How should I address you then?" Will retorted, clearly trying to de-escalate the situation.

The man suddenly lunged at Will, who, with a fighter's reflex, dodged smoothly, letting the attacker stumble past. Will then pivoted to face him again, hands raised in a practised defensive stance. Noticing movement from the corner of his eye, Will saw another group of men rising from their seats, their intentions clear.

As the train slowed, nearing Main Street Station, a large man charged towards Will with raised fists. Will ducked under a wild swing, countered with a swift uppercut to the attacker's midsection, followed by a quick jab to the chin, sending the man reeling backward into his accomplices.

Two more men lunged at Will. He sidestepped, grabbed one by the arm, and used the momentum to throw him down the aisle. The other attacker swung wildly, but Will blocked the punch and delivered a powerful hook to the man's temple, knocking him out cold.

The carriage descended into chaos, bystanders shrieking and scrambling away from the unfolding melee. Amidst the chaos, Marie and Brandon acted quickly, forming a protective circle around Jessica. They moved her skilfully towards the back of the carriage, weaving through the panicked crowd.

Will braced himself again as more of the attackers closed in. He relied on the reflexes honed in countless sparring sessions, his body reacting almost independently of thought. Each movement was precise, and each block and counterattack were a testament to his training.

In the melee, Doug was wrestling with another of the attackers. He had the man in a bear hug, his arms locked tightly around him. The man struggled, his movements becoming more desperate as Doug's grip tightened, methodically squeezing the resistance out of him.

Meanwhile, Will was suddenly overwhelmed as two more men joined the fight. They threw themselves at him with reckless abandon, forcing him to the ground. The carriage rocked as the train pulled into Richmond station, the opening doors revealing the busy platform.

Quickly seizing the opportunity, Brandon and Marie ushered Jessica off the train. Just then, two guards appeared. They were armed with guns similar to the one Doug had aimed at Richard previously. In an instant, the situation shifted dramatically. Both Will and Doug found themselves on the ground, the guards' weapons proving to be stunningly effective. The other assailants were also incapacitated; the carriage, now filled with the stunned silence of a conflict abruptly quelled.

Hours later, Will awoke in a jail cell with a massive headache. Doug lay beside him, and there was no sign of Jessica.

Doug groaned as he awoke, and Will immediately asked, "What did those guards hit us with?"

"They are called stunners," replied Doug, rubbing his head. "They shoot bolts of kappa rays that overload the central nervous system. A mild dose can leave one dazed, but we received a higher dose that knocked us unconscious."

"So where are we?" asked Will.

"I'm guessing Richmond Police Station. We'll probably be held overnight and charged tomorrow."

As they were talking, a policeman appeared at the cell door. "Gentlemen," he said, his tone formal, "since there's no judge available over the weekend, you'll be spending two nights in the cells. We'll sort everything out Monday morning."

Will and Doug exchanged a resigned look, then simultaneously let out a frustrated groan, their dismay echoing off the cold cell walls.

"I wonder where Jess is," said Will.

"I saw Marie and Brandon get her off the train unharmed, so I'm sure she's fine. There's nothing we can do while locked up here, so we'll have to wait and play it by ear. Our documentation should withstand all but a deep investigation."

****

Meanwhile, as Will and Doug lamented their situation, Jessica found herself in a far different scenario. As the train doors slid open, chaos erupted in the carriage. The station platform loomed, a blur of movement and noise, but Marie's voice was clear and focused. "This way, quickly!" she urged, guiding Jessica with a firm hand.

Brandon, right behind them, glanced over his shoulder, keeping an eye on the escalating fight. He reached back to Jessica, pulling her safely out of the train car as the doors began to close behind them. The trio moved swiftly through the crowd, the sounds of the conflict fading into the background.

Once they had put some distance between themselves and the train, they slowed, finding a quiet corner of the busy station. Marie looked at Jessica with concern. "Are you alright?" she asked.

Jessica nodded, still catching her breath. "Yes, thanks to you both. I can't thank you enough for what you've done."

From a distance, they could see local police dragging Doug, Will, and several others caught up in the scuffle, presumably taking them to the local Richmond police station.

"It was nothing. We couldn't just stand by," Brandon responded, his expression serious. "But we need to understand what just happened back there. Who were those men, and why did they attack you?"

Jessica sighed, the gravity of the situation settling in. She knew she had to trust someone, and after their actions, it seemed Brandon and Marie were her best bet. "It's going to sound unbelievable," she started, her voice hesitant.

"We're used to unbelievable," Marie said with a small, encouraging smile.

Taking a deep breath, Jessica began to explain. "I'm not from this world. I mean, I am from here, but not... this version of here. I come from a place where history took a different path—the name Williamsburg, it's from my world, and not a slur there. Those men were angered by a history they understood, one that doesn't match my own."

Brandon and Marie exchanged a look, a mix of scepticism and intrigue on their faces.

"Let's get out of here and discuss this further," Brandon suggested.

They checked into a small, inconspicuous hotel on the outskirts of the city, far enough from the chaos but close enough to remain connected to the police station where they assumed Doug and Will were being taken.

Once settled into the relative safety of their hotel lounge, Jessica began to open up about her journey and the challenges she faced, her hands moving animatedly as she spoke. The light caught the ring on her finger, drawing Brandon's attention.

"That's a remarkable stone," Brandon remarked, curiosity piqued. "I was an opal miner in Australia for years, and I've never seen anything like it. What is it?"

Jessica smiled slightly, watching his reaction. "It's called Tanzanite. My grandfather mined it and gave it to my grandmother. It's common in my world, but here..." She paused, looking down at the stone, "I guess it's not something you recognise?"

Brandon shook his head, intrigued. "No, I've dealt with a wide variety of gemstones, but I've never come across this Tanzanite. If it's unknown here, its value could be quite significant."

Feeling the weight of Brandon's words, Jessica began to consider the practicalities. "As much as this is part of my family history," she sighed, twisting the ring around her finger thoughtfully, "it might be best if we find it a new owner." Her gestures punctuated her words, adding a layer of emotion to the discussion. "It's clear that it's valuable, and right now, we could really use more resources."

Brandon mulled this over, the gears turning in his head. "Let me make a few calls. I know a couple of collectors who go crazy for undiscovered or unique pieces. They pay top dollar for the privilege of being the first to showcase a new gem."

"Thank you, Brandon," Jessica said, her hands finally stilling as she placed them in her lap, feeling a mix of relief and resignation. "This could really help us move forward with our plans."

Brandon gave her an encouraging nod, already reaching for his phone. "Let's see what we can do. This ring might just be the breakthrough you need."

The next morning, after a brief period of rest and planning, Brandon made a few discreet calls. His contacts were extensive, but he knew exactly who would be most interested in such a unique find. After explaining the potential significance of the Tanzanite ring, he arranged a meeting with a collector renowned for his passion for rare gemstones and artifacts. The collector was intrigued enough to agree to travel immediately from his Washington home for this opportunity, emphasising the importance and rarity of the occasion.

Just a few hours later, the collector, a middle-aged man with a keen eye for detail, examined the ring closely under a magnifier. His interest was piqued, and after a brief negotiation, a deal was struck. The sale provided Jessica with much-needed funds, which she knew would be crucial in the future.

With the ring sold and the newfound funds at her disposal, Jessica decided it was time to prepare herself not just mentally but also physically for the challenge ahead. She headed to a boutique known for its sophisticated and authoritative business attire. There, she selected a sleek dress suit that balanced professionalism with a commanding presence necessary for her next role.

As she left the boutique, a quaint antique store caught her eye. Intrigued, she decided to take a brief detour. Inside, amidst the myriad of nostalgic items, a particular piece stood out—an old digital camera, strikingly similar to one she had owned back home. The sight of it was unexpectedly comforting, a poignant reminder of home. She picked it up, feeling the familiar weight and the worn buttons under her fingers. On impulse, she purchased the camera, thinking it might serve as a useful tool or simply as a keepsake from a past that felt both distant and dear.

Feeling a mix of nostalgia and renewed purpose, Jessica continued her preparations. She returned to the hotel to say her goodbyes to Brandon and Marie. She found them in the lounge, their conversation pausing as she approached.

"I just wanted to say goodbye and thank you," Jessica began, adjusting the lapel of her new suit. "I wouldn't have made it this far without your help."

Brandon stood, offering a reassuring smile. "We're glad we could assist. Remember, if your travels take you to Ammon, come find us at the old Catholic mission. It's well-known around there."

Marie added warmly, "You're always welcome, Jessica. Maybe our paths will cross again someday."

After a heartfelt hug with each of them, Jessica stepped back, adjusting her new suit. "I hope they do," she replied. "Take care, both of you."

Leaving the hotel behind, Jessica headed to the courthouse with determination. She planned to pose as Will and Doug's lawyer, a daring strategy. Her only preparation was the legal knowledge gleaned from years of watching her father, an accomplished criminal lawyer, work and absorbing countless legal dramas on TV. The courthouse, an imposing structure of stone and glass, symbolised the law and order she now had to navigate.

As she approached, Jessica focused intently on her mission, her confidence bolstered by her remembered knowledge of pertinent legal terms and processes. Her new suit added an extra layer of authenticity, reinforcing her confidence as she prepared to embrace the role she had concocted.

Once inside, she moved through the bustling corridors with purpose, mentally rehearsing potential arguments and legal jargon. Upon reaching the courtroom, Jessica paused, taking a deep breath to steady her nerves. Pushing the doors open, she stepped in, ready to undertake the legal challenge ahead. Her resolve was unshakeable: she was determined to secure her friends' release, no matter the risk.

Chapter Nine

Back in Florida, Richard was still in the holo-room practising being "Evil Richard," as the group had started to call him.

"It's coming along really well," said Sela.

"Yes," said Savina, "you're even starting to scare me!"

Richard finished the speech he was working on, a particularly disturbing media conference where Prince Richard was explaining the apparent deliberate targeting of civilians during a conflict in British Congo.

"This is horrific," said Richard. "And he genuinely seems to enjoy delivering such terrible news."

"Are we closer to a plan?" asked Jim. "Time is ticking. We need to act before she goes to trial, or it'll be too late."

"Agreed," said Savina. "I think the best plan is the simplest. We show up at the Detention Centre in Jacksonville, which is essentially a glorified police station, and Richard marches in, demanding to see the prisoners under the pretence of Empire security or some such. Then we walk out with her."

"OK," said Sela, "but what if she won't come? I mean, would you agree to leave with the Director of Empire Intelligence?"

"That's where I come in," said Jim. "I'll have to convince her that her uncle has come to rescue her."

"But does she know you well in this world?" asked Sela.

"Good point," said Jim. "We'll have to hope so."

"There's too much 'hope' in this plan for my liking," said Savina.

"I think it will work," continued Richard. "From what I've observed of Evil Richard over the past few days, he generally does as he pleases, and nobody seems to challenge him."

"Do we have everything we need?" asked Jim.

"Yes. Richard's uniform is ready. We have a car prepared for the four hour drive; all we need is a go-ahead."

"Well, it's a go from me," said Jim.

"And me," said Sela.

"I'm as ready as I'll ever be," said Richard. "So, it's a go from me too."

"Well then, we leave at 8 am tomorrow. We should be at the detention centre by midday, which is a good time to arrive since the shift ends at 1 pm, and the guards should be most relaxed."

"I'll practice a bit more with the uniform," he said, his voice betraying a hint of self-consciousness.

Sela, who had been watching him with a gentle amusement dancing in her eyes, took a few steps closer. "Need some help with that?" she asked, her voice teasing yet tender. The corner of her mouth lifted in a half-smile, her eyes reflecting the soft light of the room.

Richard looked up, a playful challenge in his eyes. "Are you offering, or do you just want to see me fumble around some more?"

Sela's laughter, rich and melodic, filled the room. "A little bit of both," she admitted, her gaze softening. "But mainly, I'd like to be of help."

As they shared a lingering, charged moment, Jim and Savina caught onto the unmistakable chemistry building between the pair. Their exchanged glances were a silent conversation, a mix of surprise and approval.

Savina smirked. "Well, we'll leave you two to... 'practice'," she teased.

Suppressing a grin, Jim added, "Don't stay up too late. We've got a big day tomorrow."

As they exited, the room seemed to grow quieter, the outside world momentarily forgotten. Richard and Sela stood closer now, the atmosphere thick with anticipation.

"Guess it's just you, me, and this troublesome uniform," Richard whispered, the gravity of their closeness causing his heart to race.

Sela nodded, her fingers lightly touching the fabric of the uniform, and by extension, Richard's chest. "Let's figure it out together," she murmured, her eyes never leaving his.

****

Meanwhile in Richmond, Will remarked, "They sure are taking their sweet time," while staring at the seemingly slow-moving clock outside the cell he and Doug were in.

As hours passed, the monotony was interrupted by clanging. The ancient cell door creaked open, revealing a hallway with several rooms branching off.

A guard appeared and announced, "Your lawyer's here. Go to Room C."

Both men rose and made their way to Room C. To their surprise, Jessica awaited them, smartly dressed in a suit and holding a briefcase.

"Close the door behind you," she whispered. "I've only got ten minutes."

"How did you get here? And in that?" Will gestured to her suit.

"While the guards were busy tasing you two," Jessica began.

"They're called stunners," Doug interjected.

"Okay, 'stunning' you two," she corrected. "Brandon and Marie got me out in the confusion. And I've watched enough legal dramas on TV to know how to pass as a lawyer."

"And the suit?" asked Will. "How did we afford it?"

"What do you mean by 'we'?" Jessica replied, slightly irked. "Do you know that ring I always wear?"

"You mean the one passed down from your grandmother?" Will responded.

"Yes, that one," Jessica said, wiggling her fingers to show its absence. "The stone in it is called Tanzanite, which my grandfather found in Tanzania in the late 1960s. That valley hasn't been mined in this world, so it fetched a handsome price. Plus, I pointed the collector to the exact location in Tanzania where he could find more."

"So, what's next?" asked Will, feeling a bit guilty about her sacrifice.

"Okay, so my entire legal know-how comes from watching my father work and binge-watching old TV shows like *Law and Order*," Jessica whispered to Will, her tone a mix of embarrassment and resolve. "But that means I've got the basics down: plead not guilty, argue for bail, then use that freedom to plan our next move."

Will chuckled quietly, appreciating her resourcefulness. "It's better than nothing. Let's hope our fake IDs hold up long enough for us to make a break for it."

Doug, overhearing them, was bewildered. "Wait, are you telling me our defence strategy is based on a TV show?"

"Not just any show," Jessica replied confidently, louder this time so Doug could hear. "Top-tier legal dramas—they consult real lawyers, you know. Plus, it's not like we're flush with options here."

Doug sighed, a blend of resignation and incredulity colouring his expression. "I can't believe this is happening. Alright, let's hear this TV-inspired legal strategy of yours."

"Unfortunately, you're going to have to spend another night in the cells; our court date is tomorrow at ten," Jessica informed Will and Doug, her tone apologetic.

Will, sensing Jessica's tension, cracked a smile and said, "Don't worry, Jess, at least I can look forward to another gourmet dinner. I'm hoping for more of that delightful green swill they serve here at the 'Hilton Richmond'."

After leaving the police station, Jessica returned to the hotel, knowing that Brandon and Marie had already resumed their journey to New York. This left her alone with her thoughts, the weight of tomorrow's responsibility pressing heavily upon her.

The following day at 10 AM, Jessica entered the courtroom, her heart rate increasing as she saw Will and Doug being led from the cells. She gave them an encouraging nod, trying to mask her own anxiety. As they took their seats, the reality of their precarious situation hit her with full force.

Armed with nothing but her wits and a crash course in legal proceedings gleaned from television shows, Jessica was about to defend Doug and Will before a real judge. Despite her makeshift preparation, she felt a surge of determination. "Your Honour, my clients plead not guilty," Jessica began, her voice steady despite her inner turmoil. Doug glanced at Will, his face etched with worry and confusion as he tried to grasp the TV show angle that only Will fully appreciated.

The judge peered down at them, his gaze lingering on Jessica. "And on what basis does your defence make this plea?"

Drawing a deep breath, Jessica pieced together her response, pulling from various scenes and arguments she remembered from her favourite episodes. "We believe that when the facts are fully presented, the evidence will show that my client's actions don't warrant the charges against them."

Doug, hearing Jessica's legal rationale for the first time, was taken aback by her confidence. Despite his doubts, he found himself impressed by her ability to construct a coherent defence from fragments of fictional courtroom battles.

The prosecutor eyed Jessica sceptically, ready to dismantle her arguments. Yet, she held her ground, requesting bail with a persuasive mix of earnestness and rehearsed legal jargon.

To everyone's surprise, the judge had no issue granting bail, albeit with a stern warning about the seriousness of the charges and the consequences of failing to comply with court orders.

As they exited the courtroom, Doug shook his head, still processing the surreal strategy session and their even more improbable courtroom success. "I'll never doubt the power of a good TV show again," he muttered, half in jest, half in awe.

Jessica, Will, and Doug exchanged a look of relief and tentative hope. They had cleared the first hurdle, thanks largely to Jessica's unconventional preparation. Now, with a bit of borrowed time, they were ready to skip bail and tackle the challenges that lay ahead. With their false identities just robust enough to get them out of immediate trouble, they headed to a bustling train station, boarding a New York-bound train.

Trying to lighten the mood, Jessica quipped, "I think I'll play mute this time around."

"We can't blame you," Doug and Will responded in harmony.

"This world is perplexing," Jessica mused. "So much feels familiar, yet it's all so different."

"We should be cautious about our public discussions concerning this world," Will added, gazing out of the window. Turning to Doug, he continued, "By jumping bail we're now on a tight schedule – less than five days to reach New York, liaise with your contacts, acquire a portable X-ray, and then dash back to Florida. What do we do once we're in New York?"

"Our primary destination is an establishment in Chelsea, Manhattan Island," Doug responded. "I have some allies there. We'll strategize further after the meet."

As the train journeyed on, it briefly halted in Washington, D.C., with many travellers disembarking. As they ventured further, the train began filling with passengers who appeared to have stepped out of a scene from *The Godfather*.

Doug, sensing his companions' intrigue, explained, "The Italian population in the US is significant, especially in New York. After Mussolini's downfall post-1950, many migrated here. Just another leader," he added, "who dared challenge the Empire and failed."

Eventually, Penn Station loomed, and the trio disembarked, blending into the throngs on 7th Avenue.

"We can either walk or grab a taxi to Chelsea. Your choice," Doug offered.

Will, cautious as ever, asked, "Is it safe to walk?"

"As safe as anywhere else in this city," Doug affirmed.

"Then let's walk," Jessica decided, her eyes sparkling with curiosity. She was keen to immerse herself in this familiar but alien city's ambience.

They made their way to 5th Avenue and headed toward Chelsea. Having lived in New York for significant portions of their lives, Will and Jessica couldn't help but admire the view. Jessica, in particular, was in her element. The antique camera she had purchased was a flurry of activity, capturing the unique juxtapositions that New York City offered. She was particularly fascinated by anything that stood out as different or unusual, her lens eagerly focusing on scenes that captured the essence of the city's evolution.

Dominating the skyline, as always, was the iconic Empire State Building. It stood tall and proud, a steadfast sentinel amidst the city's constant flux. To Will and Jessica, it looked exactly as they remembered, a comforting constant in the sea of change.

They continued their stroll down 5th Avenue and passed the distinctive Flatiron Building. Its unique triangular shape and historical significance made it an enduring symbol of the city's architectural heritage.

"Most of the buildings look so different, and yet certain ones are exactly the same," commented Jessica, her camera clicking almost continuously.

They headed downtown until they reached 17th Street, where they spotted a drugstore. All three of them entered and Doug proceeded to the side of the shop, where he knocked rhythmically on a small door: knock... Knock-a-knock... knock. After a brief pause, the door opened, and a man resembling a small mountain gestured for them to enter.

"Shave and a haircut," Will murmured.

"Two bits," Jessica added, grinning.

"What are you two going on about?" Doug asked.

"Just a little other-Earth joke," Will replied.

"Well, don't," Doug said, slightly annoyed. "We don't want any repeat Patriotville incidents."

Inside, they found themselves in a large, windowless room exuding a Roaring '20s ambience adorned with Chesterfield furniture and old-fashioned wall hangings. The "bar" more closely resembled a kitchen, with countertops laden with stacks of cups and saucers.

A waitress guided them to several stylish chairs around a coffee table and inquired about their tea preferences.

"I'll handle this," Doug assured the others. "Leave it to me. I know what you like."

Turning to the waitress, he ordered, "One Rickey and two Old Fashioneds, please." Will and Jessica gave Doug a puzzled look but remained silent.

Soon, their drinks arrived in three teacups: gin for Jessica and whiskey for both Doug and Will.

"I've never had gin from a teacup before," remarked Jessica, bemused.

"They serve it this way so that if there's a raid, we can all claim we were merely drinking tea," Doug explained.

After two rounds of "tea," Phil and Tony, Doug's old acquaintances from his time in Cuba, joined them. Doug laid out their cover story: They operate a clinic in Cuba and require an X-ray machine since their only one has malfunctioned. The

Florida government mandates that all medical equipment be purchased through official channels, which charge exorbitant prices.

"So, by helping you, we'd be pissing off both Florida and the US?" Tony questioned.

"Exactly," Doug confirmed, his face set in a serious expression.

Phil chuckled heartily. "Sounds like our kind of challenge. Count us in."

Tony's expression then shifted to a more serious tone. "That leads us to the matter of payment," he began, his gaze fixed on Doug. "You know we normally go for the high-quality rum you bring in from Cuba. But my cousins run into trouble—too much heat from the Feds and an oversupply of product. We need something different this time."

Doug furrowed his brow, a flicker of suspicion crossing his features. "Tony, after everything we've been through, you're telling me you can't make an exception? Feels like you might be using the situation to push for more."

Tony held up his hands, his expression earnest yet firm. "Doug, I value our history, truly, but my hands are tied here. With the feds cracking down, moving booze is risky, and it's not just about preference—it's about practicality."

As the tension in the room mounted, Jessica intervened, sensing the need to smooth things over. "Hold on," she said, reaching for her briefcase. With a click, she opened it and revealed its contents.

Tony leaned forward, eyeing the briefcase. "How much cash is in there?"

Jessica displayed at least $30,000 in neatly stacked $100 bills. "Will this suffice?" she asked, hopeful yet firm.

Tony inspected the cash and then looked back at Doug, his expression softening. "This should cover it," he confirmed with a nod, a sense of relief washing over him. "Let's plan to meet here again around midday tomorrow. We'll sort everything out then."

"How large is a portable X-ray?" Will queried.

"Roughly the dimensions of a standard suitcase," Tony replied, "though substantially heavier. There are smaller handheld models, but they're only for hands and feet. The power Doug specified necessitates a heftier device."

"Yes, it needs to be a minimum of 32 kW," Doug added.

"That won't pose a challenge," Tony assured. "My cousin has an ample supply. Might we also interest you in any other apparatus your clinic could use?"

"Let's start with the X-ray machine," Doug suggested cautiously, "and later, we can discuss potential further transactions."

Tony and Phil finished their tea and then stood up. "See you here tomorrow, midday," Tony said as they both exited the bar.

"Well, that went better than I expected," Doug remarked. "Let's keep a low profile for now and return tomorrow."

Chapter Ten

As they approached the Detention Centre in Jacksonville, the tension in the car increased. Sela glanced at Richard; her expression filled with concern. "Are we sure this is the best way? Impersonating someone this dangerous..."

Richard met her gaze in the rearview mirror, a smirk playing at the edges of his lips. "I know we've practised this, but now that we're here, trust me, I've got this," he assured her confidently.

"Showtime," Sela declared with a resigned sigh, trying to gather her courage.

"Good luck, everyone," Savina added from the driver's seat. "Let's keep it simple and get out as quickly as possible."

The car inched forward, coming to a stop at a manned barrier. The guard, looking somewhat disinterested, leaned towards the driver's window. "Purpose of your visit?" he began but was cut off as Richard rolled down his window.

Staring at the guard with a defiant glare, Richard commanded, "Let us in," he paused for emphasis, his voice dropping to a menacing whisper, "NOW."

The guard blinked, taken aback by the intensity of the demand. "Uh, yes, immediately, sir," he stammered, fumbling to raise the barrier.

"That was easier than anticipated," Savina murmured as they drove towards the parking area.

"Now for the next step," Richard noted, his eyes scanning the surroundings as they parked near the holding cells.

"These people are terrified of you," Savina reminded him, adjusting her rearview mirror. "Maintain this attitude, and all will go smoothly."

As they exited the car, a group of officers emerged from the main entrance. One of them, a man with a rigid military posture, hurried over. "Sir! We weren't expecting you," he exclaimed, saluting sharply. "I am Captain Derarant. How can we assist you?"

"Captain, there's a prisoner here from the US protest named Josie Washington. I need to see her. She holds critical information for an investigation I'm leading."

"Of course, right away, sir!" the Captain responded, instructing an aide to bring her to Interrogation Room 3.

"Ensure all cameras and microphones are disabled," Richard added nonchalantly.

"Certainly, sir. Please, follow me."

Soon, they stood outside Interrogation Room 3. "Thank you, Captain," Richard said. "You may leave us."

"One more thing," the Captain interrupted. "Will you depart in the same vehicle or should we prepare the RAM Jet?"

Richard exchanged a puzzled glance with Savina before she swiftly interjected, "Prepare the jet. We'll head to London after our chat."

"As you wish." Captain Derarant nodded, departing.

"Savina," Jim began, "go in first. Check the cameras are disabled, as we can't predict Josie's reaction."

She nodded, entering a room where a young woman in her early twenties sat, looking terrified. With brown hair and eyes, she bore a striking resemblance to Jim, particularly in their shared nose and jaw structure.

"What do you want?" Josie whispered nervously.

"Just a moment," Savina replied, pausing to ensure the camera was disabled. She reached behind it and unplugged the cable, just to be safe.

"Who are you?" Josie asked, her voice laced with confusion. "Why am I here? I only protested for women's rights. I know nothing..."

Interrupting, Savina comforted her, "Don't be scared. There's a bizarre tale to be shared. Perhaps I'm not the one to narrate." She opened the door for Jim.

Upon seeing him, Josie's eyes widened. "Who are you? It's impossible! Who are all of you?"

"Relax, Josie," Jim comforted. "I can clarify, but why do you think it's impossible? I'm your Uncle Jim."

"But... you died a decade ago. I attended the funeral," Josie stammered.

"I did?" Jim wondered.

Savina interjected, "That's where the strange story I mentioned begins. This Jim is still your uncle, but from another Earth."

"Another Earth?" Josie asked. "How can that be?"

"It's too complicated to explain right now," Savina continued, "but did you trust your uncle?"

"Yes!" Josie responded without hesitation.

"Then trust him now because we intend to get you out of here," assured Savina.

"Get me out? I thought I was doomed, given they were preparing to throw the book at me," Josie replied, her voice tinged with a mix of hope and disbelief.

Smiling, Savina said, "We have an ace up our sleeve." She then opened the door, letting Richard and Sela in.

"Oh my god!" Josie exclaimed, her hand flying to cover her mouth as her eyes widened in sheer terror upon seeing the notorious head of Empire Intelligence. His name alone evoked a wave of fear across the planet, synonymous with ruthless suppression and cold efficiency.

Seeing her reaction, Richard's eyes briefly softened, betraying a hint of regret or perhaps understanding of the fear his reputation inspired.

"Don't be afraid. He's from the same place as your uncle and isn't who he appears to be," Savina quickly interjected, her tone urgent yet reassuring. She stepped slightly in front of Josie as if to shield her from Richard's imposing presence.

Josie's heart pounded fiercely in her chest as she tried to process the contradiction in front of her. The man she knew from holo-reports and whispered stories was now her potential rescuer? It was almost too much to comprehend.

"Now, it's time for us to depart," Savina declared, breaking through the heavy silence that had fallen.

"Right," Richard agreed, his voice firm, reclaiming the authority he was known for. "Time for my performance. Jim, fetch Captain Derarant."

As Jim hurried out, the tension in the room spiked.

Turning back to Josie, Richard's expression was all business. "Can you appear as terrified as possible? Your reaction upon seeing me earlier was spot on."

"That won't be difficult," Josie admitted, her voice a faint echo of her inner turmoil. Despite Savina's assurances, the shadow of Richard's fearsome reputation loomed large in her mind.

The wait for the Captain was fraught with silent anticipation, each heartbeat echoing in the tense air. Richard, standing with the calm certainty of command, prepared to face the Captain and reshape Josie's fate.

The atmosphere was tense as the Captain approached. Richard, exuding an air of command, addressed him firmly. "This prisoner is crucial to our understanding of the global resistance. I'm taking her with me for interrogation."

The Captain, caught slightly off-guard, quickly recovered. "Of course, sir! Immediately, sir!"

Richard, keen to expedite their departure, inquired, "Is my RAM Jet ready?"

"It's prepared and waiting, sir," the Captain affirmed promptly.

"Excellent. Lead on," Richard commanded, his voice leaving no room for dissent.

They arrived at the hangar housing the RAM Jet, a sleek, teardrop-shaped vessel with ample room for a sizable crew. The Captain gestured towards a young officer, clearly nervous, introduced as their pilot.

Richard waved him off casually. "No need. I'll take the helm."

A moment of hesitation passed before the Captain voiced another concern. "Sir, how should we address inquiries from the US about their prisoner next month?"

Richard, already moving towards the ship, replied without looking back. "Leave that to me. I'll deal with it personally."

"Understood, sir. Is there anything else you require?"

"Just your continued cooperation," Richard said, glancing at Savina's anxious face. He then raised his voice, authoritative and urgent. "Everyone, get on board. NOW!"

Once inside, Savina's concern quickly surfaced. "Are you sure you can handle this?"

Richard confidently settled into the pilot's seat. "I can manage any machine. How hard can it be?" he boasted.

"Just tell it what you want in pilot speak," Savina instructed, her tone reflecting a bit of indirect knowledge. "I used to date a commercial pilot, and while this is military, some basics overlap. Use clear, direct commands, and make sure you confirm each one with the computer."

Taking Savina's advice, Richard issued a series of voice-activated commands, articulating each one carefully. "Initiate startup sequence," he said clearly. The ship's computer responded with a series of beeps, confirming the command.

"Set course for Fort Lauderdale," Richard continued, his confidence growing as he interacted with the controls. The dashboard lit up with a route projection.

As they soared into the sky, swiftly heading towards Fort Lauderdale, Richard turned to Savina, his curiosity piqued. "Just how fast can these things go?"

Noticing his amazement, Savina replied with a hint of pride, "Remarkably fast. Imagine getting from here to New York in under twenty minutes."

Richard's eyebrows shot up as he quickly did the math. "That's roughly Mach 10!" he exclaimed, visibly impressed.

"Yes, and they're equipped with both Ion and RAM Jet engines," Savina added, leaning closer to share more details. "This allows them to operate seamlessly in both our atmosphere and outer space. Even though the technology is different, the principle of command and control is somewhat similar. But we must be cautious not to use the full speed too frequently—it would draw too much attention."

The RAM Jet soared through the skies, its streamlined design cutting through the clouds with ease. Richard's helicopter competency was coming to bear as he manoeuvred the controls, guiding them smoothly back to their base. The onboard lights cast a soft glow, illuminating the futuristic interiors of the jet.

In the main cabin, Sela and Savina, both still high on adrenaline, huddled together. Their voices melded into animated recounts of the daring escape, occasionally punctuated with bursts of laughter or a dramatic reenactment of a particularly tense moment. The atmosphere was thick with relief and the thrill of success, providing a stark contrast to the events that had unfolded only hours ago.

But, away from the others, near the viewing port, which showcased the clouds rushing by, stood Jim and Josie. Their silhouettes were cast in a half-light, emphasising their familial resemblance despite hailing from different realities.

Jim, sensing Josie's swirling confusion, gently steered her to a more private corner of the jet. The hum of the engine and the distant chatter from the main cabin provided a gentle backdrop as he began to speak.

"Josie," Jim's voice was soft, his eyes reflecting both concern and a deep-rooted affection. "I can't even begin to imagine how you must be feeling. But I promise, by the time we land, I'll try to give you all the answers you seek."

Josie's gaze, initially filled with a myriad of questions and a touch of fear, slowly melted into one of trust. They both sat, uncle and niece, from different realities, bridging the chasm of understanding, one word at a time. The gravity of their conversation formed a poignant contrast to the light-heartedness that filled the rest of the jet.

"Thanks, Uncle Jim," said Josie, her voice tinged with a mix of relief and curiosity. "It's just... a lot to process, you know? Seeing you here, after everything that's happened..."

"I know it must be overwhelming," Jim acknowledged, leaning back slightly as he searched for the right words. "We have our differences, our worlds apart, but here we are. How have you been managing with school and everything else?"

"School's been okay, just the usual stress," Josie replied, her expression softening. "But the protest... it was something I felt I needed to do. It's not just about the activism; it's about making sure I'm part of the change, however small it may seem."

"You've always been brave, just like when you were little," Jim said, a smile breaking through his concern. "I remember how you never backed down from what you believed in, even then. It's good to see that hasn't changed."

"I guess some things stay the same, no matter where we are," Josie mused, a faint smile crossing her face. "What about you? What's been the biggest challenge in your world?"

"Balancing everything is always a challenge," said Jim, his gaze drifting to the window briefly. "I work in the space industry, which demands a lot but it is rewarding. I've had the chance to work on projects that might one day change the course of humanity. But being away from family, it's tough. It makes me realise what I've missed here, with you."

"I can only imagine," Josie remarked, her eyes wide with a mix of admiration and longing. "But thinking about your adventures, travelling through alternate realities, it kinda makes me wish I could see it all for myself."

"Maybe one day, Josie," Jim said, his tone hopeful. "The universe is vast, and who knows? Maybe there's a reality where you're the engineer or the astronaut."

"That would be something, wouldn't it?" Josie asked, pausing as she reflected. "Right now, though, I'm just glad you're here. After thinking I'd lost you forever... this is like getting a second chance."

As their conversation meandered between light-hearted topics and deeper reflections, the RAM Jet continued its swift journey through the skies. Outside the viewing port, Jim observed the landscape below as they passed into Florida, noting subtle technological advancements that marked Josie's world as more advanced than his own.

Josie pointed out features of her Earth that showcased its technological edge. "See the way our cities integrate with the terrain? We've developed technology to enhance, not replace, the natural environment. Our buildings use adaptive materials that change to optimise energy consumption based on weather conditions."

Jim nodded, impressed by the harmonious blend of technology and ecology. "It's impressive," he admitted, his voice filled with genuine appreciation. "In my world, we have some similar concepts, but they're not as widespread. Here, it seems like these ideas are fully realised and integrated into everyday life."

"That's right," Josie confirmed, her eyes sparkling with pride. "Our approach is to use technology to support sustainability. It's about enhancing life without compromising our planet's health. It might not be a drastic difference from your world, but these small advancements make a significant impact."

Jim's interest deepened as he watched the seamless interaction between technological structures and natural elements. "This integration is something we've only started to scratch the surface of in my world. Seeing it in action here is incredibly inspiring. It makes me think about what we could change at home to achieve similar harmony."

Josie smiled, sensing his growing enthusiasm. "Who knows, Uncle Jim? Maybe your visit will be the catalyst for change when you return. Sometimes, seeing is believing."

"Maybe," Jim mused, his gaze returning to the landscape as the jet passed over a particularly impressive example of eco-technological architecture. "For now, though, I'm just absorbing it all. After thinking my world was at the forefront, being here is like discovering a whole new realm of possibilities."

As their conversation continued, the nuances of their respective worlds provided fertile ground for discussion. The RAM Jet cut smoothly through the clouds, its advanced design just one example of Josie's world's subtle technological superiority.

Chapter Eleven

Meanwhile, in the heart of New York, the mood was notably different. Nestled discreetly behind an unassuming storefront, the Chemist speakeasy throbbed with the beats of jazz and the muted conversations of its patrons. Will, Jessica, and Doug occupied a dimly lit corner booth, the amber glow from the overhead lights casting deep shadows over their faces. The sounds of soft music and clinking glasses served as the backdrop for a mounting tension. The ornate clock on the wall, with its intricate hands moving steadily, was the silent witness to the trio's growing impatience. Jessica, with her blonde hair neatly tied in a bun, seemed particularly restless. She exhaled audibly, her fingers drumming a rhythm of impatience on the wooden table.

"They're late," she said, the irritation evident in her tone.

Will, attempting to defuse the situation, leaned back against the plush velvet of the booth. "It's only been fifteen minutes," he said, his hazel eyes scanning the entrance every now and then. "They'll show up."

But as the hands of the clock seemed to crawl, the air filled with a quiet tension. Finally, thirty minutes past the scheduled time, the entrance door creaked open, revealing Tony. He stepped in, removed his hat, and scanned the room until his gaze met the trio's expectant faces.

Jessica, never one to mince words, got straight to the point. "You're late," she remarked, her tone cold.

Tony, becoming accustomed to her directness, replied without missing a beat, "Ran into a slight problem on the way. Nothing too major."

Doug leaned forward, his broad shoulders tense with anticipation. "What's the hold-up?"

Tony hesitated for a moment, then said, "My cousin's getting a bit greedy. Wants another 10K for the item."

Will, who had been silent till then, spoke up, his voice tinged with frustration. "How much more?"

"Another 10K," Tony reiterated.

Doug's face flushed a shade of crimson. "Tony," he said, trying to keep his voice steady, "You and I, we've been through a lot. I can't believe you'd let your cousin pull something like this on us."

Tony, sensing the rising tension, quickly held up his hands in a placating gesture. "Listen, I'm not trying to pull a fast one here. There might be a workaround – a temporary fix, at least until we get things sorted."

Doug's piercing gaze didn't waver as he challenged, "What's on your mind, Tony?"

Taking a deep breath, Tony began, "I've heard that Bellevue Hospital over on 1st Avenue has at least six units in their teaching section. We could, let's say, 'borrow' one for the time being. It buys us time while I figure out a permanent solution."

"The Bellevue?" mused Will. "I'm familiar with it. My sister trained there."

"So, what's the plan? Just walk in and take it?" Jessica asked in disbelief.

"Pretty much," Tony said, smiling at Jessica. "I have a cousin who works there. He can get us some hospital gear, and we simply walk in, pick one up, and walk out. With so many people in the hospital, no one will question us if we look the part."

"Sounds crazy," Jessica remarked, looking to Will and Doug for validation.

"It's crazy enough that it might work," observed Doug after a moment of contemplation.

"Okay, let's do it," said Will, a hint of sarcasm in his voice. "Before we change our minds and it costs us another 10K." He glared at Tony.

"Come on, guys," Tony interjected. "I'm on your side, and I'm risking as much as any of you by going in."

"What's this going to cost us?" Will inquired cynically, still sceptical of Tony.

"I can procure the uniforms and ID cards with what you've already given me. Plus, it'll cover incidentals."

"Incidentals?" Will questioned. "You mean your fee?"

"A man's got to make a living," Tony responded with a shrug.

"How long before we can proceed?" Jessica asked, warming up to the plan.

"We'll reconvene at 6 pm tonight at a small hotel on East 28th Street where I know the desk clerk. We'll change into our uniforms and enter during the 7 pm shift change, grab a machine, and exit through the river entrance. Phil will be waiting with a van, and then we'll be on our way."

"What could possibly go wrong?" Will pondered aloud.

"It's a good plan. It will work," Doug noted. "Besides," he added, "we don't have many alternatives."

"Agreed," said Will.

"See you at 6; we will meet in the coffee shop across from your hotel," Tony confirmed.

The hotel Tony had pointed them towards was a nondescript building, its facade weathered by time, with an interior that spoke of better days long gone. The muted tones of the wallpaper, the slightly worn-out carpet, and the aging chandeliers all hinted at a once-grand establishment now in decline.

Inside their room, the trio found themselves trapped in an agonising dance with time. The clock, an old-fashioned piece with hands that ticked audibly, sat on the nightstand, its monotonous rhythm a constant reminder of their anxious wait.

Jessica, her legs crossed, frequently glanced at the clock as if willing the hands to move faster. Doug, in an attempt to distract himself, flipped through the few channels the hotel TV offered, but his mind was clearly elsewhere. Every so often, he'd throw a sidelong look at the clock, his jaw clenching with impatience.

Will, seemingly the most restless of the lot, paced the floor. The weight of their plan and the uncertainty of what awaited them at Bellevue Hospital pressed heavily on his mind. Every tick of the clock seemed to stretch into eternity, amplifying their collective anxiety. The day felt longer than any they'd experienced as they waited for the right moment to act.

"I'm going mad just sitting here doing nothing. Let's talk about something," Jessica suggested, her voice echoing slightly in the sparse room.

"What's on your mind?" Doug asked, sensing her need for a distraction, his face showing a mix of concern and curiosity.

Leaning forward, Jessica's expression turned thoughtful. "I really want to understand why all those people were so upset about me saying Williamsburg instead of Patriotville. That guy who attacked Will said it had something to do with a King

141

William bombing Atlanta, but I don't really understand why. What happened?"

Doug sighed, his gaze lowering briefly before meeting Jessica's eyes. "It's a heavy piece of their history," he began, his voice steady but filled with the weight of the past. "King William VI was a particularly nasty ruler of the Empire who, during a brutal conflict with the US, ordered the destruction of Atlanta. It was an act intended to break the will of the US. He then threatened to bomb New York if the US didn't allow California to secede, aiming to fracture the country significantly."

Jessica's eyes widened in shock, her previous irritation replaced by a growing understanding. "That's horrifying. I had no idea."

Nodding, Doug continued, "Yes, and so when the decision was made to rename Williamsburg, it was laden with emotion. Despite the town being named after a mill owner, Jonas Williams, the prevailing sentiment in the country was that it had to go. Choosing 'Patriotville' was a deliberate rejection of everything King William represented. It was about erasing any possible link to his legacy from their country and honouring the resilience and suffering of their citizens instead."

Jessica let out a slow breath, her mind racing with the implications. "I see why it stirred so much emotion then. It's not just a name; it's a statement... a reminder of resilience and, in a way, a form of healing."

"Exactly," Doug agreed, his tone reflecting a mix of pride and sombreness. "Names carry power, Jessica. They evoke memories and emotions. For many, changing the name to Patriotville was an act of reclaiming history and asserting control over their narrative as survivors and fighters."

Jessica nodded, the weight of the discussion settling over her as she glanced out the window. The shift from their intense conversation to the scene outside seemed to pull her thoughts back to the present. She turned back to Doug and Will. "Understanding the past helps us navigate the future," she said, her voice steadier. "And right now, we need to focus on what comes next."

Will looked between Jessica and Doug, sensing the shift in mood. "Right," he agreed, checking his watch. "We've got a meeting in a few minutes, right?"

The trio gathered their things, and at 5:30 pm, they were seated in a bustling coffee shop, gazing anxiously at the imposing Bellevue Hospital across the way. The place was alive with the chatter of patrons and the whirring of espresso machines, a lively backdrop to their serious conversation.

"It looks nearly identical," Will observed. "The main difference is that new front entrance with the helipad. In our reality, helicopters had to land further up the FDR Drive at the TSS Heliport. The teaching section is on the left," he indicated, pointing at the hospital's oldest section. "It was built in the late 1700s and probably untouched since. I remember it being bloody cold whenever I visited."

"You rarely mention your sister," Jessica remarked, her eyes probing Will's face, filled with curiosity and concern. Her coffee sat untouched, the conversation more gripping than the hot beverage.

Will paused, his expression turning reflective. The sounds of the café seemed to fade as his mind travelled back to a time filled with pain and loss. "She was finishing training when the Coronavirus hit New York in 2020," he finally said, his voice filled with a mixture of pride and sadness. "Hospitals were overwhelmed, and PPE was scarce. It was inevitable that frontline staff would contract the virus."

Jessica's breath caught in her throat as she listened. The details were painting a vivid picture, and she felt a lump forming in her throat.

"We didn't know her childhood pneumonia had compromised a lung. She battled for over a month before succumbing." Will's eyes were misty, and his voice trailed off. The memories were still raw, even after all this time.

"I'm so sorry," Jessica whispered, her hand reaching out to offer a comforting touch. Her fingers lightly squeezed Will's arm, a small gesture filled with empathy.

Will exhaled a deep and heavy breath that seemed to release some of the weight he carried. "It's been years, but revisiting the past is surreal. This is my first time back in New York since she was here." He glanced out of the café window, the city's skyline a stark reminder of his sister's dreams and their abrupt end.

Doug, who had been quietly observing the exchange, chimed in, his voice gentle but focused. "Well, hopefully your familiarity will help us get the X-ray machine." He looked between Jessica and Will, understanding the gravity of the moment but also recognising the importance of their mission.

Will's face hardened, determination replacing the sorrow. "There are only so many ways to lay out a hospital, so I'm guessing it will be pretty similar."

As the sun began its descent, casting the city in shades of amber and gold, Tony made his timely appearance at the coffee shop. He carried with him a neatly packed bundle, which, upon closer inspection, revealed itself to be a set of hospital maintenance uniforms. The fabric was rough but appeared authentic, complete with name badges and the hospital's insignia embroidered on the left breast.

The group returned to their hotel and swiftly retired to their respective rooms to change into their uniforms, glancing in mirrors to ensure they looked the part. The outfits were a surprisingly good fit, making them look every bit like the hospital employees they intended to impersonate.

By 7 pm, the streets outside started to buzz with activity, the changeover between shifts filling the surroundings with hospital workers both coming and going. Among the throng, the quartet emerged from the hotel – Will, Jessica, Doug, and Tony. Their demeanours were calm and professional, their strides purposeful, every bit mimicking the evening shift workers they were emulating.

To any observer, they were simply another group of maintenance workers headed for a night's work. Their uniforms bore no discrepancy, and their body language reflected nothing but routine.

As they approached the hospital entrance, Phil's van became visible. Parked in the prime spot within the hospital car park, it was strategically positioned for a quick getaway. Phil, a seasoned collaborator in such endeavours, gave a subtle nod from behind the wheel.

"Okay, act like we belong here," advised Tony, casting a concerned glance at Jessica, who appeared on the verge of a panic attack.

"I'll be alright," Jessica assured. "Let's just get it over with."

They walked into the hospital, ready to flash their badges to security. However, the guard didn't even glance their way as they joined the crowd.

"Head to the basement," Tony directed, guiding them towards the elevators on the left.

"Why the basement?" Will asked. "The machines are on the second floor in the training wing."

"We need to grab some equipment to look the part of fixing an issue," Tony explained. "The workshops are in the basement."

"Right, good thinking," Will acknowledged. "Let's move."

As the elevator door opened to the basement, they sighed in relief at the absence of people.

"Let's get some wheeled trolleys, buckets, mops, and brooms," Tony instructed.

Quickly assembling typical cleaning gear, they summoned the elevator again. Once inside, Tony pressed the button for the 2nd floor. As the doors slid open, they quickly assessed their surroundings before heading towards the "Training Unit" sign. Suddenly, a door swung open, revealing two nurses.

"That was fast. We just called," one commented.

"We were nearby," Tony improvised smoothly.

"Good, it's a mess in there," the nurse said, motioning them inside.

Upon entering, the group was met with a ghastly sight and odour.

"What happened?" Jessica gasped; her face contorted in disgust.

A toppled stack of bedpans answered her question. "We'll step out for some air. Thanks for handling this," one nurse said, grateful.

Once the nurses departed, Tony motioned for the group to abandon the cleaning effort. "We're not cleaning this. Let's move."

The training unit, nestled in a quieter section of the hospital, was dimly lit with overhead fluorescents that buzzed intermittently.

Rows of training equipment lined the room, but it was the supply room at the back that was their main interest.

Will cautiously approached the door, his brow furrowed with concern as he surveyed its sturdy metal frame. He reached out, turning the handle with a gentle pull, but it resisted—firmly locked. Tony, observing the failed attempt with a smirk, rummaged through their stash of cleaning supplies and pulled out a hefty sledgehammer.

Brandishing it with confidence, he announced, "Plan B," and added with a wry smile, "I've got the key." Without another word, Tony swung the sledgehammer with considerable force. The door groaned ominously under the first blow. A second, more powerful strike followed, and the lock yielded with a loud, definitive crunch, granting them access.

The eerie silence that followed hung heavily in the air. Jessica glanced nervously around the dimly lit corridor and whispered, "Did no one hear that?" The possibility of alarms blaring and hospital security swarming the area filled their minds with dread.

"Maybe," Tony responded tersely, his eyes scanning the interior of the supply room they had just breached. He stepped inside first, his expression firm. "But we've come this far. No turning back now."

Once inside, they quickly located the compact X-ray machines, each about the size of a suitcase, making them surprisingly manageable. Working swiftly and silently, they loaded two of the machines onto the trolley, securing each unit carefully to avoid any unwanted noise. Once everything was in place, Tony cautiously peeked out the door. He immediately noticed a security guard standing by the doorway, his back partly turned as he spoke into his radio, likely alerting his team about the disturbance they had caused.

"Security to the second floor. Possible break-in at the training unit supply room. Requesting backup," the guard relayed into his radio with a steady, alert tone.

Tony gestured to the others to remain silent and gave a reassuring nod, signalling he had a plan. They watched, holding their breath, as the guard finished his call and started to turn towards them.

Jessica whispered urgently to Will, "We need a distraction or something. We can't just barge through him."

Will nodded, quickly scanning their makeshift arsenal of cleaning supplies for anything that might be useful. Meanwhile, Tony edged closer to the doorframe, his gaze locked on the guard's movements. As the guard clipped his radio back onto his belt and turned fully towards them, Tony seized the moment.

"Now!" Tony hissed under his breath.

With a burst of energy, Tony pushed the loaded cleaning trolley directly into the path of the guard. Caught unawares, the guard instinctively stepped back, but the momentum was too much. The trolley clipped his side, knocking him slightly off balance and forcing him to grab onto it to steady himself.

"Sorry! Equipment failure," Tony called out loudly, pretending to struggle with the trolley's direction.

The guard, now slightly disoriented but quickly regaining his bearings, shook his head and demanded, "What's going on here?"

Seeing that the guard wasn't fully convinced and was poised to act, Tony made a split-second decision. He pushed the trolley harder, using it as both a shield and a battering ram. This time, the force was enough; the guard was knocked down, landing hard on the floor with a heavy grunt.

"Move, now!" Tony urged, his voice low and urgent.

With the guard temporarily incapacitated, they quickly maneuvered past him, their movements swift and coordinated. As they left the supply room, Jessica glanced back with a twinge of guilt but knew they had no time to dwell on the ethics of their actions.

They hurried towards the elevator, the urgency of their mission intensifying with each step. The faint sound of the guard stirring in the background only hastened their pace.

The elevator ride down was fraught with tension. As the doors opened, they were met with the stern faces of two security guards waiting for them. "Stop and show us your IDs," one of the guards ordered firmly. "We have a report of a disturbance."

Tony, with a look of sheer desperation, jabbed at the "close" button while simultaneously pressing a random floor button. The guards began to reach for their weapons, their fingers twitching near the triggers. But the doors slid shut just in time, the elevator unexpectedly ascending to the fourth floor.

As the doors opened, they hurried out, the wheels of their trolleys squealing against the polished hospital floor as they raced away from potential capture, their hearts pounding with the adrenaline of the escape.

Jessica's voice, shaky from adrenaline, broke the silence. "Where are we headed? They'll have this place swarming in no time."

Tony's response was quick, his eyes darting around, "The back entrance. We can slip out there."

Doug, incredulous, gazed at the heavy X-ray machines. "You seriously think we can make a quick escape with these?"

"Better than being locked up," Tony shot back, abruptly leaving the trolley behind and sprinting ahead.

With no other visible option, the group trailed Tony, pushing the weighty trolleys. Their hasty entrance into a ward shocked a few nurses.

Will, quick on his feet and sensing the urgency of their situation, seized the moment to create a diversion. With a voice that cut sharply through the ambient noise of the bustling facility, he shouted, "Cleaning emergency! Out of the way!" The assertiveness in his tone conveyed an urgency that sent staff members scurrying aside, allowing Will and his companions an unobstructed path.

As they hurried along, the dim, flickering light of the emergency exit sign became a beacon at the end of the long corridor. Tony, with his hand pressed firmly against the door, was already positioned as their lookout. As the group neared, he barked out commands to hasten their escape. "Move, move, move!" he yelled, his voice echoing off the walls.

The group picked up speed, their footsteps a rapid staccato against the tiled floor. But in their haste, a misjudged step or an ill-timed push caused chaos. The door which Tony was holding suddenly slipped from his grasp. It swung shut with a resonant thud, the sound magnified in the confined space. Almost immediately, the sharp wail of an alarm filled the air, its piercing cry signalling their attempted escape.

Peering through the door's small, reinforced window, they saw Tony's expression transform into one of regret and panic. His eyes met theirs briefly, full of apologies, as he mouthed a hasty "Sorry." With no time to waste, Tony turned and vanished into the stairwell, his footsteps fading as he descended, leaving the group to recover and plan their next move quickly. The alarm echoed through the corridor, amplifying the urgency of the situation. Will's voice was stern. "We need cover. Now."

Jessica's eyes darted around. "Where?"

Will, attempting to recall the hospital's layout, snapped his fingers. "Supply rooms. There should be one down this hall. Bellevue has them on every floor."

With a shared sense of purpose, the trio made their way to the supply room, barricading themselves inside, praying they had bought enough time.

"Now what?" Jessica whispered, anxiety evident in her eyes.

"We wait and hope things calm down," Doug suggested.

"We should inform the others about our situation," Jessica said, her voice steadying.

"We agreed to maintain radio silence unless it's an emergency," Will reminded her. "We've already reached out once to brief them on our plan to raid this hospital. Remember, it's a high risk—Doug mentioned the US actively monitors all cell phone calls."

"I believe this qualifies as an emergency," Jessica countered. "We're on the brink of capture."

"All right," conceded Will, pulling out his phone. Dialling Savina's number, he switched to speaker mode. "Savina, we've hit a snag. We're in the hospital but are now cornered in a storage room."

"Is everyone okay? ...and the machines?" Savina's inquiry cut through the tension.

Doug, taking the phone from Will, responded with a mix of relief and concern, "We're all intact, Savina. And yes, we managed to get two machines. But we're cornered. Exiting directly will only get us into the hands of security."

Savina's thoughtful pause was almost tangible through the line. Then, with a burst of inspiration, she inquired, "Can you make it to the roof?"

Doug's eyebrows furrowed in confusion. "We might be able to, but what good would it do?"

"Just trust me." Savina's voice had an undertone of excitement. "Get to the roof, and we've got a way out for you."

"Way out? What do you mean?" Doug pressed.

"We've managed to get our hands on a RAM Jet!" Savina exclaimed.

Doug's eyes widened, and he almost laughed in disbelief. "A RAM Jet? Seriously?"

Savina's chuckle echoed through the phone. "Yeah! So hustle up; we'll be overhead in fifteen minutes."

"We will be there," said Doug, hanging up the phone.

Savina hung up the phone and rushed over to where Richard, Sela, and Josie were waiting. Her face conveyed urgent concern as she blurted out, "They're in trouble—we need to launch immediately."

As they hurried to the RAM Jet, Savina instructed, "Richard, you'll have to fly it manually," and strapped herself in. 'We're going to push the jet beyond its programmed traffic control limits, and the automatic systems will kick in to slow us down. Don't spare the engines; we need to get to the roof of Bellevue Hospital as fast as possible."

Richard nodded, his face a mix of determination and anxiety. "I've been practicing," he reassured the team, though his hands moved hesitantly over the controls, still not fully accustomed to the layout. "But don't worry, I'm on it," he added, his voice tinged with focus as he carefully flipped a series of switches to power up the RAM Jet. "I'm getting the hang of this," he said, trying to project more confidence than he actually felt.

A moment later, Richard engaged the engines. They roared to life, the ground trembling slightly under the power of the jets. Within moments, they were airborne, the hospital coordinates locked in. The aircraft sliced through the sky at an unprecedented speed, racing towards the rescue, each moment critical.

****

Back at the hospital, Will surveyed the room and proposed, "I have an idea. Since they're looking for four maintenance workers, let's have Doug lie on that patient gurney over there. We can place the X-ray machines on its base shelf and cover everything with a sheet. Jess and I will wear those hospital coats and transport it to the roof."

"Do you think that'll work?" Jessica inquired.

"Any other ideas?" Will asked impatiently.

"Nope. Let's go with it," agreed Doug. "We've only got fifteen minutes."

Minutes later, they exited the supply room, pushing the gurney towards the elevators. Two security guards blocked their path, and one demanded, "Where are you going?"

"Taking this patient for an emergency appendectomy," Will replied authoritatively. Doug groaned for emphasis.

The security guard pressed the button for Floor 3 and said, "OK, proceed."

Relieved, they entered the elevator, descending to the third floor. Once the doors opened, they quickly pressed the button for the top floor. As the elevator doors shut behind them, they were relieved that, for the moment, there were no hostile eyes on them. Upon reaching the top floor, they pushed the gurney to the door marked "To the Roof". Following a signal from Will, Doug disembarked, and they each lifted an X-ray machine. But as Jessica opened the door, an alarm blared.

"Hurry!" Jessica urged as she dashed up the stairs.

"We're trying," Doug gasped. "These machines are heavy!"

"Right behind you," Will panted, keeping pace.

"We're almost there," Jessica encouraged, nearing the rooftop door.

Emerging onto the rooftop, the sight that greeted them was straight out of a science fiction novel: a teardrop-shaped aircraft cutting swiftly through the sky, its approach almost silent. Jessica, her eyes wide with a mix of awe and urgency, pointed towards the descending craft. "That must be them," she said, her voice laced with a hope that bordered on desperation.

Doug merely nodded, his attention fixed on the gear they'd hastily gathered for their escape. "I hope so," he muttered, placing his equipment on the ground with deliberate care, mirroring Will's actions. The urgency of their situation was unmistakable, the weight of their mission pressing down on them with each passing second.

As the aircraft made a smooth landing, its rear chute opened, revealing Sela and a woman they hadn't seen before. Both were motioning frantically for them to board. Without hesitation, Jessica broke into a sprint towards the ship, pausing only to ensure Doug and Will were close behind. Their escape was so near, yet the sudden burst of the roof access door and the appearance of four security guards threatened to shatter their hopes. The guards didn't hesitate, opening fire with kappa rays, their shots sizzling through the air.

"Hurry!" Jessica screamed, a sharp contrast to the almost serene descent of the aircraft moments before. She dove into the ship, with Doug and Will not far behind, their steps fuelled by adrenaline.

As they hurled themselves into the safety of the aircraft, Sela's voice cut through the chaos, "We've got them! Go! Go! Go!" The chute sealed with a hiss, and the craft ascended sharply, leaving the chaos of the rooftop—and the sprawling cityscape of New York—far behind.

Inside the RAM Jet, the atmosphere was electric, a vibrant mix of relief and the buzz of shared stories and emotions. The ship's engines hummed softly in the background, providing a soothing backdrop to the lively discussions unfolding among the passengers.

Doug, gazing out the window, found his thoughts drifting to his friend who was now missing. "Tony was caught in an impossible situation," he said, the weight of his concern evident in his voice. "Everything happened too fast—the alarms, the locked doors. He's the kind of guy who always has a plan, but sometimes... it's just not enough. I hope he got out okay."

Jessica, ever empathetic, nodded. "From what you've told me, Tony sounds like the kind of person who's always there for you." There was a pause, a shared moment of silence for their absent friend, before she added with a lighter tone, "Plus, he's incredibly sexy."

Doug blinked, taken aback, while Will let out an incredulous laugh. "He is? Can't say I've noticed."

Jessica's cheeks tinged with a hint of pink, her earlier tension easing into a shy smile. "Just an observation," she demurred.

Will, still chuckling, shook his head. "Well, I'll have to take a closer look next time."

The cabin grew quiet for a moment, but Josie's voice soon filled the space. "If you think that's mind-bending, wait until you hear my story with Jim!" She laughed, casting a knowing glance at Jim.

Jim, with a twinkle in his eye, picked up from there, "She's not kidding. Josie isn't just some stranger we decided to help; she's my niece."

Jessica's eyes widened, "Really, your niece, family ties across dimensions? Now that's a tale I want to hear!"

Will, equally intrigued, added, "And let's not forget this incredible RAM Jet."

"I've named her *Stardust II*," came a voice from the cockpit.

"Good name!" they all concurred.

"It's one of Prince Richard's special ships," continued Richard. "Fully armed, holding cells replacing cargo bays, plus lots of special places for hiding things —ideal for a despot."

"Charming," Jessica remarked. "Hopefully we never cross paths."

The craft flew down the coastline and, upon reaching Florida, slowed for a landing on the airstrip where they'd parked the *Stardust* just a few weeks earlier.

Chapter Twelve

Early the next morning, as the first light washed over their makeshift war room, the team reconvened in a charged atmosphere, detailing their strategic plans to locate the Dimension Stone near Ammon. Maps and digital interfaces were sprawled across the central table, flickering under the soft glow of the room's lighting.

"Do you think you can trust them completely?" Savina questioned, eyeing the maps but alluding to their newfound Catholic allies who had offered their sanctuary.

"Normally, I'd liken the Catholic Church to House Slytherin," Will joked, trying to lighten the mood. His comment drew puzzled looks from Josie but chuckles from Jessica and Sela.

"It's their alternate-world humour," Savina explained with a wry smile to Josie.

"You'll get the hang of it," Jessica added, her voice tinged with gratitude. "We've already put our lives in their hands. After that debacle in Williamsburg, I wouldn't have escaped without their help. When they demanded answers, I had to be honest about who I am and where I come from."

Piqued by this, Will asked, "How did they react to your story?"

Jessica hesitated, her gaze drifting to the interplay of light and shadow on the walls, with memories flickering in her eyes. "At first, they thought I'd lost my mind," she began, her voice laden with the weight of her recollection. "But then, Brandon noticed the Tanzanite ring. You know, the one I sold. He used to be an opal miner back in Australia and he could tell straight away that it was unlike any stone he'd ever seen. That revelation changed everything. It not only shifted their opinion of me but also secured us the funds to get you out of prison."

"So, back to the plan," Will interjected, tapping on the map that pinpointed their next major step. "The mission is here near Ammon, or what we know in our world as the Siwa Oasis. It's about 470 kilometres from Alexandria, but most of the space ore is stored in the desert between Al Elanin and Ammon, which is almost ideal for our operation. We'll fly the *Stardust II* to Ammon, hide on the mission grounds, scan for our meteorite, retrieve it, and return to our Earth."

"That's it?" Jessica quipped, raising an eyebrow. "It sounds simple enough! What could possibly go wrong?"

"Indeed, it sounds straightforward," Jim noted, his tone steady yet wary. "But there's much planning left to do. The desert is unpredictable, and our approach must be meticulous."

The crew nodded in agreement, the weight of their task evident in their solemn faces. They resumed their tasks with renewed vigour, each member absorbed in their specific roles. Meanwhile, Jessica, her brow furrowed with lingering concern, quietly slipped away from the group. She found Doug intently examining some navigational charts.

"Doug, have you heard anything from Tony?" she asked hesitantly, her voice low.

Doug paused, looking up and noting Jessica's anxious expression. "I was going to tell you—I managed to get hold of Phil this morning. He confirmed that Tony escaped the hospital and has now left the country for a while, just in case he was spotted."

Jessica let out a relieved sigh, the tension in her shoulders easing slightly, though her mind remained clouded with concern for his ongoing safety.

Later the next day, after the crew had scavenged anything they might need from the original *Stardust*, they gathered again for a heartfelt goodbye to Savina, Doug, and Josie. The mood was sombre, not only because of their departure but also due to the complicated legal issues Doug and Josie now faced.

"Are you sure you can't take me with you?" Josie asked, her eyes brimming with tears, reflecting her mixed feelings about staying behind.

"You know we can't," Jim responded softly. "You have a life here, and my Josie has a life in our world. It wouldn't be fair to bring you into a situation where everything seems familiar but is actually entirely different."

Jessica then stepped in, her voice carrying a mixture of concern and pragmatism. "There's another option. We could drop you all off somewhere like Cuba, where U.S. jurisdiction won't reach easily. It might give you a fresh start away from all this trouble."

Doug gave a small, reassuring smile, and shook his head slightly. "It's nothing I can't handle. We'll be okay. The important thing is staying together and facing whatever comes our way. Plus, Savina's life is here; we can't just uproot everything on a whim."

Jessica nodded, understanding his perspective. "We're truly sorry that our actions have led to this situation for you both. But remember, we're all in this together, no matter the distance or dimension. We'll find ways to support you."

Savina noticed Jim's worried expression as he contemplated leaving this version of his niece behind. "We'll look after her," she affirmed, her gaze meeting Doug's, who responded with a reassuring nod. We will ensure her safety, no matter what," she added, her voice resolute, leaving no room for doubt.

They shared a moment of heavy silence, filled with mutual understanding and unspoken promises. The group then embraced, a long, lingering hug that spoke volumes about the deep bonds they had formed.

Finally, the crew made their way to the *Stardust II*. As they boarded, Richard headed straight to the flight deck to begin the systems check. "OK, folks, it's a four-hour trip, and Egypt is seven hours ahead of us, so we will arrive around 10 PM Alexandria time," he announced, his voice projecting a calmness that belied the emotional weight of their farewells.

As the engines of the Stardust II hummed to life, each crew member settled into their seats, their thoughts lingering on Doug and Josie, the challenges ahead, and the enduring ties that bound them across worlds and circumstances. With a final glance at the receding lights of the base, the aircraft soared into the night sky, carrying them toward an uncertain future.

PART FOUR

Chapter Thirteen

Hours into their journey, the vast expanse of the Atlantic Ocean stretched beneath them like an endless tapestry. The *Stardust II* cruised smoothly at high altitude, its path aligning with the equator and mirroring the routes of cargo planes bound for Casablanca. Inside the cabin, a quiet resolve settled among the crew as they reviewed the plan: cross over Morocco, navigate through Algeria, and approach Ammon via Libya.

The journey was uneventful until they neared the African coastline, gliding over the azure expanse of the Atlantic Ocean. The Canary Islands had just come into view, a picturesque sight from above, characterised by rugged landscapes and the promise of exotic lands beyond. It was a moment of serene beauty, abruptly shattered by the harsh, insistent sound of a warning buzzer that pierced the calm.

Richard, who had been monitoring the controls with a practised eye, felt a jolt of alarm. "We've lost power!" he shouted over the din of the alarm and the sudden, uneasy murmur among the crew. His hands moved swiftly over the console, attempting to diagnose the issue in real-time. "Something is interfering with the systems. We're going down!"

"Can we make it to the islands?" exclaimed Will.

"We are pretty close to Tenerife," replied Richard. "That's the largest and most populated."

"It's probably easier to hide in numbers rather than on one of the smaller ones," said Jessica.

"Agreed," said Will. "Take us in."

"Will do, Captain," replied Richard. "Hang on, it could be a bumpy ride."

"Where are you going to land?" asked Jessica as she slid into the co-pilot seat.

"Tenerife Airport," replied Richard. "Luckily, it looks almost exactly the same as the one on our Earth, and I've landed my helicopter there many times."

"Of course you have," replied Jessica. "The playground for all the rich playboys."

"That's Ibiza," corrected Richard. "This is for the rich and famous. Hang on, we're going down."

Richard skilfully guided the *Stardust II* towards the main airport and landed alongside a number of other aircraft. Almost immediately, an airport security car pulled up next to them. Two female officers exited the vehicle and approached the rear chute of the airship.

"I'll go and talk to them," said Will. Turning to Richard, he added, "We'll keep you in reserve, but listen in," pointing to his earpiece.

"Good idea," replied Richard. "I'll get Jim and Sela to run a diagnostic on what has gone wrong and figure out how to fix it."

Will exited the airship and approached the two officers. They introduced themselves as Sergeants Letitia Wills and Ashleigh Williams. Will introduced himself, but Letitia immediately interrupted him, saying, "What sort of idiot flies during a Dead Zone alert?"

"Dead Zone alert?" replied Will. "I don't know what you mean."

"I need to speak to your pilot," said Ashleigh.

"Sure, I'll just get him. But first, I'm just a passenger," said Will. "What is a Dead Zone alert?"

"It's a smuggler defence system. Ships and airships leaving the port of Casablanca sometimes get attacked by smugglers. When there is credible intel that a smuggler attack is likely, we activate the Dead Zone field, which kills the power to all ion engines from here to the coast of Morocco," explained Letitia. "Can you explain what you're doing flying over Tenerife during a Dead Zone alert?"

"We were just on our way to the Catholic mission in Ammon," replied Will.

Both officers immediately drew their weapons, pointing them directly at Will.

"What did I say?" said Will, a bit nervously.

"That's a well-known smuggler's route. I need to speak to your pilot. Now!" replied Ashleigh.

"I'll get him, just hang on. But I don't think he wants to be disturbed."

"I don't care what he wants," said Ashleigh. "Just get him here now before we arrest you as a smuggler."

"Arrest who as a smuggler?" echoed a deep voice. Richard appeared, descending the chute with an imposing presence.

Instantly recognising him, Ashleigh and Letitia snapped to attention, hastily holstering their weapons. Their faces drained of colour as they stammered out their apologies.

"Sir, we had absolutely no idea you were in the area. We're deeply sorry. The Governor hadn't even formally requested Empire Intelligence's intervention, and now you're here," Ashleigh explained, her voice trembling.

Richard fixed a stern gaze on them, his authority unmistakable. "I was in the neighbourhood and decided to detour here. Apparently, no one informed me there was an active Dead Zone. This seems like a serious oversight," he stated, his tone icy as he shot a "WTF" look at Will.

"It was activated when smugglers attacked the Super Yacht *Umberto* as it left Casablanca yesterday," replied Letitia.

"The *Umberto*?" said Richard. "What did they want?"

"That's above my security level. I need to take you to the Governor," said Letitia.

"Alright," Richard responded, quickly adding, "I need to notify my crew." He then pivoted towards Will, stating, "You're coming with me."

"Yes, sir," said Will, with just a trace of irony.

Richard and Will returned to the ship. Will grabbed one of their communicators and told the rest of the crew to monitor and be ready to leave immediately before the real Richard or his agents showed up.

They both went outside and got into the vehicle with Ashleigh and Letitia, where they made their way through the streets of Santa Cruz to the Plaza de Espana and the President's Palace.

Will and Richard were immediately rushed into the President's Office, where they were introduced to President Juan Carvo, a short, balding man with a very concerned look on his face.

"Prince Richard," he said, holding out his hand. "A pleasure to meet you."

"You too," said Richard, returning the handshake.

"I'm amazed you're here, as I was just about to call your office. How did you know to come here?"

Thinking quickly on his feet, Richard said, "The department intercepted chatter relating to the *Umberto*, and I was on my way to investigate when the Dead Zone field hit."

"I didn't expect you to be personally involved," said the Governor, "but I guess when royalty is involved, the Empire reacts quickly."

"Yes, royalty," said Richard, thinking quickly. "So, obviously, I am here personally. I need you to send me as much information as you've gathered before my team launches a rescue attempt."

"At once, sir," replied the Governor, summoning one of his aides.

"Turn the Dead Zone alert off so that we can continue our mission," replied Richard.

"Of course, Director," said the Governor. "As soon as you're ready to leave, we will open a window to let you through."

"Very good," replied Richard. Turning to Will, he added, "Let's return and come up with a plan. They'll regret ever crossing the Empire," he said menacingly.

Richard and Will left the Governor's palace and were driven back to the *Stardust II,* where they found the others had been busy.

"I got hold of Doug," said Jessica, "who contacted Tony about what he knew was going on in Libya. Libya is still Italian," she added, "and the Mafia has a strong presence there."

"Are you sure we need to involve them? We could use the local police," said Jim.

"The risk of someone talking to the Empire is just too great," said Will. "If word gets back to the real Richard, we're in trouble."

"Agreed," said Jessica. "Our best hope is to get an introduction from Tony."

"We could just leave and continue our mission," said Sela.

"That is an option," said Will, "but Richard has already been exposed here. If we just disappeared, I'm sure it wouldn't be long until the real Prince Richard heard about it."

"Jess, can you call Tony directly rather than through Doug?" asked Will. "I think he has a bit of a crush on you."

"OK," she replied, chuckling, "I can't help being irresistible to handsome Italian men."

She called Tony, and he immediately answered.

"Hi," she said, "we need another favour."

"Another?" Tony replied. "I'm still feeling guilty about leaving you in the hospital."

"Water under the bridge," Jessica replied. "But if you're feeling that guilty, we need a contact with your 'Family' in Libya."

"Libya? What are you doing there? I thought you were heading to Cuba."

"We're in Tenerife at the moment, but things are a bit more complicated than that. We need some help with a situation we have here."

"Well, I happen to be in Milan now. It seemed like a good time to leave New York for a while, so I guess I could pop down to you."

"I think we can do better than that. Our new friend, the Governor, has offered his private airship," Richard announced with a hint of satisfaction.

"Friends in high places," Tony chuckled. "Impressive!"

"Get to the airport; the airship will be waiting."

"OK, see you soon," Tony signed off with a casual "Ciao."

Jessica turned to Richard, sighing, "Do you think the Governor would spring for a shopping trip? I lost most of my clothes when we escaped from New York, and I'm sick of wearing this outfit."

Sela chimed in eagerly, "Me too! I really need something nice."

"And I should look good for Tony," Jessica added, a mischievous sparkle in her eye.

Seeing an opportunity to boost morale, Richard quickly spoke with the Governor, who was only too happy to assist. "Anything you want," he assured them. "While the airship heads to Milan to pick up your man, I'll arrange for Sergeant Williams to help your team out."

Grateful for the break, Jessica and Sela, accompanied by Ashleigh, ventured into the heart of Tenerife's shopping districts. The warm Canarian sun promised a delightful day ahead.

"Finally, no more jumpsuits!" Sela exclaimed as they entered a chic boutique, her eyes lighting up at the sight of the fashion-forward attire.

Jessica laughed, flipping through a rack of vibrant dresses. "I'm thinking something daring for tonight. Tony won't know what hit him." She winked at Ashleigh, adding, "He's Italian, you know." Ashleigh shook her head with a smile.

"Remember, we're looking for fun, not a fashion felony," Ashleigh quipped as she pulled out a particularly flamboyant sequined dress and held it up to Jessica. "This might just be a bit too much sparkle."

Jessica mock-gasped, "Too much sparkle? No such thing!" But she laughed and set the dress back on the rack, opting for a sleek red gown instead.

Sela tried on a series of outfits, each more extravagant than the last, until she found a floral maxi dress. She twirled in front of the mirror, making the fabric billow. "I feel like a goddess in this. What do you think, Ashleigh?"

Ashleigh nodded approvingly. "Goddess level confirmed. You're killing it, Sela!"

As the afternoon progressed, they tried on a myriad of outfits, from elegant evening gowns to playful beachwear. They joked about how each outfit could be used in their "spy wardrobe", creating hilarious backstories for each ensemble.

"Imagine negotiating in this power suit," Jessica said, striking a pose in a sharp blazer.

"Only if you pair it with those absurd sunglasses," Sela countered, handing Jessica a pair of oversized, glittery shades.

By sunset, both women had found not only a new wardrobe but also a rejuvenated sense of camaraderie. Ashleigh's initial reserve had given way to bursts of laughter and shared jokes.

As they left the final store, bags brimming with new purchases, Jessica nudged Sela with a grin. "Who knew the Governor's idea of support would be so... chic?"

"Best mission ever," Sela laughed, swinging her shopping bag. "Now, let's find a place to show off these new outfits!"

Later that evening, Tony was making his way to the *Stardust II*, with Jessica and Will waiting outside to greet him. Jessica stood confidently, the sleek red dress from their shopping spree in Tenerife hugging her figure, adding an air of elegance and allure to the evening. The dress was bold, daring, exactly what she had envisioned for this moment.

As Tony reunited with the group, his opening line was tinged with a mix of relief and regret. "Great to see you guys again," he began, scratching the back of his head in an all-too-familiar gesture of awkwardness. "And about the whole 'abandoning you' saga—still drafting my apology letter in my head."

Will clapped him on the back with a laugh. "Forget it, my friend. What else could you have done? Anyway, look at us now, all part of a grand reunion special."

The moment Tony's gaze found Jessica, something in the air seemed to shift, charged with a different kind of electricity. His eyes momentarily widened as he took in her appearance, clearly taken aback by the stunning transformation. She radiated a mix of confidence and casual grace that seemed to captivate him entirely.

He moved in for a hug, a simple gesture that somehow lingered longer than either of them had intended. As they pulled away, their eyes locked, a silent conversation passing between them, filled with words neither had yet found the courage to utter.

Then, in a moment of awkward levity, Tony cleared his throat and flashed a sheepish grin. "Well, that was... longer than your average hug," he chuckled, scratching the back of his neck.

Jessica couldn't help but laugh, a lightness washing over the charged atmosphere. "Yeah, just a bit," she replied, her cheeks tinted with a hint of pink. She gave a playful twirl in her dress, adding a flirtatious flair to the moment. "Thought I'd dress up for the occasion."

Tony's smile deepened, his eyes lingering on her just a moment longer before turning his attention to the imposing form of the *Stardust II*. "Wow! How do some doctors from Cuba wind up piloting a Secret Police RAM Jet? Last I checked, med school didn't offer courses in grand theft aero," he quipped, his eyes wide with admiration and a hint of incredulity.

Jessica, still caught in the aftermath of their prolonged embrace, managed a smile. "Well, Tony, let's just say our resumes are a bit more... eclectic than you remember. Come aboard, and I'll spill the beans. It's quite the story."

Will and Jessica walked Tony onboard the *Stardust II* and introduced him to Jim and Sela.

"Where do we start?" said Will.

"At the beginning, I guess," said Jessica.

"OK, let's do this," said Will. "Eight months ago, we were on a spaceship called the *Stardust,* heading out past Mars to investigate a glowing cometoid that was heading towards Earth."

"A glowing thing heading towards Earth?" said Tony. "I'm sure I would have heard something about that."

"Well, that's where it gets interesting," said Jessica.

"Let me continue," replied Will. "When we got to the cometoid, we sent a probe down that confirmed the object was made of a chemical we had never seen before. The boffins back at NASA said we should fire an X-ray onto it."

"NASA? Who's NASA? And X-rays? Why would you have an X-ray machine on a spaceship? Does this have something to do with our hospital break-in?"

"All will be explained soon," replied Will. "What we didn't know is that exciting the compound with an X-ray beam opens the door to a tunnel that leads to other dimensions."

"Other dimensions?" said Tony, incredulously.

"Yes," replied Jessica, "We are from another dimension."

"Another dimension?" said Tony. "Am I being pranked? Where are the cameras?"

"No joke," replied Jessica.

"Some things are different in our dimension, but some things and people are the same," said Will.

"Like this guy," said Jessica, introducing Tony as Richard walked out of the cockpit. "Tony, I'd like you to meet our dimension's Richard Coburg."

"You bastards!" yelled Tony as he lunged at Richard. Luckily, Will and Jim were prepared and grabbed him before he could attack Richard.

"One day we'll meet someone who is pleased to see me," said Richard, ironically. "Hi, Tony. I'm not the Richard from Empire Intelligence. I'm Richard Coburg, an electronics expert from what we call Earth One."

The revelations whirled around Tony like a storm, each one seeming to weigh him down further. His shoulders drooped as he murmured, "I... I need to sit."

Jessica gently guided him to a chair. "It's a lot to take in," she whispered soothingly.

Sela, her brow furrowed in thought, finally spoke up. "Maybe we should show him the highlights from Savina's memory recovery video. It could help him see things more clearly."

Jessica nodded, digging into her bag to retrieve a sleek VR headset. "Here, this might make things easier to understand," she said, handing it over to Tony.

Tony hesitated, the headset in his hands. "So, Doug and Savina—they believe all of this?"

"Yes," Jessica confirmed, her tone firm. "Doug helped us get back to Earth. Without him, we'd still be out there in space."

"This better be good," Tony muttered, still not fully convinced but slipping on the headset.

As the video played, a montage of their extraordinary experiences unfolded before Tony's eyes. When it ended, he removed the headset slowly, his expression contemplative. "Okay, let's say I believe you. Things do start to make more sense. You all seemed so at ease in New York, yet occasionally looked puzzled by the simplest things."

Will chuckled, leaning back in his chair. "Good observation," he acknowledged. "We've lived in New York too, in our own dimension. It's vibrant and bursting with life. But the New York you know seems quite restrained to us; the nightlife and freedom we're accustomed to just wasn't present."

"And I've known Doug and Savina for years," Tony continued thoughtfully. "If they believe you, I guess I can as well. Which leads me to the obvious question—how did you get a RAM Jet?"

"We had a mission in Jacksonville and had to play the doppelganger routine. The Commander took one look at me and asked if he could ready my RAM Jet" answered Richard.

"That explains a lot," Tony said, a mix of intrigue and concern in his voice. "We've always suspected the Director has several off-the-books, top-secret missions worldwide. This one in Florida must be for covert operations within the US. We usually never see them because of the cloak."

"Cloak?" Jim frowned, his curiosity piqued.

"Yes," Tony continued. "These ships have a cloaking device that makes them invisible to both the naked eye and our most advanced tracking systems. It also functions as a force field— nothing can penetrate it."

Richard's eyes lit up with excitement. "Ah, computer," he called, turning toward the ship's console. "Activate the cloaking device."

"Of course, Director," the computer replied smoothly. "Cloak activated."

"Maybe we should rename our ship the Defiant," Richard mused, grinning at the Star Trek reference.

"Enough with the Star Trek references," Will laughed,

half-exasperated, half-amused. "Deactivate the cloak; we don't need it here at the airport."

"Computer, deactivate cloak," Richard said, still chuckling at his own joke.

"Cloak deactivated," the computer confirmed.

Sela, who had been silently observing, finally spoke up with a bemused smile. "What's this about Star Trek now? Are we on a spaceship or a sci-fi convention?"

Jim laughed, understanding the confusion. "It's just Richard being Richard. But honestly, the technology is straight out of sci-fi. Makes you wonder what else the Director has hidden away."

"Okay, now that we've had our fun with that, why am I here?" Tony asked, shifting the focus back to the purpose of their gathering.

Will took a deep breath before responding, sensing the seriousness of Tony's question. "We're on our way to Ammon to find the Dimension Stone," he explained. "But we got caught in a Dead Zone field because of the hijacking of the Super Yacht Umberto. According to the information given to us by the

Governor, onboard was the second in line to the Danish Throne, Prince Viggo, and his wife.

"To maintain our cover, we had to agree to mount a rescue mission. The best way to avoid Empire security was to request help from you and your friends in the Libyan Mafia."

"Not a bad plan," said Tony. "I have a cousin in the organisation, and I'm sure they would like the Danish Royal Family to owe them a favour."

"Another cousin?" joked Jessica.

"I'm Italian," replied Tony. "I have a lot of cousins."

The group then discussed various plans to liberate the *Umberto*, and after a while, a plan emerged.

"So, the plan is," started Will, "we fly to Benghazi, pick up your cousin and some of his well-armed friends. We then fly to where we last knew the *Umberto* to be. Under the cloak, we use the onboard sensors to locate the hostages and the hijackers. Then, under cover of darkness, we land and take over the ship."

"That sums it up," agreed Tony. He turned to Richard and said, "We'll have to disguise you somehow; my cousin won't be as understanding as I am."

"Good idea. We don't want to have to explain where we're from to everyone we meet," added Will.

Soon after, the *Stardust II* left Tenerife, heading towards the city of Benghazi. As they approached, the city's buildings were outlined against the setting sun. Old structures stood beside new skyscrapers, showcasing the city's blend of past and present.

From the deck, Tony pointed out a specific compound. "That's the place," he said, his voice carrying a note of familiarity. "That's where my cousin is based."

Will quickly directed Richard, indicating where to land. "There," he instructed. Richard nodded, acknowledging the command, and began the descent.

As the *Stardust II* touched down, there was immediate movement outside. Clearly, they were expected. Tony stepped out first, his expression determined. Inside the ship, the rest of the crew waited anxiously, feeling the tension rise.

After a brief period, Tony returned with a team of eight following him. They looked ready and focused, each displaying a demeanour that spoke of preparedness and resolve. Tony introduced them to the crew, pointing to one person in particular.

"This is Marcos, my cousin. He's vital to our plan."

Marcos surveyed the group, his gaze assessing, then firmly shook hands with Will, sealing their newfound alliance.

"Good to meet you all," Marcos said. "I'd like to introduce Luca," he added, gesturing to a woman standing beside him. She had sharp eyes and an air of quiet confidence. "She's our tech expert—she'll handle the technical aspects of the mission."

Sela looked at Luca with curiosity. "Pleasure to meet you," she said. "What kind of tech work do you specialise in?"

Luca offered a subtle smile. "I deal with communications, systems infiltration, surveillance—anything that requires a digital touch."

"Impressive," Sela replied, genuinely intrigued.

She then glanced at the rest of Marcos's team. "And what about the rest of your crew?" she inquired.

Marcos's expression turned serious. "They're specialists in their own fields," he said tersely. "It's better you don't know the details.

An uneasy silence settled over the group. Will cleared his throat. "Well, we're glad to have you all on board. Let's focus on coordinating our efforts."

With introductions complete, the crew and Tony's team began discussing the plan in detail. Richard, seated in the open cockpit of the Stardust II, was careful to remain unrecognized by Marcos's team. To conceal his identity, he had donned a hoodie pulled low over his face and wore a medical mask covering his nose and mouth.

Marcos glanced toward the cockpit, noticing the figure at the controls. "Who's that?" he asked casually.

Sela quickly responded, "That's our pilot. He's been dealing with some severe allergies and prefers to keep to himself."

Richard turned slightly, giving a brief nod without making eye contact.

Marcos nodded in understanding. "Ah, allergies can be tough out here."

"Especially with all the different climates we've been through," Will added smoothly. "But don't worry, he's the best there is."

Marcos seemed satisfied with the explanation. "As long as he gets us where we need to be."

"Trust me, he will," Sela assured him.

The rest of Marcos's team paid little attention, focusing instead on the mission ahead.

A few minutes later, with everyone briefed and positions assigned, they were airborne again. The Stardust II soared silently under cloak, heading toward the coast of Western Africa on the hunt for the Umberto.

Chapter Fourteen

The crew's search for the Umberto took longer than expected. They scoured the waters off the coast of Western Africa; Jessica and Sela took turns at the radar, scanning for any sign of the yacht, while Jim tweaked the sensors, trying to sift through the maritime traffic cluttering their screens.

"Nothing yet. Let's expand the search grid," Jim suggested, adjusting settings after settings, hoping for a breakthrough.

As evening approached and the sky turned a deep orange at sunset, a small but significant signal finally appeared on their radar. "Got something!" Jim exclaimed, excitement breaking through his earlier frustration. "That's definitely our target; it matches the Umberto's size and speed, heading northeast toward the shipping lanes."

Richard promptly altered their course, bringing them closer to the yacht, now just a silhouette against the ocean's expanse. As they approached, Jim prepared to deploy a new tool in their arsenal—the cloaked drone. They had found it among other sophisticated gadgets on board the Stardust II, and this would be its first field test.

"There she goes," Jim said, as he released the drone, watching it disappear into the dusk sky. The drone, virtually invisible and silent, began its descent towards the yacht, its advanced scanners activated to map out the exact positions of the people on board. This crucial information would be key to their planned rescue.

Twenty minutes later, the crew, plus Tony, Marcos, and Luca, gathered around the main screen.

"From what I can make out," Jim said, "it looks like the passengers are in the bar area at the back of the yacht with a guard at each of the three exits. The crew seems to be held near the bridge with at least two guards, and the cabin crew is locked in on Level One, also with two guards. Plus, there are a number of guards patrolling around the deck."

"How can you tell how many guards there are?" asked Jessica.

"They are the ones with big metal objects, which the sensors indicate as guns, whereas the rest don't have any. "We believe they're heading to a rendezvous location with another boat, where they'll transfer the passengers," explained Jim.

"We need to act fast," Jim added. "If they're planning to transfer the passengers, we might not have much time."

"The plan is to shoot a sleep canister through that window on the bridge. The gas takes effect almost instantaneously and will knock everyone out for at least an hour. Marcos and some of his men will then enter Level One through the back service door. With the element of surprise, we aim to keep casualties to a minimum," Tony outlined.

"Let's aim for zero," said Will.

"What about the passengers?" asked Jessica.

"How are your acting skills?" replied Tony.

"Acting?" queried Jessica.

"Yes, we will drop you off under full cloak at the lifeboat area on Level Two. On our signal, you and Sela will pretend to stumble along to the bar, posing as two tipsy passengers who've lost their way. As soon as you've distracted the guards, my men will incapacitate them."

"Wouldn't that be dangerous?" asked a concerned Sela.

"We don't think so," said Tony. "The hijackers want all passengers alive and well for ransoming, so two seemingly drunk women won't raise suspicions."

"It's a good plan," agreed Will. "I am particularly nervous about freeing the passengers in the bar. Is there any way we can draw the guards away from them instead of going in shooting?"

"Couldn't we send in a sleep capsule, like we're doing with the guards on the bridge?" asked Jessica.

"We could," replied Tony, "but some passengers are in their 80s and might not survive the gas."

"From what we've learned about this group," began Marcos, "the experienced smugglers are the ones guarding the crew on the bridge and the cabin crew on Level One. Therefore, the smugglers guarding the passengers aren't as battle-hardened. They expect resistance from the crew, not the elderly passengers, as Tony mentioned."

"It sounds like a reasonable plan," Will remarked. "It's almost 6 p.m. Let's wait a couple of hours. It should give us the element of surprise when they're finished feeding the passengers."

Jessica and Sela donned their newly acquired party attire that befitted their role as luxury passengers, a stark contrast to their usual, more casual clothes. Jessica slipped into a glamorous, sequined gown that shimmered with every movement, reflecting the cabin's light in captivating patterns. Sela opted for an elegant satin dress that complemented her poised disposition.

"I knew these outfits would come in useful," Jessica laughed, admiring herself in the mirror. The dress accentuated her silhouette, making her feel both powerful and graceful. She turned to Sela, who was meticulously adjusting her dress, ensuring every detail was perfect. "And you look stunning," Jessica added as Sela walked around the room, the fabric flowing smoothly with her steps.

Sela grinned, giving a mock bow. "Why, thank you, darling. You're not too shabby yourself," she teased back, her eyes twinkling with mirth. "Feels good to dress up for a change, doesn't it?"

"It does," Jessica agreed, her smile brightening. "Especially when it's for a cause as daring as this. Who knew our shopping spree would gear us up perfectly for a covert mission?"

Their smiles briefly converged into a light, nervous chuckle—a fleeting moment of levity amidst the mounting tension. As they reviewed their plans, their elegant dresses seemed to empower them, blending the lines between their undercover personas and their true selves.

However, Sela's smile faltered as she mentally rehearsed the mission details again. "Jess, I'm not sure I'm ready for this. It's one thing to play dress-up, another to face what's out there."

Noticing the sudden shift in Sela's expression, Jessica moved closer, placing a reassuring hand on her shoulder. "Sela, look at me," she said gently. "We've prepared for every scenario. We're not just playing parts; we're skilled, and we're ready. You're ready. And remember, Tony and his team will be right there with us, ensuring our safety every step of the way."

Sela took a deep breath, her anxiety visibly easing under Jessica's calming presence. "You're right. It's just the jitters, I guess."

"Alright, let's make this operation as successful as our shopping trip," Sela said, her confidence creeping back. She clinked her bracelet against Jessica's as if toasting to their imminent adventure.

"Agreed," Jessica replied, her gaze firm and her voice filled with determination. "Let's show them that style and substance can go hand in hand. And with Tony and his team watching our backs, we have nothing to fear."

As the sun disappeared from the sky, Richard piloted the Stardust II to the lifeboat area. There were no signs of guards. Upon decloaking, Jessica, Sela, Tony, and two of Marcos's men quickly disembarked. Richard cloaked the ship again and positioned it near the Umberto's bridge, preparing for their strike.

The crew split into two distinct teams, each with a critical mission to accomplish. Jim took the lead of the first team, whose main goal was to secure the bridge. Luca, joined this team, ready to take control of the yacht's systems. Meanwhile, Will, flanked by Marcos and a few others, focused on rescuing the cabin crew.

Moving like shadows themselves, Will's team approached from behind and swiftly took down the rear guards using stunners. The element of surprise was on their side as they edged closer to the hostages.

Simultaneously, Jim's team prepped their sleep canisters. With a synchronised nod, they released them into the bridge area. A hazy mist quickly filled the room. Moments later, they stormed in, their movements precise and coordinated. Some pirates tried to retaliate, but they were overwhelmed both by the effects of the canisters and the swift response of Jim's team.

As they secured the bridge, Luca immediately moved to the control panels. Her fingers danced over the keys with practised ease.

"Once I get into their mainframe," Luca said, her eyes focused intently on the screens, "I can control the yacht's door locks, alarms, and surveillance systems."

"Good," Jim replied. "We need to make sure no more surprises are waiting for us."

"Already on it," Luca responded. "I've locked down all access points to our location and disabled internal alarms. The pirates won't be able to move freely now."

Nearby, Marcos approached the door next to the bridge, his senses on high alert. He listened intently, then signalled the all-clear to Will. With skilful hands, he managed the lock, revealing the yacht's frightened crew, bound and obviously traumatised. "It's okay," Will whispered reassuringly. "You're safe now."

Yet, their mission was far from over. An alarm suddenly wailed, its red lights casting an ominous glow over the corridors.

Jim turned to Luca with a questioning look. "I thought you disabled the alarms?"

"I did," Luca replied, her fingers flying over the keyboard. "This must be a manual override from another location."

Jim's voice came urgently over their radios, "They know we're here. Everyone, hold your ground. We must secure this position."

Marcos, thinking quickly, shouted, "We need a diversion. Maybe trigger a fire alarm or lifeboat alert."

"Already on it," Luca interjected. "I can send out a false fire alarm to confuse them."

Acting on her idea, Luca accessed the yacht's internal systems, sending out a fire alarm. The blaring sirens and flashing lights added to the pirates' confusion.

Using the ensuing chaos as a cover, the team ushered the freed crew members toward their planned exit. But just as they saw an escape route, a group of pirates blocked their path, guns raised. What followed was a fierce firefight. Luca and Marcos took defensive positions, covering the hostages. At the same time, Will, Jim, and the other members of the team returned fire, pushing back against the attackers and ensuring the crew's safety.

Just a few minutes later, the decisive words crackled through the secure radio channel. "Bridge secure," announced Will, confirming they had taken control of the yacht's command centre swiftly and quietly.

From the cockpit of the Stardust II, Richard responded calmly, "Aye, Captain. I'm just awaiting the report from Tony's team."

While the other teams were securing the bridge and crew decks elsewhere on the yacht, Tony was briefing Jessica and Sela. "Alright, we're in position. I need you both to pull off that spectacular act of yours. Distract the guards so we can locate the passengers. And for the love of all that's holy, be quick about it!"

Jessica ruffled her dress and smeared her lipstick, transforming herself into an all-too-familiar caricature. "The 'flamboyantly drunk heiress' gig? Oh, it's a classic."

Feeling a resurgence of her usual daring, Sela adjusted a deliberately skewed tiara with a confident smile. "Why can't business and pleasure mix just a little? Lighten up, Tony." Her confidence seemed to return as she embraced the role they were about to play.

Tony rolled his eyes. "This isn't an improv night, ladies. Remember what we're here for."

True to their word, Jessica and Sela walked down the corridor toward the bar with dramatic flair, stumbling and swaying as if they'd had one too many martinis. The opulent hallway was lined with ornate mirrors and gilded fixtures, reflecting their exaggerated antics. As they approached the entrance to the bar, two guards stood watch outside the heavy double doors.

One guard stepped forward, his expression stern. "What are you doing out of the holding area?" he demanded.

Jessica hiccupped loudly, batting her eyelashes. "Holding area? We were looking for the ladies' room," she slurred. "Got a bit turned around."

Sela giggled, leaning heavily on Jessica. "Is this where they keep the good champagne?" she asked, pointing vaguely toward the bar doors.

The second guard narrowed his eyes. "All passengers are to remain inside. How did you get out?"

Before they could answer, a voice from inside the bar barked, "What's going on out there?"

Taking advantage of the distraction, Jessica and Sela pushed past the guards and stumbled into the bar. The room was filled with anxious passengers seated around tables or standing in clusters, all under the watchful eyes of several armed guards positioned strategically throughout the space. Eyes turned toward the newcomers, a mix of surprise and curiosity flickering across the passengers' faces.

"Well, look at all these familiar faces!" Jessica exclaimed, throwing her arms wide. "We thought the party was elsewhere!"

Sela spun around unsteadily. "And here it is! Time to celebrate!" she declared, making her way toward the centre of the room.

The guards inside exchanged confused glances. One barked, "Who let them out? Get them back with the others!"

"Oops, our mistake," Jessica said, pretending to trip over her own feet. She grabbed a nearby table to steady herself, sending glasses and utensils clattering to the floor.

Sela, meanwhile, had reached a grand piano in the corner. "A little music to lighten the mood!" she announced, standing at the piano and striking a cacophonous chord.

"Stop that!" a guard shouted, marching toward her.

The passengers watched with a mix of confusion and dawning amusement. The guards' attention was fully on Jessica and Sela now, their orderly control of the room beginning to unravel.

Outside, Tony and his team moved into position. "They're creating the distraction. Time to move," Tony whispered.

Silently, they slipped through a service entrance that Luca had unlocked remotely. Inside the bar, the chaos escalated as Jessica began to sing an off-key rendition of 'Girls Just Want to Have Fun' while Sela pretended to accompany her on the piano.

"Enough!" the head guard roared. "Grab them!"

As two guards advanced on the women, Jessica feigned a sudden bout of nausea. "Oh no... I don't feel so good," she moaned.

Before the guards could react, she leaned forward and vomited all over their shoes. The guards recoiled in disgust, one of them slipping and nearly falling.

"Sorry!" Jessica said weakly, wiping her mouth.

At that moment, Tony and his team sprang into action. "Now!" Tony signalled.

They burst into the room, stunners raised. "Everyone, stay calm!" Tony commanded.

The passengers remained seated as blue energy pulses shot across the bar, striking the guards with unerring accuracy. The guards attempted to return fire, but the surprise attack left them disorganised.

One guard managed to aim his gun at Sela, who stood exposed at the piano. His finger tightened on the trigger.

"Watch out!" a passenger screamed.

Sela dove behind the piano as a shot rang out, the bullet embedding in the wall behind her. Tony pivoted and fired his stunner, hitting the guard squarely in the chest. He collapsed, his weapon clattering to the floor.

In less than a minute, all the guards were incapacitated. The passengers looked around, uncertainty etched on their faces.

Tony surveyed the room. "It's okay now. The yacht is secure, and you're all safe," he announced.

Jessica helped Sela to her feet. "That was a close one," she said, her tone more serious.

Sela nodded, brushing dust from her clothes. "Too close. Thanks for the assist."

An elderly woman cautiously rose from her seat. "Are... are you with the authorities?" she asked hesitantly.

"We were sent by the Director himself to help you," Tony replied, offering a reassuring smile. "Is anyone hurt or in need of medical assistance?"

A murmur spread through the crowd as passengers began to stand, relief evident on their faces.

A middle-aged man approached, extending his hand. "Thank you. My wife twisted her ankle during all this," he said gratefully.

"Just doing our duty," Tony replied with a steady handshake, his tone warm but modest. He gestured toward Jessica and Sela, who were already scanning the cabin with alert eyes. "There should be medical supplies on board—we'll see to her."

For a moment, there was a hush. A few passengers exchanged glances, the strain of fear giving way to relief at the sight of someone taking charge. Jessica had already slipped her pack from her shoulder, checking the compartments with crisp efficiency, while Sela crouched beside the injured woman, speaking softly, her touch both gentle and professional.

The atmosphere in the cabin shifted—uncertainty yielding to a fragile sense of order. People began to stir, emboldened by the crew's calm presence, and then the first voices rose:

- "I think I've bruised my arm."

- "My daughter's feeling faint."

- "Does anyone have something for anxiety?"

Sela rose and moved among them, her manner calm and unhurried. "We'll help everyone," she said reassuringly. "Please, take a seat, and we'll make sure each of you is looked after."

At that moment, a distinguished man stepped forward from the crowd. He had piercing blue eyes and carried himself with an air of quiet authority. Dressed in an understated yet elegant suit, he approached Will, who, along with Marcos, had just entered the bar.

"Excuse me," the man said. "May I speak with you?"

Will turned to face him. "Of course," he replied.

"Allow me to introduce myself. I am Prince Viggo of Denmark."

Will blinked in surprise. "Your Highness," he said respectfully. "It's an honour."

"The honour is mine," Prince Viggo replied. "Your team's actions have been extraordinary. Please convey my deepest gratitude to the Director for his prompt response."

"I will, Your Highness," Will assured him. "Our priority is your safety.

"Let me introduce you to Tony and Marcos. Their team will be accompanying you to Casablanca".

Prince Viggo nodded appreciatively. "That is most reassuring. Knowing that such capable individuals will be with us eases many concerns. I am grateful to have them by our side."

As the pleasantries continued, Will turned to Marcos and whispered, "We need to get moving. Have you seen Jess?"

Sela, overhearing the conversation, chimed in with a mischievous twinkle in her eye. "She and Tony seemed to be exploring the cabins together. They left, oh, about 20 minutes ago?"

Will raised an eyebrow, a smirk playing at the corners of his mouth. "Guess we can afford a small delay."

When the time was closer to an hour than minutes, the door to the bridge slid open. Jessica walked in, her hair slightly tousled, followed by a slightly out-of-breath Tony.

Will, suppressing a chuckle, inquired, "Is everything alright?"

Flashing a sly smile, Jessica responded, "Oh, everything's more than alright."

Trying to maintain a straight face, Tony added, "Just making sure all the cabins are, uh, safe and secure."

"I'm sure they are," replied Will.

PART FIVE

Chapter Fifteen

With their goodbyes exchanged, a mix of anticipation and nervousness permeated the atmosphere among the crew. Within the hour, the *Stardust II*'s engines hummed to life, setting a course for the predetermined rendezvous point. The journey was swift, and under the veil of their advanced cloaking technology, they arrived unnoticed. Their destination was an area steeped in history, nestled next to an old Catholic mission lying quietly near the Libyan border. Amidst whispers of the past and the shadow of ancient walls, they touched down in a place that seemed untouched by time.

The mission was a grand spectacle, a relic of ages past. Its sandstone walls, weathered by time, stood defiantly tall. Stained glass windows, though faded, still captured the essence of the stories they depicted, filtering light into kaleidoscopic hues. Spires reached towards the sky, a testament to the architectural ambitions of a bygone era. Here and there, creeping vines claimed the old stones, draping the structure in a mantle of serene coexistence with nature.

Jessica was the first to disembark, her smile bright and welcoming as she introduced Will, Jim, and Sela to the waiting Australian couple. Brandon, with his easy-going manner and sun-kissed skin, extended a firm handshake, while Marie, with her warm eyes and welcoming aura, greeted everyone with a nod.

"And as I told you back when we first met, here is our pilot, Richard Coburg," Jessica announced, gesturing towards the spacecraft's open hatch. Richard emerged into the light, his appearance not just similar, but identically that of the notorious Director of Empire Intelligence.

"Oh, wow," Marie exclaimed, stepping back slightly in instinctive caution before catching herself. "He is the spitting image of the Director. That should certainly aid in your mission."

"What, no gun?" Richard joked as he descended the last step, his tone light but tinged with darker expectations. "I can't believe it; finally, someone who doesn't flinch at the sight of me."

"Well, we were warned," Brandon replied, smiling broadly as he shook Richard's hand. "Welcome, Richard. It's good to finally meet you."

As they walked away from the ship, Jessica sensed a weight lifting from Richard's shoulders—here, he was merely a pilot, not the feared figure from this world. Her eyes darted around the surroundings. "We should cloak the ship," she suggested, noting the openness of the area that left them vulnerable to prying eyes.

Brandon pointed to one of the mission's sturdier structures. "Better yet, let's shelter it in there. It keeps it out of sight and ensures nobody accidentally stumbles into it."

They maneuvered the *Stardust II* into the suggested building, concealing it from view. As they did, Marie began sharing the mission's rich history. "This place, built in the 18th century, has always been a beacon of faith. Though it's seen its share of abandonment due to political turmoil over the years, we've made it our home for a while now."

With the ship safely tucked away, the group congregated in the mission's spacious kitchen, which Richard immediately dubbed the War Room. Here, with cups of freshly brewed tea in hand, they began to lay out the details of their pressing mission.

"It's fortunate you arrived during Ramadan," Brandon noted. "Fewer people around during the day will make it easier to remain hidden."

Jessica's voice, firm and clear, cut through the dimly lit room. "We're here on a mission," she began, her fingers tapping impatiently on the table's surface, "to locate and secure the Dimension Stone."

Brandon raised an eyebrow and chuckled. "The Dimension Stone? That sounds like something out of a children's fantasy book. What's our grand strategy to find this mythical rock?"

Jim took a deep breath. "When we were in Miami," he began, recalling Doug's obsession with tracking the stone, "Doug was engrossed in data, trying to predict the Space Rockers' paths. He was confident he had pinpointed three potential landing spots for the stone, all within this sprawling complex."

The words stirred a mix of excitement and trepidation. "So, we're basically on a cosmic scavenger hunt?" Brandon smirked. "Sounds simple enough."

Jessica reached into her bag, producing three sleek "all-access" ID cards. "It might be simpler than you think," she smirked, waving them for emphasis.

Marie's eyes widened as she took in the cards, her fingers brushing the edge of one. "Where in the world did you manage to get these?" she asked, her voice filled with wonder and a hint of concern.

Jessica leaned in, her lips curling into a conspiratorial smile. "Let's just say I have some friends in high places who were more than willing to help our cause."

Brandon's face turned sombre, realisation dawning. "Santa Paola Mafia," he murmured. "You've got connections there."

Marie gave a half-laugh, her tone lightening the mood. "And they're good Catholic boys, too!"

"They've given us more than just these," Jessica added. "We have the override codes for the base and all the storage bins."

Brandon responded with a grin. "Excellent. I think this mad plan of yours might actually work."

By the time dawn painted the sky with shades of pink and orange, the *Stardust II* crew, clad in their signature uniforms except for Richard, were ready to embark on their quest. Richard was wearing a carefully chosen disguise, ready to blend seamlessly into the background. They departed from the Catholic missionary compound, a place that had provided them with much-needed sanctuary, in one of the compound's workers' vans.

The facility's entrance loomed before them, a silent testament to the secrets it held within. Thanks to the observance of Ramadan, the usual hustle and bustle typically associated with the facility was conspicuously absent. It was as if the universe itself was aiding them in their endeavour.

Inside the facility, Sela swiftly accessed a computer terminal. "Our target is bins located in Sector 44," she informed the group, her fingers flying over the keys. "Specifically, bins number eight, nine, or ten."

The group made their way to a garage-like area, where an array of golf cart-type vehicles awaited them. Without hesitation, they hopped onto one, setting their course straight for Sector 44. As the vehicle hummed to life and began its journey, a sudden, deafening sonic boom echoed through the vastness of the facility.

Startled, they looked up to see an imposing airship. Attached to it was a carriage, eerily familiar in its design. With grace and precision, the airship descended, releasing its carriage cargo before ascending rapidly, disappearing against the backdrop of the vast sky.

Jim, always one to appreciate engineering prowess, murmured, "Impressive," as he watched the spaceship become a speck in the distance. "But we have a job to do. Let's find this rock."

As they approached Sector 44, an urgent alarm blared, halting their vehicle abruptly. A security drone, bristling with machine guns, emerged from the shadows, its camera lens fixating on them. "Identification, please," a mechanical voice demanded. One by one, they presented their IDs, which the drone scanned along with their faces. The tension in the air was intense as each second passed, their fates hinging on the authenticity of the counterfeit IDs.

When it came to Richard, the drone paused, lingering on him longer than it had on the others. The machine's scanners hummed ominously as Richard stood, trying not to betray his growing anxiety under its scrutinising gaze. After what felt like an eternity, the drone finally beeped affirmatively.

"Identification confirmed. Proceed." The alarm ceased, and the drone retreated into its recess. They exchanged looks of relief and gratitude, particularly Richard, who took a deep breath, his relief evident.

"Thank Marcos and his team for these IDs," Jessica whispered, a wry smile playing on her lips as they resumed their journey. The close call had injected a fresh dose of urgency into their mission, emphasising how critical stealth and caution were in their search.

With renewed focus, they disembarked at Sector 44. The first bin they accessed was Bin 8. As anticipated, it was crammed with large rocks, each rivalling the size of a small car. They scrutinised each rock carefully, hoping to find the Dimension Stone amid the geological giants. However, despite their meticulous search, the stone eluded them.

Pushing forward with a mix of determination and rising anxiety, they checked Bins 9 and 10. Both bins stood mockingly empty, offering nothing but hollow echoes of their hopes. The silence of the empty bins seemed to laugh at their efforts, intensifying the sting of disappointment.

A wave of frustration washed over the group. Will, however, maintained a spark of optimism. "We were prepared for this possibility," he reminded them, his voice steady and confident. "Let's return to the computer. With Doug's program, we can tap into the *Stardust II's* system and pinpoint the exact location of our bin.

"Back at the computer terminal, Richard took the lead, connecting a device that looked much like an advanced USB stick. Its edges glowed faintly with a soft, bioluminescent light, hinting at the sophisticated technology encased within. The stick interfaced seamlessly with the terminal through a wireless quantum connection, initiating the software installation. The progress indicators flickered and merged on the holographic display, casting eerie shadows on their determined faces.

As the software silently loaded, a sense of urgency enveloped the room. Every member of the group was fixated on the changing display, aware that every second counted.

"All right, that's our cue," Richard announced once the installation was completed, breaking the tense silence. They gathered their gear swiftly, their movements practised and precise and made their way back to the van, each step quick and purposeful. With their exit strategy firmly in mind, they left the complex, the weight of their unfulfilled mission heavy on their shoulders, but their resolve to find the Dimension Stone and return home undeterred.

****

Three days passed in a whirl of activity, the mission's demands blurring the hours into a relentless stream of challenges. However, during a rare pause in their hectic schedule, Will, Jessica, Brandon, and Marie found themselves gathered around a small table. A bottle of wine was shared among them, its contents softly glimmering in the dim light of the makeshift command centre. As they sipped their wine and enjoyed the brief respite, Brandon seized the moment to delve into a more introspective topic.

"Amid all our focus on the mission, I've been pondering something more personal," Brandon began, his voice carrying a mix of curiosity and contemplation. "I'm really intrigued by how religious institutions might evolve differently depending on their world. Could you share how the Catholic Church operates in your world? The differences could be quite enlightening given our unique histories."

"Sure," said Will. "In our world, after the devastation of the World Wars, there was a significant push for the Church to address the modern world's challenges. This led to the Second Vatican Council in the 1960s, which modernised the Church significantly, altering the liturgy, improving relations with other religions, and addressing issues of social justice."

"Exactly," Jessica added. "Historically, these changes were partly a response to the cultural and ethical crises of the mid-20th century. The Church needed to remain relevant and maintain its influence in a world that was rapidly secularising and grappling with the aftermath of global conflict."

"That's intriguing," Brandon noted. "Here, without the catalyst of global wars, the Church didn't face the same pressures. Our historical trajectory was more about maintaining the status quo. European empires continued their colonial influence well into the 20th century without the disruptions of your wars, which meant that the Church's role in society remained more or less consistent with how it was in the early 1900s."

"Yes," Marie agreed, "and because our society was more stable but less dynamic, the Church focused on reinforcing traditional values. It's been a stronghold against the tide of change that never quite hit us the way it appears to have happened in your world."

"It's fascinating to see how historical events—or the absence thereof—shape religious institutions," Will reflected. "For us, Vatican II was a turning point, redefining the Church's mission to be more inclusive and outward-looking."

"Speaking of inclusivity," Jessica queried, "how does the Church handle Jerusalem being an international city in your world? That must bring unique challenges and opportunities for interfaith dialogue."

"It does indeed," said Brandon. "Jerusalem, as an international city, is a focal point for global cooperation and conflict resolution. The Vatican plays a significant role there, advocating for Christian interests while also supporting efforts to promote peace and understanding between all faith groups."

"It's a unique arrangement that forces different religions to collaborate more closely," Marie explained. "The Church is part of a larger international body that manages the city, which has become a symbol of global unity rather than division."

"That's a stark contrast to our Jerusalem," Will observed, "which remains a hotbed of geopolitical strife. The Church in our world tries to mediate, but the challenges are immense given the political and religious tensions."

"It sounds like your version of Jerusalem could be a model for what many hope to achieve in our world—actual, functional interfaith harmony," Jessica mused. "It's enlightening to see how different circumstances lead to different approaches in handling such a sensitive and significant place."

"Absolutely," Brandon agreed. "It makes you appreciate the complex interplay between history and faith."

As the conversation drew to a close, the group felt a warm sense of camaraderie in the air, enhanced by their reflective dialogue. Brandon glanced around appreciatively. "This has been incredibly insightful," he said. "It's late, though, and we should get some rest for tomorrow."

Marie nodded in agreement. "Good idea," she responded, signalling the end of the evening. "Let's call it a night. We need to be sharp for the day ahead."

Jessica pushed back her chair and stood up. "See you all in the morning," she said with a smile, grateful for the night's exchange.

Will gave a brief nod as they tidied up the table. The room darkened with the flick of a switch, and they dispersed quietly, each pondering the evening's discussions as they headed to their quarters, ready for the next day's challenges.

Chapter Sixteen

Early the next morning, the mission resumed with a heightened sense of urgency. The group had transformed an entire room into a makeshift command centre. The walls were adorned with sprawling maps, graphs, and charts illustrating the intricate labyrinth of Space Rocker flight paths and the schedules of the grand Space Elevators. Multiple monitors flickered with data, streaming live updates of airship movements and pinpoint locations where Space Rocker carriages were scheduled to unload. Amidst this technological marvel, the crew worked tirelessly, cross-referencing data, debating theories, and mapping out the next steps.

Jim adjusted his glasses and meticulously traced a flight path on one of the maps. His fingers paused at Sector 46. "All the evidence suggests that the Space Train meant to transport our Borange variant was delayed. I am near certain that its cargo was diverted, resulting in the unloading taking place in either Bin 6 or 7 of Sector 46."

Will, poring over a different set of data, nodded in agreement. "That aligns with what we have," he said, his voice filled with urgency. "We need to act swiftly and head back to the complex. The longer we delay, the more at risk we are. Our covert rescue operation isn't going to stay under wraps for long, especially with the *Umberto* nearly at the port."

Before they left, Jessica pulled Will aside, her grip firm on his arm. "Remember the last time we were in Sector 44? When the alarms went off just as we arrived?" Her voice was tense, reflecting the gravity of their previous misadventure.

Will nodded, his expression solemn and eyes darkened with the memory. "I haven't forgotten. This time, we have to be even more cautious."

"The way the drone stopped on Richard's ID has me concerned," Jessica added, her brow furrowing deeper with worry. "Let's leave him in the van this time. We can't afford any complications."

Will agreed with a curt nod. They both knew the stakes were higher than ever.

The second visit to the complex was a tense rerun of their first. The ambience was thick with apprehension as they snaked their way through the sprawling facility, dodging prying eyes, avoiding unscheduled patrols, and making their way to their objective: Sector 46. The air was stale, carrying a faint, metallic scent that seemed to cling to the cold concrete walls. Dim overhead lights flickered sporadically, casting long shadows that danced eerily along the corridors.

Each step echoed ominously in the silence, amplifying their anxiety. Jessica's heart pounded in her chest as she scanned their surroundings, ever alert for any sign of danger. Will moved with practised stealth beside her, his senses heightened, muscles tensed for action.

As they approached Sector 46, the tension grew. The corridor seemed to stretch endlessly before them, an oppressive tunnel of uncertainty. The metallic scent mingled with a faint whiff of oil and machinery, a reminder of the relentless industrial activity that powered the facility.

Will whispered, his voice barely audible, "Almost there. Stay close, everyone."

Jessica nodded, her eyes narrowing as she focused on the path ahead. They slipped into the shadows, blending seamlessly with the dim, flickering light. The cold concrete walls felt like they were closing in, pressing down with an almost tangible weight.

Finally, they reached the entrance to Sector 46. Will paused, his hand raised to signal a halt. He glanced back at Jessica, their eyes locking in silent understanding. This was the moment of truth.

As they approached Bin 6, memories of their last interrogation by the drone played back in their minds. Each step seemed to echo ominously around them, amplifying the silence that hung heavily in the air.

"Please let it be this one," Sela whispered under her breath as they neared Bin 6. Jim quickly tapped in the master code they had acquired, unlocking the door. As it swung open, they were instantly greeted by a breathtaking sight. Dominating the expansive room was a rock they recognised, its surface shimmering in a vibrant shade of orange. It basked in a beam of sunlight that slipped through the door left slightly ajar, creating a spectacle that left them in awe.

"Close the door! Now!" Will's voice rang out, shattering the momentary stillness. Jim didn't need to be told twice. With a sense of urgency, he lunged at the door, pulling it shut. As darkness engulfed them, the stone's once radiant luminosity began to fade, dimming down to a gentle glow after a few long minutes.

Jim expertly chiselled two sizable chunks from the now-inert stone; his movements were practised and precise. "One can never be too prepared. A little extra won't hurt," he remarked, his voice echoing slightly in the cavernous space. However, as he bent to lift one of the chunks, it slipped from his grasp with a heavy thud. "Jeez, that's heavy!" he exclaimed, rubbing his hands together. "Makes sense though—when 35% of it is an element with 164 protons, it's going to weigh more than your average rock."

Jessica nodded in agreement. We can't just carry these rocks back to the van; their glow would attract everyone on the base. Luckily, we have that steel chest in the van.

Sensing the urgency, Will quickly opened his communicator. "Richard, do you copy?" There was a moment of static before Richard's voice came through, clear and affirmative. "Loud and clear, Captain."

"We need the van here immediately," Will directed with urgency. "We've secured the stone, but it's highly reactive to sunlight, more so than we expected."

"Understood. I'm on my way," Richard responded, his voice firm and resolute.

As they waited outside for Richard to arrive, their nerves were strained further when a truck roared into view, dust billowing around it. It skidded to a halt, blocking their path, and four guards clad in full regalia dismounted swiftly. The lead guard, a burly man with a scar running down his face, stepped forward imposingly. "This area is off-limits. What business do you have here? There have been no clearances issued for today."

With a respectful nod, Jim addressed the guard. "I understand you're just doing your job," he said calmly. "We're here under direct orders from the Empire. Here are our credentials."

The guard's eyes narrowed suspiciously. "Empire or not, I've got no records of any clearance. What project are you referring to?" he demanded, his tone indicating that he was not one to be easily fooled.

It was at this moment that Richard made his appearance, stepping out of the van with an air of undeniable authority.

"I am the clearance," he declared, his voice dripping with authority.

The shift in the guards' demeanour was almost comical. Their once assertive stances crumbled, replaced by a mix of surprise and deference. "Sir! We did not realise you were on site today."

Richard's gaze was icy as he retorted, "If you needed to know, you would have been informed. Your insubordination speaks volumes. Leave. Now."

Not needing to be told twice, the guards scrambled into their truck and retreated hastily, leaving the group to continue their mission.

After the guards left, the team regrouped, their relief evident yet tempered with the urgency of their situation. They quickly packed and loaded the pieces of the Dimension Stone into the van, its weight a solid reminder of the day's success and the challenges that lay ahead.

As Richard closed the van doors, his posture relaxed slightly, a sign of satisfaction at having asserted his authority so effectively. "That should keep them at bay for a while," he remarked, allowing himself a brief smile.

A short time later, the setting sun cast the desert in a golden hue, bathing everything in a serene light. The crew, victorious from their recent endeavours, made their way towards the Catholic mission, the ancient stones of the edifice promising solace and the hope of a return to their own dimension.

Eager conversations filled the van as it bounced along the rough desert terrain. Will kept the discussion grounded by carefully reviewing their mission's success and outlining their next steps. "We need to stay alert. There's still a lot we don't understand about the forces we're dealing with," he advised, keeping the tone serious and focused. Jim added technical insights about the dimensional travel mechanics, while Sela interjected with questions, her youthful energy bringing a lighter tone to the strategic planning.

Jessica, however, remained noticeably quieter, her gaze fixed on the horizon with a look of deep concern. Her instincts, sharpened by years of training, sensed an unusual calm that seemed out of place in the desert's vast emptiness. The unsettling drone incident from four days ago lingered in her mind, its abrupt halt and focused sensors igniting her suspicion that they were being closely monitored.

As the mission's silhouette appeared in the distance, the team's progress was abruptly halted by a dramatic blockade. Six black SUVs, bearing the stark Double Eagle emblem of the Empire, roared out from behind the dunes and swiftly encircled the van. The menacing growl of their engines filled the air as they skidded to a stop, enveloping the van in a cloud of dust and tension.

The door of the lead SUV opened slowly, revealing a figure clad in tactical armour. His authoritative presence cast a long shadow across the desert floor. Holding a sophisticated weapon, he surveyed the scene with a calculated gaze. Then, in a voice that boomed across the sands, he commanded in Arabic, "اخرج الجميع!" before repeating in English everyone out! ensuring his command resonated with chilling clarity.

The team exited the van with evident reluctance. Will maintained a calm exterior, hands raised in a gesture of peace, while Jim and Sela's expressions mixed curiosity with concern. But it was Richard who took a bold step forward, his bearing confident, even defiant.

"I am Prince Richard, Director of Empire Intelligence," he announced clearly, trying to command the situation with the authority of royalty. "There has been a grave mistake. You are detaining a superior."

The commander, masked and unyielding, responded with a short, cynical chuckle. "Are we now?" he replied dryly, his voice laced with disbelief. He made no move to acknowledge Richard's claim, signalling his men instead to proceed with their operation. "Secure them," he ordered dismissively, his attention already shifting away from Richard's protests.

Seeing the commander's focus shift, Jessica quickly assessed the situation. Noticing a temporary lapse in the soldiers' formation, she seized the opportunity to dash toward the nearby mission. Her movements were swift and decisive, each step echoing against the cobblestones as she made her escape. The soldiers momentarily faltered, caught off guard by her sudden sprint but hesitant to fire near the sacred grounds of the mission.

Jessica slammed the mission's heavy wooden doors behind her, bolting them shut with trembling hands. Inside, the cool and quiet nave offered a stark contrast to the chaos erupting outside. Sunlight filtered through the stained-glass windows, casting colourful patterns on the stone floor. Her breaths came quick and heavy as she leaned against the door, her heart pounding in her chest. Her mind raced to devise a plan of action, but panic threatened to overtake her.

The echo of the door slamming reverberated through the silent hall, bringing Brandon racing to her side from a nearby alcove. "What's wrong?" he asked urgently, his eyes wide with concern.

"They've been captured, but I escaped. They're outside," Jessica replied, her voice barely above a whisper as she struggled to catch her breath.

"Don't worry," Brandon reassured her, placing a comforting hand on her shoulder. "You're safe here. This is a place of sanctuary; they will not dare come in without being invited."

Outside, Richard continued to insist on his identity, frustration evident in his voice, but with Jessica's escape, the commander's patience wore thin.

"Take them all," he commanded briskly, his tone final and unforgiving. The soldiers moved in with practiced efficiency, escorting the remaining team members toward the waiting SUVs, their faces expressionless behind dark visors.

The journey to the unknown destination was tense and enveloped in silence, broken only by the low hum of the SUV's engines. Each member of the team was left to their thoughts, pondering their next moves and the implications of their capture. Richard, though outwardly calm, was internally grappling with confusion. He wondered why his usual tactics, which had previously navigated them through dangerous waters, had suddenly failed to influence this commander. What was different this time? His mind raced as he tried to piece together any missed details that could explain the change in his fortune.

Chapter Seventeen

As the miles stretched and the familiar silhouette of the mission disappeared behind dunes and dust, the four exchanged fleeting looks, words unnecessary. Their eyes conveyed a mix of fear, determination, and a silent promise to one another that they would find a way out of this.

Suddenly, the surroundings became all too familiar. The base. It stood there, unchanged, but its meaning was now tainted with dread. They continued on past the base for around thirty minutes before arriving at a massive, imposing concrete structure. There, casting a shadow of audacious superiority, sat a black RAM Jet. Its design, a mirror image of their own *Stardust II*, was a sleek embodiment of menace, its surfaces catching the dying light of the sun in a sinister display. It was clear that they were about to meet the real Prince Richard.

Will, Jim, Richard, and Sela were yanked out of the vehicles and taken into a dark room where they were strapped to chairs.

"What do you want from us?" demanded Sela, her voice shaking with fear.

"We want information," replied one of the masked men. "And we're going to get it from you, one way or another, but first," he said, looking at Richard, "there is someone who really wants to meet you."

Richard was roughly dragged into a dimly lit room and bound to a chair in the centre. His pulse raced as he stared at the door, bracing for what was to come.

The door swung open, revealing this dimension's version of Richard—an uncanny mirror image of himself with a face hardened and chiselled by years of ruthless ambition and unchecked power. He strode confidently to the desk facing Richard, his gaze piercing.

"I've been looking forward to this moment," he began, his voice low and menacing, each word carefully articulated to maximise the sense of looming threat. "Imagine my surprise when I received a call from the Captain of the Jacksonville Detention Centre, his tone filled with righteous indignation. He demanded to know when I planned to return a prisoner he accused me of releasing. Such insolence could not be tolerated."

He paused, letting the silence hang heavy in the air. A cruel smirk played on his lips as he continued, "After ensuring the captain's termination for his insubordination, I scrutinised the logs. What did I find? There was me, inexplicably authorising the release of this supposed nobody. A perplexing blunder, wouldn't you agree?"

His eyes narrowed as he leaned closer, the smirk now replaced by a predatory grin. "And just as I was tying up that particular loose end, another surprise call came through. This time it was from the Danish King himself, overflowing with gratitude for what he believed was my personal intervention in his son's release. You've been quite the busy actor, haven't you?"

He straightened, folding his hands behind his back, his voice dropping to an even more sinister tone. "And then, merely four days ago, I was spotted entering Sector 44 here in Ammon, a place I had no recollection of visiting... It seems you've been playing quite the elaborate game."

The air between them crackled with tension, his presence dominating the space. "I suppose I should be thanking you for these unexpected diversions. But instead, you've cost me a competent captain, and now," he leaned in again, his breath cold against Richard's ear, "you've piqued my deadly curiosity. Who or what the hell are you, and what are you doing with my RAM Jet?"

Before Richard could answer, he leaned forward, his eyes narrowing. Then, as if things weren't intriguing enough, he continued, "I find you here with this." He gestured towards the chest on the desk, which he opened with a deliberate, taunting motion. Inside lay the shimmering fragment of the Dimension Stone they had recently extracted. His eyes fixed on Richard, he picked up the fragment, his voice dropping to a cold, menacing whisper, "Do you know what this is?"

Richard tried to remain calm and called on the role he had been playing. "No idea, it was in the ship when we stole it. You could ask your Captain, but oh, you can't, as you killed him."

Prince Richard's eyes narrowed. "Don't lie to me," he growled. "I know you've gone to a lot of effort to find this piece of rock."

Richard swallowed hard. He knew he had to be careful with his words. "I honestly don't know anything about it."

Prince Richard chuckled. "You expect me to believe that?" he asked incredulously. "You've been looking for this rock for weeks. You must know something."

Richard shook his head. "I swear, I don't know anything. Please, just let me go."

Prince Richard leaned in close to Richard, his eyes boring into him. "I don't believe you," he said softly. "But I'm feeling generous today. I'll give you one more chance. Tell me everything you know about this and who you are, or I'll make you regret it."

Richard summoned every bit of self-control he had and snarled, "Well, I will just have to regret it then!"

Prince Richard's expression hardened, and with a flick of his hand, he signalled the guards. "Take him away and hook him up to the neuraliser. Then we will have some answers," he commanded coldly.

The Captain of the Guard stepped forward hesitantly, his expression tense with apprehension. "Sir, one of the women managed to escape into the Catholic Mission. My men refused to follow, respecting their sacred grounds," he explained, his voice betraying a hint of fear about the reaction this news might provoke.

Prince Richard's gaze was icy as he regarded the Captain with visible contempt. "Let her be," he responded curtly, his voice dripping with arrogance. "Her and her pathetic church friends pose no threat to my plans. They are inconsequential. He paused, then dismissed the Captain with a disdainful wave. "Dismissed," he concluded contemptuously.

"The remaining guards were swift and efficient as they partially dragged Richard through a stark, dimly lit corridor to a room that chilled Richard to the bone—not just with its cold metallic surfaces, but with the ominous presence of a large machine that loomed in the centre. It was eerily similar to the device Savina had used to record their memories, a connection that did not escape Richard's notice.

As they strapped him into the neuraliser, Richard felt a rush of adrenaline mixed with profound dread. The machine was intricate, with wires and electrodes soon attached to his head, a cold, impersonal invasion of his most private sanctum—his mind.

The process was invasive and thorough. As the machine whirred to life, Richard felt a tingle at the base of his skull, a prelude to the deeper probe that would soon map their every thought, memory, and secret.

The other crew members were then brought in one by one. They looked at Richard with a mix of pity and fear as they, too, were hooked up to the machine. The atmosphere was tense, the only sounds being the soft electronic hum of the machine and the occasional shuffle of feet.

Prince Richard watched from a distance, his expression unreadable, waiting to sift through the extracted memories and information that he believed would unlock the mystery of the two pieces of rock sitting on his desk.

What seemed like days later, the *Stardust II* crew were dragged into a much larger room, where they were pushed roughly into waiting chairs. On the left side of the room, a giant holo screen displayed an image of the original *Stardust*.

Prince Richard entered the room, smiled at them all and said, "Hello, Dimension Travellers."

The *Stardust* crew looked at each other despairingly, knowing that their secrets had now all been revealed to one of the nastiest pieces of human scum imaginable.

"Here is another piece of footage that might interest you," he said as he showed soldiers in the same Double-Eagled uniforms as the ones that had captured them storming the Florida compound. The footage clearly showed Doug's body lying on the ground, but thankfully, there was no sign of Savina or Josie. The hangar door lay open, revealing the original *Stardust*.

He looked at Richard. "I can't really have you parading around, being me."

"That wasn't the plan," Richard replied, his voice steady despite the circumstances. He could feel the eyes of his friends on him, their hope resting on his shoulders.

"No?" Prince Richard smirked, "Then what was?"

"We just want to go home," Sela interjected, her voice a soft plea in the harsh surroundings.

Prince Richard walked deliberately toward the metallic table in the centre of the dimly lit chamber. His eyes were riveted on one of the enigmatic stone fragments that lay there as if it held untold secrets. Slowly, he circled the table, closely examining the stone's seemingly nondescript appearance, taking in its subtle hues and textures.

"An exceptional piece of rock you've presented us with," he finally said, breaking the silence. "My team of experts has been wrestling with its mechanics, trying to decipher how to unleash whatever it is that lies within. Regrettably, they're at an impasse."

He paused and looked up, locking eyes with his guests. "I find it particularly interesting that even after delving into your memories, courtesy of our advanced neural interface, there remains an unexplained gap. One moment, you are in contact with this stone in your own universe, and the next, you're in what you refer to as the dimension corridor."

The air seemed to thicken with tension as if the stone itself was absorbing the words spoken around it. The Prince leaned closer to the table, his eyes narrowing. "This anomaly, this missing link in your memory, suggests that the stone is far more than it appears. And it seems to hold a power that even you, who brought it here, do not fully understand."

Prince Richard turned his gaze to Sela, seemingly contemplating her earlier statement. After a moment of silence, he chuckled, "And you think I'll just let you walk out of here with a weapon of such immense power? I think not."

Richard stiffened at his words, "It's not a weapon. It's a gateway. To our home."

"You see," Prince Richard began, leaning on the table, "that's where you're wrong. It's a weapon. A gateway to other dimensions, other worlds. The power to conquer, control, and dictate. And it's going to stay right here."

He paused again, allowing his words to resonate. "I have already spoken with Queen Victoria, and she is rather keen on the idea of expanding the empire into different realities. Imagine—an empire that spans not only the globe but multiple dimensions."

Will spoke up, his voice filled with defiance. "You can't keep us here forever. We're not from this dimension. We don't belong here."

"Ah," Prince Richard responded, "but that's where you're wrong. As long as I have this—" he gestured towards the stone—"you're not going anywhere."

His icy gaze turned back to Richard. "Tell me, how does it work? How can I unlock the power within this stone?"

Richard met Prince Richard's gaze. "I'm not telling you anything."

The Prince smirked again, a cold and ruthless expression. "We'll see about that. Guards!"

At his command, four guards entered, their stony expressions matching the harshness of the room. Prince Richard pointed at Jim. "You two," he said pointing at two of the guards, "take him. Let's see if his friends' safety encourages some cooperation."

"No!" Sela cried as Jim was pulled away from them. His reassuring smile was the last thing they saw before the door shut, plunging them back into the chilling silence.

Prince Richard's command was chillingly calm. "Take these two," he said, pointing at Richard and Sela, "back to their cells," he ordered the remaining guards, his voice devoid of warmth. "I wish to speak more with the Captain."

As the guards escorted Richard and Sela away, Prince Richard turned his icy gaze back to Will. "Now, Captain," he began, his tone deceptively soft, "we are going to have a little chat."

The room was stark, the air thick with tension as Prince Richard produced a syringe from his pocket. "This," he said, brandishing it before Will's eyes, "will help loosen your tongue." Without waiting for a response, he injected Will with the contents, a potent cocktail designed to disorient and weaken his resolve.

With Will's senses clouded, Prince Richard activated a screen showing a loop of the footage they had captured earlier—the lifeless body of Doug lying on the ground at the Florida compound. Each replay was a calculated torment, a reminder of the fate that could befall all of them.

"You see, Captain, no one here is leaving alive unless I get what I want," Prince Richard continued, his voice low and menacing. "Think about your crew—about what will happen to them if you do not cooperate. This could be any one of them next."

As the drugs coursed through his veins, Will's vision blurred, but the images of Doug and the sound of Prince Richard's threats echoed relentlessly in his mind. The psychological assault was relentless, each word from Prince Richard designed to erode Will's mental defences.

"No!" Will struggled to speak, his voice a hoarse whisper, but his captor's face remained impassive, the smirk never leaving his lips.

"We'll see how long your defiance lasts," Prince Richard remarked coldly, signalling to the returning guards. "Take him back to his cell. Let him ponder his choices."

As Will was dragged away, the last image he saw was Prince Richard's satisfied grin, a stark reminder of the power he wielded and the dire circumstances they were all in.

Under the lingering effects of the drugs, Will's reality twisted into a relentless torment. The compound's walls seemed to close in on him, the echo of his own breathing unnervingly loud in the charged silence. Each thought was a battle, his mind foggy, his senses dulled. The drugs now played cruel tricks on his perception, amplifying his guilt and helplessness.

He was haunted by images of Jim, his friend and confidant, being subjected to unspeakable torture somewhere within the same desolate compound. The vivid flashes of Doug's lifeless body replayed mercilessly behind his closed eyes. Doug, who had been more than a colleague, a steadfast friend whose death now weighed heavily on Will's conscience. And Jessica—brave, resilient Jessica—was unaccounted for, her fate unknown. Each of these thoughts bore down on him with crushing force.

Guilt gnawed at Will, the insidious whisper in his mind telling him that he had failed them all. It was his plan, his decision, that had led them here to this moment of despair. As the leader, he had promised to keep them safe, to guide them through whatever challenges they faced, but now, imprisoned and powerless, he felt he had let them down in the most fundamental way.

In the dimming light of the cell, with the night encroaching, Will's figure slumped against the cold wall. His usually resolute eyes, now blurred by the drug's effects, were clouded with doubt. Yet, as the hours passed, a faint glimmer of resolve began to stir within him. He could not undo the past, but he could shape the future. Will knew that succumbing to despair would not honour Doug's sacrifice or aid his crew. He needed to gather his strength, clear his mind, and forge a plan. No matter the odds, he owed it to those who were suffering, to those who had fallen, to fight back, to reclaim control from the grasp of their cruel captor.

In the silent solidarity of their shared cell, Richard and Sela noticed the subtle shift in Will's demeanour. Despite the drugs and the despair, a leader's spirit began to re-emerge, flickering like a flame in the darkness. This silent resurgence gave them a much-needed spark of hope. Together, they would endure the night, and with dawn, they would begin to piece together their escape, their resilience fuelled not by certainty, but by the necessity to act against the injustice imposed upon them.

Chapter Eighteen

Meanwhile, back at the Catholic mission, the early morning light filtered through stained glass, casting colourful patterns on the stone floor. Jessica's mind was a whirlwind of strategy and concern. The mission, with its tranquil corridors and silent prayer rooms, offered a stark contrast to the urgency pulsing through her veins. She needed more help than the mission's peaceful walls could provide.

Her thoughts frequently turned to Tony. Just a few days ago, they had said what they believed to be their permanent goodbyes, an emotional farewell that had left her feeling both bereft and fortified. They had shared deep vulnerabilities and an intimacy that had transformed their relationship. Now, the thought of drawing him back into danger after such a definitive parting felt like a betrayal of their last moments together. Yet, involving Tony—and his resourceful friend Marcos—was perhaps her best shot at orchestrating a successful rescue.

Walking through the mission's quiet hallways, every step felt heavy with the gravity of her decision. She reached the small, secluded alcove where the mission's old communication panel was installed, her heart pounding with apprehension and resolve.

Standing before the panel, Jessica hesitated, her finger hovering over the call button. She whispered to herself, "I need their help," her voice a mix of determination and trepidation. Taking a deep breath, she pressed the button with a resolute push.

The line crackled to life, and soon Tony's voice filled the space, surprised and slightly guarded. "Jessica? I... I wasn't expecting to ever hear from you again," he said, his tone a mixture of confusion and concern.

Jessica's voice trembled slightly as she responded, "I know, Tony, and I'm sorry to call after our goodbye. But it's urgent. Will, Jim, Sela and Richard have been captured by the Empire. I managed to escape back here to the Mission and I need your help to rescue them. It's risky, and I hate dragging you back into this..."

"You don't have to apologise, Jess," Tony replied, his initial surprise softening into the warmth of their shared past. "Tell me everything. I'm here for you, no matter what."

Heartened by his response, Jessica quickly briefed him on the situation, her voice steadier with each detail shared.

Tony's reply was immediate and decisive. "Jessica, I understand how important this is to you. They're more than just your crew; they're family. I'm still in Casablanca as a guest of Prince Viggo. Although Marcos returned to Libya after the Umberto docked two days ago, I can reach out to him. I'll go to Libya myself, and I'm sure Prince Viggo will help me with transport. We'll assemble a team, and we'll do everything we can to bring them back safely."

As the call ended, Jessica felt a surge of hope mixed with fear. Tony's commitment reassured her, but the stakes were incredibly high. She glanced around the mission's peaceful interior, a silent prayer forming on her lips for the safety of all involved.

As Tony prepared to depart for Libya, Jessica couldn't help but feel a mix of anxiety and hope. She knew that their rescue mission was a risky endeavour, but with Tony and Marcos on their side, they had a fighting chance to free their friends from the clutches of their captors. The clock was ticking, and everyone's fate hung in the balance.

Brandon and Marie sat with Jessica in their well-equipped War Room, poring over detailed maps of the region. The room was a blend of modern technology and historical significance. Advanced communication equipment lined one wall, while the others were adorned with simple religious icons, a testament to the mission's century-old presence. The atmosphere was thick with determination, the walls seeming to echo silent prayers for the success of their daring plan.

"Most of the compound's supplies come from this route," Marie pointed out, her finger tracing a narrow path on the map. "The delivery trucks always stop at the old market here for refuelling. It's a potential weak point."

Brandon, who had spent the last few years building relationships with the local community, nodded in agreement. "The market is often bustling. It could provide good cover for surveillance or even for planting tracking devices on the trucks."

Jessica relayed this information to Tony and Marcos via a secure line. "Brandon and Marie suggest using the market for intel gathering. It's a regular stop for compound supplies."

Tony's voice crackled through the speaker. "That's a solid lead. We can use it to our advantage. Maybe even plant a bug on one of the trucks to get a layout of the inside."

Marcos chimed in, "We also need eyes on the ground. Brandon and Marie, can you handle observing the compound's supply routines? Any pattern you find could be key to timing our approach."

"We can do that," Marie confirmed. "We know people who can help without raising suspicion. Discretion is a way of life here."

Brandon added, "And we've got old radio equipment. It's not the latest tech, but it's reliable and off the grid. We can use it for communication during the operation."

Tony's voice, tinged with unmistakable concern, asked, "How safe are you there?" Pausing, as if weighing his next words, he added, "Is there any chance of them coming back to search for you?"

Jessica held the device closer, her voice steady but her heart racing. "I don't think so," she replied, trying to sound more convinced than she felt. "Brandon believes they wouldn't dare attack a religious compound, not one under the protection of the Jerusalem Accord. Even the Empire isn't reckless enough to violate that."

"Good," Tony responded, a sigh of relief barely concealed in his voice. "Just stay out of sight, and we'll be there soon."

"It's a shame we can't just fly in there under cloak," said Jessica.

"It is," replied Tony, "but the whole compound is protected by a Dead Zone field, so old tech and combustion engines are our only way in."

As the plan grew more intricate, the roles of each participant became clearer. Brandon and Marie would serve as the eyes and ears on the ground, using their deep understanding of the area to gather crucial information and assist in communication.

Tony and Marcos, with their tactical expertise, would handle the more dangerous aspects of the mission, infiltrating the compound and leading the escape. Jessica, torn between her concern for the safety of her friends and her affection for Tony, knew her role was to bridge these two worlds, coordinating and supporting both teams.

A cloud of dust heralded the arrival of Tony and Marcos at the Catholic mission just as twilight deepened. Three rugged, sand-covered SUVs came to a gentle stop outside the imposing structure. Stepping out from their vehicles, Tony and Marcos scanned the surroundings with practised caution, alert to any sign of danger.

The other two SUVs contained the rest of Marcos's team, each member prepared and focused, embodying the same determination as their leaders.

"Alright, team," Marcos addressed his crew, his voice steady. "Let's stay sharp and follow the plan to the letter."

Tony nodded in agreement, his eyes never leaving the horizon. "We've got this. Everyone knows their roles. Let's move out."

As they approached, Tony glanced at Marcos, recalling the long conversation they had during the drive. He had explained everything—the dimension travellers, the critical nature of their mission, and what was at stake. Marcos, ever the sceptic, had listened intently, his initial disbelief gradually giving way to a grave nod of acceptance.

The door of the mission opened, and Jessica emerged, her expression a mix of relief and apprehension. She hurried towards them, her steps quickening as she closed the distance. "You made it," she said, her voice a whisper lost in the vastness of the desert.

Tony nodded, his gaze lingering on her for a moment, a silent exchange of worry and resolve passing between them. "We're here, Jessica. Marcos is up to speed. He knows who you are and where you come from. Let's get to work."

Jessica looked at the assembled team and turned to Marcos. "Where is Luca?" she asked?

Marcos glanced around, his expression unchanging. "She is on another mission. We'll just have to do without her."

Jessica sighed, accepting the answer. "Understood.

Inside the mission, the air was thick with anticipation. Brandon and Marie greeted Tony and Marcos with a mixture of reverence and gratitude, having heard of their exploits.

The group gathered around an old wooden table, maps and satellite images spread out before them. Marcos took the lead, outlining their approach. "Thanks to your intel," he said, nodding to Brandon and Marie, "we've adjusted our plan. We'll use the market as a staging area for surveillance and track the supply trucks to get a better understanding of the compound's routines."

Tony added, "Timing is critical. We'll need to synchronise our movements with the guards' shifts and the desert's conditions. Sandstorms can provide cover, but they're unpredictable."

Brandon chimed in, "We've been monitoring radio chatter. There's a storm expected tomorrow night. It could be your best window."

As they pored over the details, Brandon leaned forward. "There's something else. This morning our surveillance spotted the real Prince Richard's RAM Jet being moved into a private hangar nearby. It seems he's here personally, which complicates our approach."

Tony's eyes narrowed. "Does he have his usual entourage?"

Brandon shook his head. "No, it appears he's only brought a few of his most trusted agents. He doesn't trust easily, which means those agents are highly skilled and extremely loyal. We need to be extra careful not to tip them off."

Marcos rubbed his chin thoughtfully. "That means our approach has to be even more covert. Any direct confrontation could escalate quickly out of our control."

The group nodded in agreement, the gravity of the situation settling in. They returned their focus to the maps, their strategy evolving with each new piece of information, weaving a more intricate web of plans to navigate the impending storm and the guarded secrets of Prince Richard's presence. Marie unfolded a local map, pointing to several trails. "These old smuggler routes are rarely patrolled. They could serve as an escape path once you get them out."

Jessica listened intently, her mind racing with the details of the plan. She knew her role was to coordinate their efforts, keeping communication lines open between Tony's team and the mission.

As the evening wore on, the group drilled down into the specifics. Every potential obstacle was discussed, and every contingency plan was laid out. Tony and Marcos exuded a calm professionalism, their confidence reassuring to the others.

Finally, as the first stars began to twinkle in the night sky, the meeting concluded. There was a sense of cautious optimism in the air. The plan was set, the roles were clear, and the stakes were higher than ever.

****

Meanwhile, back at Prince Richard's compound, the atmosphere was charged with a sense of impending dread. Jim was roughly escorted into the interrogation room, his hands bound tightly behind him. The room was stark, illuminated only by a harsh overhead light that cast deep shadows across Prince Richard's face, giving him an even more menacing appearance.

Prince Richard paced before Jim, his steps echoing ominously in the cold, hard space. Stopping abruptly, he leaned in close, his voice low and dangerous. "Tell me, Jim, how does this stone work? How can I unlock the power within?" he demanded, his icy gaze piercing.

Jim remained silent, his jaw set, trying to resist. In response, Prince Richard nodded slightly to the guards. One of them stepped forward, delivering a sharp, painful blow to Jim's abdomen. Jim grunted, doubling over as much as his restraints would allow, pain clouding his vision.

Breathing heavily, Prince Richard watched Jim struggle. "I have all the time in the world, and my methods can become much more... persuasive," he whispered threateningly. "Think of your friends, Jim. Their safety depends on your cooperation."

Jim's resolve wavered, but he held firm, lifting his head to meet Prince Richard's cold stare. The thought of his friends suffering similar or worse fates was unbearable, but he remained silent.

Seeing Jim's defiance, Prince Richard's expression darkened. "Very well," he said quietly. "Let's see if a more personal incentive encourages you to talk." He leaned in closer, his voice dripping with malice. "If you don't start talking, I will test my next methods on the pretty Asian girl." His lips curled into a cruel smile. "I haven't used my chair for a while."

At this, Jim's composure broke. His eyes widened in panic, and he struggled against his restraints. "No, leave her out of this!" he shouted, his voice cracking with desperation.

Prince Richard smirked a cold and ruthless expression. "Then tell me how the stone works," he demanded.

Breathing heavily, the weight of the threat against Sela pressing down on him, Jim felt a surge of panic. Suddenly, memories that had been repressed, locked away by Savina's machine, began to surface. Flashes of the discovery and the accidental activation all came rushing back. He finally spoke, the words almost a whisper, "X-rays. It's activated by X-rays. We discovered its power accidentally."

A slow, satisfied smile spread across Prince Richard's face. "X-rays, you say?" He stepped back, his demeanour shifting to one of triumph. "Fascinating... and so simple."

He turned to an aide standing by the door. "Prepare the lab for immediate testing. We may have just found our key to unlimited power," he ordered, not taking his eyes off Jim. Then, with a chilling calmness, he added, "Thank you, Jim. Your cooperation is most... valuable."

As Jim was led back to his cell, each step heavy with regret, he couldn't shake the feeling that he had just made a deal with the devil. The burden of his forced cooperation, coupled with the ominous threat against Sela, was a torment he knew he would carry with him, haunted by the potential consequences of unleashing such power.

****

Back at the Catholic mission, it was decided that Tony, Marcos, and the rest of their team would spend the night there, resting before the challenging operation ahead. As they settled in, the desert around them seemed to hold its breath, waiting for the storm that would signal the beginning of their daring rescue.

The next day, the mission—usually a place of peace and reflection—transformed into a hub of strategic planning. Its walls echoed with whispered plans and fervent prayers as the team meticulously prepared for the operation. They spent the entire day refining their strategy, knowing that the success of the mission depended on every detail.

As night fell once more, the hours passed slowly, each tick of the clock a reminder of the impending action. Under the cloak of the following night, with the desert wind whispering secrets across the sands, Tony, Marcos, and their handpicked team approached the compound. They moved with the stealth and precision of shadows, each step carefully placed to avoid detection. The looming sandstorm, a swirling dance of nature's fury, provided the perfect cover.

In the distance, the compound stood, a solitary fortress in the desolate landscape. The team paused, taking a moment to survey the area through night-vision goggles. The guards, mere silhouettes against the dimly lit compound, moved with a routine laxity born of long, uneventful nights.

Marcos checked his watch and nodded to Tony. It was time.

The controlled explosion, meticulously planned to be a safe distance from the compound, detonated with a muffled thud. As expected, it drew the attention of the guards, who hurried towards the source of the disturbance.

With the guards distracted, the team made their move. They approached the less fortified section of the wall, where their intelligence had revealed a vulnerability. Using quiet, efficient tools, they quickly and silently created an entry point, just large enough for one person at a time to slip through.

Tony was the first to enter, his body tensed for any unexpected confrontation. The compound, now a maze of shadows and uncertainty, seemed to hold its breath. He signalled for the others to follow, each member of the team disappearing into the darkness like wraiths.

Inside, the compound was eerily quiet. The diversion had worked better than they had hoped, drawing most of the security personnel away. Tony and Marcos, with practiced coordination, split the team into two groups. One headed to disable the surveillance and control systems, while the other, led by Tony, moved towards the cells where their friends were held.

The team moving towards the control room encountered minimal resistance. A lone guard, surprised and disoriented by the sudden intrusion, was quickly and silently neutralised. With a deft touch, Marcos disabled the surveillance system, plunging the compound into a state of blind confusion.

Meanwhile, Tony's group navigated the dimly lit corridors, moving towards the detention area. The lack of guards was both a blessing and a concern – it made their advance easier, but it also suggested that the compound might have other, unseen security measures.

As they reached the detention area, Tony's heart raced. Behind these doors were their friends, unaware that their rescue was at hand. He signalled his team, and they prepared to breach the cells.

Reaching the grim, steel-enforced door that marked the entrance to the prisoners' cell, Tony took a deep breath, his eyes burning with purpose. "Open it," he commanded, and the air was filled with the sharp, agonizing groan of metal bending to human will. The door buckled and shattered, sending echoes throughout the compound.

Emerging from the darkness of captivity, Richard, Sela, and Will blinked in the sudden flood of light. Their eyes, filled with a mix of despair and hope, met those of their saviours. Words failed them, but the relief evident in their nods spoke volumes.

Will's voice, hoarse with emotion, cut through the momentary silence. "Jim? Where is he?"

"They dragged him that way," Richard said, pointing left.

"And where is Prince Richard?" Will demanded.

"That way," Richard said, pointing straight ahead.

"You guys get Jim and leave that bastard Prince Richard to me," Will snarled, moving with a determined purpose back into the heart of the compound. The anger and resolve in his eyes were as fierce as the storm. He was not just on a rescue mission; this was personal. The image of Doug's body lying on the ground and what Jim and the others had gone through fuelled his every step.

Inside the command room, Prince Richard's voice, thick with authority and arrogance, filled the air. He was issuing commands to his subordinates, unaware of the imminent threat lurking in the shadows. "I want those intruders found and eliminated," he barked. "Do you understand who I am? I am Prince Richard! I am untouchable!"

Will, hidden in the shadows, listened, his resolve turning into steel. This man, this so-called prince, was the source of his crew's suffering. The thought of what this monster had done to Doug and his crew's ordeal—the beatings, the humiliation—ignited a fire in Will. This was more than a rescue; it was a reckoning.

With a burst of energy, Will emerged from the shadows, startling Prince Richard and his guards. Clenching a combat knife, its blade glinting ominously in the dim light, he declared, "Your not untouchable now Richard," his voice ice-cold, his presence dominating the room.

Prince Richard, visibly shaken by this unexpected confrontation, tried to maintain his royal composure. "How did you get out? You dare challenge me? You dare to lay hands on a prince?"

But Will was undeterred. His voice was firm, his intent clear. "You're going to pay for what you did to Doug and my crew."

The two guards, fiercely loyal to their prince, rushed to defend him with a level of discipline and training that marked them as no ordinary adversaries. Will tackled the first guard with military precision and a burning need for retribution.

As the first guard advanced, swinging a raised baton, Will deftly sidestepped the initial lunge. Utilising his combat knife, he expertly disarmed the guard, sending the baton clattering to the dusty floor. With a quick manoeuvre, he neutralised this first threat, pinning the guard down with a swift and controlled hold.

Meanwhile, the second guard attacked with a flurry of punches, his movements sharp and calculated. Will, engaged with the first, was momentarily on the back foot. Just as the second guard aimed a critical strike, Marcos burst onto the scene. With a powerful and precise move, he blindsided the guard, delivering a knockout blow that sent him sprawling unconscious beside his partner.

"Nice timing," Will said, catching his breath as he acknowledged Marcos's help. Together, they turned their full attention to Prince Richard, who, realising the gravity of the situation, began to retreat in panic.

"You can't do this... I am a prince!" Richard stammered, his voice trembling as his usual confidence crumbled under the pressure.

"To me, you're just the man who killed my friend," Will retorted, advancing with the knife held ready, its blade a silent threat. "No title can save you from that." His grip on the knife tightened, his eyes never leaving Richard, ready to end it, once and for all.

Will advanced toward Prince Richard, the combat knife in his hand a clear threat. The prince backed away, his eyes wide with fear as he tripped over his own feet, collapsing against the wall. The cold metal of the blade reflected the fear in Richard's eyes, and for a moment, Will was tempted to end it all here—to avenge Jim and the rest of his crew.

But as he stood there, blade poised, the weight of his responsibility settled upon him. Killing Richard would be easy, but it wouldn't truly right the wrongs or heal the wounds Richard inflicted. It would only perpetuate the cycle of violence they were all caught in. With a deep, steadying breath, Will lowered the knife, his decision made.

"You're not worth it," he hissed at the prince, his voice thick with disdain. Instead of using the knife, Will grabbed a heavy-duty zip tie from his belt and quickly secured Richard's hands behind his back. As the prince struggled, Will tightened the tie, ensuring it cut slightly into Richard's wrists—a small reminder of the discomfort his crew had endured.

With the prince now restrained, Will leaned close, his voice low and commanding. "Where is the Dimension Stone?" he demanded. Prince Richard hesitated, fear flickering in his eyes, but Will's intense gaze compelled him to speak.

"It's in the lab," Prince Richard murmured, his voice barely audible above the howling wind.

"Take us there. Now," Will ordered, his tone brooking no argument. Marcos reinforced the command with a stern nod and a raise of his weapon, standing ready to act should Prince Richard attempt any deceit.

Reluctantly and with evident trepidation, Prince Richard led them through a series of dimly lit corridors until, finally, they reached the lab. The door slid open with a hiss, revealing a scene of scientific chaos—equipment strewn about, papers scattered, and multiple displays flickering with incomplete data. In the corner of the room, almost blending into the shadows, was a dentist's chair, Prince Richard's favourite method of torture, casting an ominous silhouette.

Amid this disarray, at the centre of the room, lay pieces of the Dimension Stone, each meticulously labelled and arranged on a stainless steel table.

Will's heart sank at the sight, yet a wave of relief washed over him when he realised something crucial. "They haven't started the experiments," he observed aloud, noticing the absence of essential equipment.

"Thankfully, they didn't have an X-ray machine. They aren't that easy to find," Marcos added, his voice a mixture of relief and frustration. "They couldn't activate it."

"Let's collect all the pieces," Will decided his voice firm. "We need to make sure there is nothing left behind that they can use."

Quickly and efficiently, Will and Marcos moved to gather all the pieces of the Dimension Stone from the table. They placed each fragment carefully back into the original container, which, fortunately, had been left untouched in the lab. Their actions were precise, ensuring that nothing was overlooked in their haste to secure the valuable remnants.

Chapter Nineteen

Emerging from the compound into a howling storm, Will and Marcos saw the off-road vehicles in the distance, the rest of the team, and the freed captives waiting. They looked on in a mix of shock and awe as they approached with Prince Richard in custody.

The team quickly loaded up and returned to the sanctuary of the mission, each member lost in sombre reflection.

Later that day, the mood was unusually quiet. The solemnity in the atmosphere was thick enough to be cut with a knife. At the heart of the *Stardust II*, Will, Jessica, Jim, and Sela gathered around a holographic map, its soft blue glow illuminating their intent faces. Their captive was safely restrained in the adjacent holding chamber.

Will broke the silence. "Prince Richard is now our prisoner. He's securely confined in a cell aboard this vessel – quite a twist of fate, considering it's his ship. That's a win for us and a blow to the Empire, but we've got a bigger problem."

Jessica nodded. "His uncanny resemblance to Richard. It's unsettling. It's as though the multiverse is playing some kind of sick joke on us."

Jim frowned. "And the fact that the Empire is bent on subjugating all dimensions is not a joke we can laugh off. We know he has shared the information with their Queen Victoria, and we can only imagine the havoc that this could cause."

Jessica said, "What if we can use this to our advantage?"

All eyes turned to her. "Go on, Jess," Will encouraged.

"We take Prince Richard with us back to our dimension as a prisoner," she started, watching her companions' faces for reactions. "And we replace him with our Richard here."

For a moment, no one spoke. Then Sela asked, "Are you suggesting that we leave our Richard behind? To play prince and possibly deter the Empire from their ambition?"

"Yes," Jessica affirmed. "It's a risk, but if we play our cards right, it could buy us enough time to figure out how to prevent the Empire's conquest."

"And to find Savina and Josie," Jim added.

Will stood still, rubbing his stubbled chin in contemplation. It was a daring plan. High risk, high reward. But they were accidental travellers, and they'd been taking risks since they stumbled into this universe.

Jim turned to the Captain. "Will, it's not just about buying time. If Richard can convince them that their Prince is against the conquest, we might not just slow them down. We could stop them."

Will let out a long sigh. It was a daunting idea, and the implications were massive. But, if successful, it would strike a significant blow to any of the Empire's plans. He glanced at the rest of his team, his family. Their expressions mirrored his feelings – apprehension, hope, determination.

"You're right," he finally conceded. "But we'll only do this if Richard agrees. It's his life we're gambling with."

"Where is Richard anyway?" asked Jim.

"He was on the bridge looking at the footage of the compound where Doug was killed," replied Jessica.

"Let's go and talk to him, then," said Will as the crew moved to the bridge. When they found him, Will focused his gaze on Richard. "This is a bold plan; it won't work unless you're all in. We need you to replace your doppelgänger, to infiltrate the Empire."

Richard squirmed, his eyes flicking from Will to the video he was watching and back again, the absurdity of the situation slowly sinking in. "You're asking me to stay here and impersonate him? Are you out of your minds?!" he exploded, his normal composure shattered by the audacious proposal.

Jessica leaned in, her gaze intense. "It's the only way we can buy time, Richard," she reasoned, her voice calm and steady, "We're the only ones who know the horrors the Empire can unleash if they get their hands on the Dimension Stone. There is so much of it left in that storage area. If they succeed, everyone and everything we know will be in danger. We cannot let that happen, especially now we know that Queen Victoria has been told about the stone."

Jim and Sela exchanged glances, the weight of the situation reflected in their shared gaze. They had all been working tirelessly to protect the secret of the Dimension Stone that had brought them here, the very thing that the Empire was now lusting after.

"We can assist you," Sela finally broke the silence. "You already do a pretty good impersonation of him. Now that we have secured the compound and Marco's team has captured all of Prince Richard's men, we can get more information from him using the same machine he used on us."

Richard looked around the room at the faces filled with desperate hope. He took a deep breath, looking at the video feed of his doppelgänger locked in one of the cargo hold cells, a perverse reflection of himself in a world where right and wrong had been flipped. He turned back to Will, his face resolute. "All right," he conceded, "I'll do it. For us, for our home, for all the dimensions that could fall victim to the Empire, and for Doug," he added, looking back at the footage on his screen.

"And with all the resources you command, hopefully you can find Josie and Savina," added Jessica.

"And you won't be on your own," said Jim as Tony, Marcos, Brandon, and Marie came into the room.

"We can help you," said Brandon. Marie nodded.

"And us too," added Tony. "So we can help our world."

"You're right," sighed Richard. "This is the only option. There is just too much damage the Empire can do with this bit of rock."

"And without Prince Richard on our back, we can help you get prepared before we try to go home."

In the coming days, the interior of the compact *Stardust II* buzzed with activity. Jim, working closely with Jessica, suddenly paused and said, "Back at the compound, I remembered something about the Dimension Stone, but as soon as we were safe, it's all gone again."

Jessica gave him a reassuring smile. "Don't worry, I remember everything." As the sole repository of the memories detailing the activation of the Dimension Stone, she was able to guide the crew members as they hustled about. They meticulously checked systems, installed salvaged devices from the original *Stardust*, and prepared the ship for departure with great care. What was once a quiet environment now reverberated with the hum of machinery and the purposeful cadence of footsteps resonating in the confined space.

In one of the ship's briefing rooms, Richard sat surrounded by screens displaying information about Prince Richard. Images of the prince at various functions, audio recordings of his speeches, and holographic simulations of his mannerisms played in a loop. Every detail, from the way he tilted his head when he was amused to the particular cadence of his speech, was dissected and studied.

Sela, acting as his primary guide and coach, would often sit with him for hours, quizzing him on personal anecdotes, preferences, and habits of the prince. "Remember," she'd reminded him, "you're not just mimicking his actions. You have to think like him, feel like him."

Richard nodded, sweat forming on his brow from the intensity of the training. "Tell me about his favourite foods again," he'd asked, or "What's the name of his childhood pet?" Every scrap of information was vital, and there was no room for mistakes.

"He really is a nasty piece of work," Richard remarked, thinking aloud, a hint of distaste evident in his tone.

Sela searched his eyes, her own filled with concern and a depth of understanding. "Are you afraid you might become him?" she questioned softly.

Richard hesitated, then let out a deep breath, vulnerability clear in his eyes. "A little. The line between who I am and who I could become is so thin, Sela. But I've found possible allies, voices in the Empire who want peace, who want to break away from this expansionist madness. Previously they've been silenced by... well, by me."

Sela raised an eyebrow, a ghost of a smile on her lips, "So you are planning on having a dramatic revelation? Going to turn everything around, just like St Paul on his way to Damascus?"

Richard chuckled, the sound tinged with a melancholy undertone. "Something like that. But without the martyrdom bit at the end."

The levity of the moment faded quickly, replaced by the bitter realisation that their paths were soon to diverge. Sela reached out, her fingers brushing against Richard's cheek. "Promise me you'll fight for what's right, that you won't lose yourself in that other version of you."

Richard held her hand with a gentle yet firm grip, bringing it to his lips for a tender kiss. "I promise, Sela," he murmured, the weight of his emotions evident in the quiver of his voice. "And in turn, promise me, you won't let our moments fade into oblivion. Remember us, what we shared. Remember me like this, not what I might become."

Sela's eyes, shining with tears, met his, searching for an anchor amidst the storm of their emotions. "It's etched in my heart, Richard. How can I ever let go?" Her voice trembled. "Why can't I stay, Richard? Why can't we make it work?"

Richard sighed, his heart heavy with the weight of their circumstances. He looked deeply into her eyes, his expression serious. "Sela, I want you to stay with me more than anything. But without a doppelganger in this reality, you can't get identification papers or a full life history. It would put us both in danger. Without proper documentation, you wouldn't be able to integrate into society, and any connection to me would raise suspicions."

Sela's eyes filled with tears, and she whispered, "But Richard, there must be a way. I don't want to leave you."

"I know," Richard replied softly, his voice thick with emotion. "The risks are too great."

Drawn together by an invisible force, their foreheads touched, their breaths intermingling in the space between. "Please," she whispered, the hint of desperation evident, "Stay with me tonight. Let's hold onto this moment, if just for a little while longer."

Richard nodded, eyes closing, absorbing the raw intensity of the situation. "Tomorrow is uncertain," he conceded softly, "but tonight, in this very moment, there's only us."

The world outside, with its ebbs and flows, seemed to fade into insignificance. Their lips met, the urgency of their situation translating into a fervent embrace. The room, initially a backdrop to their rendezvous, transformed into a sanctuary from the world's chaos. Hours slipped away as they clung to each other, fully aware that dawn's first light would herald the close of their shared chapter.

The following morning, the crew gathered outside the ship for the last time. Sela and Richard joined them, walking hand in hand. Reaching the bottom of the ramp, Sela paused, glancing at Richard. She then slowly began her ascent, the weight of her impending departure evident in every step. Richard remained rooted to the ground, his gaze fixed on her retreating figure.

Jessica, having earlier parted from Tony in a cascade of tears, watched the poignant scene unfold from the top of the ramp, her heart heavy with goodbye. She then stepped forward, her movements slow, as if wading through the thickness of their shared memories, to meet Sela halfway down. The ambient thrum of the spaceship's engines, a low and comforting hum, filled the space between them, weaving a soft soundtrack to their reunion. Words were unnecessary as they came together in an embrace, a silent testament to the deep bonds they formed and the painful farewells they endured. In this quiet moment, amidst the gentle purr of technology and the vastness of their journey ahead, they understood each other perfectly. Pulling back slightly, Jessica looked deep into Sela's eyes, searching for the emotions behind them. "Are you alright?" she asked gently, her voice filled with concern.

Sela tried to smile, her eyes glistening with unshed tears. "As good as I can be," she murmured, her voice wavering.

Below them, Will approached Richard, a serious expression on his face. "Richard," he began, hesitating for a moment as if searching for the right words. "I know this is necessary. But are you certain this is the path you wish to follow? To wear the face of a monster... It's a heavy burden."

Richard's gaze remained on Sela, his voice barely above a whisper. "Sometimes, the hardest choices are the ones we must make to protect the ones we love. And to bring down this tyrant, we have to use every tool at our disposal, even if it means becoming him. I've always been good at playing roles, haven't I? Just remember, every action I take is to weaken his regime from the inside."

"And what if you get caught? They won't show you any mercy, Richard."

"I've taken every precaution," said Richard. "But if they do catch me, promise me you won't try to come back. The mission is bigger than any one of us."

"It doesn't feel right, leaving you like this," said Sela softly. "Alone in this twisted dimension."

Richard replied, echoing his previous thought, "Sometimes, to save the ones we love, we must make impossible choices. But you have a universe to save. I trust you'll do it."

The crew descended from the ship and all shared a group embrace with Richard, the weight of their impending separation pressing down on them. They exchanged final words of encouragement and affection, and then, with one last look, they made their way up the spaceship's ramp.

The spaceship's engines roared to life, drowning out the mournful wind. As the ship ascended, Richard watched, a lone figure in the desert, resolute in his mission.

PART SIX

Chapter Twenty

A few hours later, the *Stardust II*'s control room was bathed in a soft, dim light. The only source of natural illumination came from the sun's blue reflection off the Earth, contrasting with the room's otherwise artificial lighting. The crew huddled around a console, a fragment of the Dimension Stone floating nearby, tethered by a diamond rope.

"The last time we ventured through," said Will, "we were thrown off-course. We can't let that happen again."

Sela, looking at a hologram of the stone's structure, replied, "This isn't just about navigation. The stone's reaction to the X-ray beam was unexpected. We're still figuring out its properties."

Jim smirked, a playful glint in his eyes. "You mean we're still figuring out how not to get lost in the infinite abyss of space-time. Maybe we should just try opening each door until we find one that squeaks."

"Squeaks?" Jessica echoed, her tone a mix of curiosity and confusion.

"It's a reference from the TV show *Sliders*," Will interjected, unable to hide a smile.

Jessica, rolling her eyes: "Very poetic, Jim. But we can be a bit more scientific. We've made modifications. I've synced the X-ray frequency to match the stone's resonance. And we blew up the whole cometoid last time, but now we have calculated exactly how much we need."

"Alright." Will nodded. "But we do this together. Every step, every decision. No lone heroics. Agreed?"

"Lone heroics are overrated anyway," replied Sela with a slight smile.

"Agreed, but if there's a dimension with an endless supply of ice cream, I'm claiming it." Jim chuckled.

"Only if it's mint chocolate chip," Jessica said, smiling broadly. "Alright, everyone ready? Firing in 3... 2... 1..."

The X-ray beam shot out, striking the Dimension Stone. A blinding luminescence expanded, forming the multidimensional corridor, a whirlwind of shifting colours and fragmented realities dragging the *Stardust II* into it.

The humming of the engines subsided as it came to a halt inside an ethereal mist. Will, Jessica, Jim, and Sela gathered in the cockpit, gazing out at a corridor that seemed to stretch infinitely in both directions. Giant, towering doors lined the corridor, each guarded by a massive five-headed snake, their iridescent scales shimmering and reflecting colours unknown to the human eye.

"Looks like we've returned," Sela announced, her voice tinged with awe. "It's reminiscent of the Hindu multiverse concept my parents used to describe."

As she spoke, a harmonious chime resonated, slicing through the air. Emerging from the surrounding mist, a figure materialised. Unlike the towering blue entity they had encountered previously in the corridor, this being possessed a different yet equally majestic aura. With multiple arms, a prominent belly, and an unmistakable elephant head, the figure seemed to embody an ancient, mystical presence.

"It's Ganesha," Sela whispered, recognition dawning in her eyes.

Approaching them, the figure's grand yet kind demeanour held the crew in rapt attention. Accompanying him were eight spectral figures, the Dikpalas, guardians of the directions. Each was clad in robes that shimmered with cosmic energy, their forms almost translucent.

The elephant-headed deity addressed them with a voice that resonated with timeless wisdom. "Greetings, travellers of the Stardust II. Welcome to the corridor of the multiverse. You know me as Ganesha. In ages past, I have worn many names — Vighneshvara, Vinayaka, Pillaiyar — but 'Ganesha' will serve. It carries enough truth. He lifted his gaze, and even the Dikpalas bowed faintly as he spoke again. "You find yourselves within the realms of creation and destruction, realms overseen by the deities Brahma, Vishnu, and Shiva." His words enveloped the crew, imbuing them with a sense of awe and reverence for the mysteries they were about to unravel.

Jessica, her mind racing with questions, managed to find her voice. "How do we get back to our own Earth?"

One of the Dikpalas, a tall figure with a deep voice, replied, "I am Agni of the Southeast. Your ship's portal tapped into the fabric of our multiverse. Without guidance, you might remain trapped here forever."

Jim gulped, his usually jovial disposition absent. "So, how do we get back?"

Ganesha motioned towards the myriad of doors lining the corridor, his words seeming to echo through the space, imbuing it with a sense of purpose and urgency. "Each door is a passage to a different reality. To find yours, you must journey through this corridor, accompanied by the Dikpalas," he instructed, his voice carrying the weight of centuries. He then reassured them, adding, "Please leave your ship. The atmosphere in the corridor is breathable." With a final note of resolve, he concluded, "We have much to do."

The crew of the *Stardust II* exchanged uncertain glances, their faces a mix of apprehension and curiosity. The concept of traversing realities was daunting, yet Ganesha's assurance and the promise of guidance from the Dikpalas lent them cautious optimism. With a collective sense of determination, they disembarked from their vessel, stepping into the corridor that seemed to stretch into infinity.

As their feet touched the ground, they immediately noticed the air—crisp and fresh, unlike anything they expected in such a place. It was as if the corridor itself was alive, breathing a life-sustaining atmosphere into its vast expanse.

Before them stood the first door, majestic and imposing. It was adorned with intricate carvings that depicted cosmic dances and celestial events, a testament to the universes that lay beyond. The imagery was so vivid, it seemed as if the stars themselves were dancing, celebrating the mysteries of the cosmos.

Guarding this threshold was a serpent with five heads; each one focused on the newcomers with a fixed intensity. The serpent, Ananta, swayed gently, its movement in harmony with the unseen rhythms of the universe. Ganesha's introduction of the Dikpalas as their guides through this journey added a layer of solemnity to their mission. These guardians of the directions, each with their own strengths and wisdom, were to be their companions in the search for their own reality.

Will approached cautiously. "What lies beyond this door?"

Aruna of the East, her voice soft like a whisper, replied, "A universe where time dances in circles. Past, present, and future are one."

Jim shook his head. "That's not our reality."

The crew moved on. At the next door, the air felt thick, almost electric. The serpent's eyes sparkled, each head emitting a soft hum.

Sela asked, "And this one?"

"A universe where sound is the essence of existence," Aruna explained. "Every entity communicates through vibrations."

Jessica, ever the curious, wondered aloud, "These universes... Are they stable?"

Apara, another of the Dikpalas, responded, "Some realms are stable, while others are in a state of flux, awaiting either preservation by Vishnu, destruction by Shiva, or creation by Brahma."

Door after door, the crew encountered realms that defied their understanding of physics and reality. Some doors were cold to the touch, others pulsated with life, and some were so ethereal they seemed to fade in and out of existence.

As hours melted into days, the relentless march of time seemed to mirror the crew's fading spirits. Every few hours, they would retreat to the sanctuary of the *Stardust II*, seeking brief respite within its familiar confines. These moments of rest were crucial, offering them a chance to refresh their weary bodies and minds before returning to the precise location where their exploration had paused. This rhythm became their lifeline, a cycle of hope and despair, exploration and reflection.

With each door they encountered and each new universe they glimpsed, the weight of their quest grew heavier. The infinite possibilities, rather than inspiring wonder, began to sow seeds of doubt. The myriad worlds they encountered were diverse beyond imagination, yet none bore the comforting familiarity of home. Each return to the *Stardust II* served as a reminder of what they sought and yet seemed increasingly out of reach.

Fatigue wormed its way into their bones, a relentless tide that eroded their resolve. The excitement and curiosity that had once fuelled their journey waned, leaving in its wake a pervasive sense of exhaustion. Sleep, when it came, was fitful and filled with dreams of endless corridors and doors that led nowhere.

Doubt began to cloud their minds, a fog of uncertainty that made them question their mission. Was their reality truly among the ones they had yet to discover, or was it a fool's errand, a chase after a shadow? The vastness of the corridor, once a beacon of hope, now seemed a mocking reminder of their plight. Conversations turned introspective, as the crew grappled with the possibility that their quest might be in vain.

It was Jim, during a moment of quiet reflection, who posed a question. "What if our reality... our universe... has been altered or erased?"

Ganesha, hearing the question, materialised in front of them and replied, "Realities are vast and intricate. Whether they are destroyed or not is up to the will of Shiva. Your universe exists, but the path to it is a testament of faith, understanding, and acceptance. But do not dally for too long; time passes differently in the corridor."

Encouraged by Ganesha's words but aware of the urgency, the crew's focus sharpened. Door after door, they looked for signs, for any indication of a path back to their own reality.

Jessica, who had been silent, letting the others voice their theories and concerns, felt a pull as they approached a door that, to her, felt different from the rest. "This feels... familiar," she murmured, stepping closer. Her hand hovered near the serpent, almost touching it as if drawn by a magnetic force.

"Check the symbol," Will suggested, his tone insistent yet tinged with hope.

Jessica peered closely at the door. "It matches the one we've recorded," she replied, her voice a blend of caution and curiosity.

Jim, rubbing his temples, let out a weary sigh. "As have about a dozen others we've encountered," he remarked, his voice heavy with the frustration and exhaustion that had settled over the entire crew.

In the background, Sela, her hand gently resting against the cool surface of the door, whispered almost to herself, "It's like... like home."

Ganesha appeared and said, "With every journey, may you gather wisdom," he intoned, his deep voice resonating throughout the space. "May your paths always lead you back. But remember this: the world you have travelled to is not for your time or realm. Your kind is not prepared for the tidal wave of progress it brings. Knowledge," he paused, letting the weight of his words settle, "is a treasure that must be earned, step by step."

Will stepped forward, desperation evident in his stance, "But Ganesha, our mission, our purpose, was to gather knowledge. How can we return to Earth with empty hands? We need our ship."

Ganesha inclined his head slightly, acknowledging Will's plea. "I understand the depth of your dedication. Thus, I will grant you passage. Your ship, the *Stardust II*, will be at your disposal. However," he added with a note of finality, "the rich history and advanced technology of the realm you've seen will remain locked away from you. I shall restrict your systems, leaving only the navigation operational."

Jessica's voice trembled with a mix of relief and frustration. "If that's the price to see our home again, so be it."

Ganesha's gaze softened, and there was a hint of mystery in his eyes. "Time has its own flow, and circumstances change. If in the future you prove yourselves worthy, perhaps the veils over this knowledge might be lifted."

He took a step closer, his tone dropping, filled with intrigue. "And remember, your journey might not end here. I might have tasks for you, roles you've never imagined." From within the folds of his robe, he produced a small device, its design intricate and unfamiliar. Its surface shimmered with a metallic sheen, its design both archaic and futuristic. "Take this," Ganesha instructed, placing the device into outstretched hands. "Lock it somewhere safe along with what you have left of what you call the Dimension Stone."

A soft rumble echoed, and a massive door behind Ganesha began to open slowly. "Your ship awaits," he announced. "The Dikpalas, guardians of the directions, have unsealed the way. Travel safely, travellers of this Earth."

The Dikpalas, their task complete, began to fade into the mist, their forms becoming one with the corridor.

The relieved crew made their way to the familiar confines of the *Stardust II*. The ship's deck pulsated with a gentle rhythm beneath their feet. Before them, the gateway that would hopefully take them home beckoned them onward. It shimmered and gleamed, a vast aperture set against the infinite tapestry of this giant corridor, promising both the known comforts of home and the endless mysteries of space.

Guarding the entrance, a magnificent creature loomed. Its five serpent heads swayed hypnotically, each pair of eyes tracking the crew's movements with an intelligence that was both ancient and piercing. The scales that covered its form shimmered with an iridescent glow, capturing the ambient light in a dance of colours. The creature, though seemingly formidable, radiated an aura of calm curiosity rather than menace. Its gaze held no malice, only a deep sense of understanding and perhaps a touch of amusement.

As they neared the gateway, the world around them began to shift. The muted tones of the ship's deck, the gentle hum of its engines, and even the feel of the metallic floor underfoot seemed to blur and fade. A rush of energy, like a gust of cosmic wind, enveloped them, and with a resonant whoosh, they were propelled forward through the gateway and out into space.

Chapter Twenty-One

As the *Stardust II* cut through the void of space, the cockpit was bathed in the glow of various instruments, each LED and display adding a subtle hue to the atmosphere. The digital readouts scrolled continuously with real-time data, while periodic beeps signalled system checks and alerts. Outside the main viewport, the vastness of space extended indefinitely, dotted with distant stars. Yet, the crew's eyes were drawn to the more immediate and awe-inspiring sight of Earth. Its vibrant blues and lush greens were vivid against the backdrop of space, indicating their proximity to the home they had left behind.

Jessica, her face pale under the ship's artificial lighting, let out a soft, almost reverent whisper. "We've actually made it back." Her hand reached out tentatively, her fingers dancing over the console's interface, betraying the tension gripping her.

Will glanced from the mesmerising view of Earth to Jessica, clearing his throat to break the poignant silence. "It seems we've returned, but we need to confirm this is our Earth. And, more critically, we need to determine just how long we've been gone."

Jim, his focus anchored to the screens in front of him, toggled through various displays. His brow furrowed in concentration as he muttered, "Sela, cross-reference our last known coordinates with the current stellar alignment. We need to verify everything."

Sela, poised at her station, responded without looking up, her fingers moving swiftly over her controls. "On it. I'm aligning the data now."

The silence that followed was filled with the soft hum of the ship's systems and the distant chorus of celestial bodies on the navigation scanners. After a moment, Sela broke the silence. "The alignments are off... by years, not just days or months."

Jim paused, a hint of frustration colouring his tone. "Shame we didn't have this technology the first time around—it would have made figuring out where, or when, we were so much easier."

The implications of Sela's findings hung in the air, thickening the tension. "It's a small miracle that Ganesha's modifications haven't rendered all our systems inoperative," Jim continued, trying to find some humour in their predicament. "At least we still have the core of our navigation intact."

As Sela continued her calculations, her voice wavered slightly, tinged with disbelief and hope. "Ten years... Can it truly have been so long? Are you certain?"

Jim, who had been cross-verifying the data, finalised his input with a heavy sigh. With a few more keystrokes, he pulled up a star chart overlaid with Earth's current position relative to their last known timestamp. "The celestial map doesn't lie," he confirmed solemnly. "We've been away for a full decade."

The revelation hit each member of the crew differently, sending a wave of shock through the cabin. Jim leaned forward from his seat, adjusting his glasses as he pondered the implications. "It felt like just a few months to us. Time dilation, parallel dimensions, or something weirder. Ganesha mentioned that time moves differently in the corridor—seems he was right."

Will, sitting at the helm, ran his hands through his hair, a gesture of perplexity and concern. "We can speculate all we want about the science of it later. First, we need to get back on solid ground and figure out what the world thinks happened to us. How much has changed back home?"

Jessica, ever practical, voiced the next immediate concern, "Does the cloak function still operate? We might need to approach discreetly."

Sela checked the systems and shook her head, her voice carrying a note of disappointment. "No, that part of our system is currently offline."

"Well, let's hope for a friendly response, then," Jim said, trying to lighten the mood with a hint of optimism amidst their precarious situation.

He then tuned the old radio to the frequency they hoped might still be monitored by someone, somewhere on Earth. The static crackled through the cockpit like a distant storm, breaking the heavy silence. As Jim initiated the call, the crew leaned in, a collective breath held between them.

"Edwards Air Force Base, this is *Stardust* requesting permission to land," Jim announced, his voice steady but tinged with an undercurrent of hope he couldn't completely conceal.

The moments that followed were filled with the tense hiss of static. Then, suddenly, the static cleared, and a voice broke through, clear and startlingly present, mirroring the crew's surge of emotions.

"*Stardust*? Is that really you?" The operator's voice crackled with disbelief. "We lost contact with you ten years ago. Stand by to transmit your landing clearance code."

The crew was momentarily stunned, then sprang into action, galvanised by the realisation that they were remembered, not merely lost to time and space.

With a mixture of relief and urgency, Jim responded to the crackling voice over the radio, "Stand by for transmission." He quickly tapped the sequence for their landing clearance code into the console, a series of familiar yet strangely distant actions.

"Landing clearance code is AQP1789V," Jim broadcasted, his voice steadier than he felt. The tension in the cockpit was palpable as they awaited confirmation.

There was a brief pause—an eternity in that moment—before the radio crackled to life again. "Code accepted; welcome back, *Stardust*," the operator replied, his voice imbued with a mix of professionalism and astonishment.

Will, taking the helm as captain with a sense of solemn duty, replied, "Thank you. It's been a long journey with more than a few unexpected detours. Can you confirm the current Earth date for us?" His tone was calm, but the undercurrent of anxiety was detectable to anyone who knew him well.

After another suspenseful pause, filled likely with the operator consulting their records or confirming details, the voice came back. "*Stardust*, welcome back to the fold. It's October 12, 2045. Where have you been?"

The simplicity of the question seemed absurd, given the complexity of their experiences. "We've been... beyond," Will answered after a brief hesitation, the enormity of their journey hanging in each word. "Details upon landing. For now, know that we're grateful to be coming home."

"Roger that, *Stardust*. Preparing your landing coordinates now. There's going to be a lot of debriefing, but first and foremost, welcome back to Earth. You've been missed," the operator concluded, a formal end to an extraordinary reconnection.

"Missed." The word echoed through the cabin, touching each crew member differently. It was a reminder of the life they had left behind, of the time that had marched on without them. They were returning to a world that was both familiar and irrevocably altered, ready to reintegrate into a society that had mourned their loss and moved on.

As the coordinates for their landing streamed through the navigation system, the crew busied themselves with the final preparations. Each member was lost in their thoughts, pondering the world they were about to re-enter.

Will leaned back in his captain's chair, a thoughtful frown creasing his forehead. "It's like stepping back into a forgotten life," he murmured, almost to himself.

Jim, who had overheard, raised an eyebrow sceptically. "Is it wise to tell them everything? Some truths might be too hard to bear."

Jessica, who had been silently overseeing the systems check, nodded thoughtfully. "Ganesha's words weren't just for theatrics. There's knowledge that humanity isn't prepared to handle."

Sela, usually the voice of calm, added her perspective. "But keeping secrets also has its risks. We could be painted as traitors or conspirators."

Will shifted uncomfortably in his seat. "I don't like the idea of holding back, but I trust Ganesha. If he believes we should keep the Dimension Stone and the device a secret, then there's a reason."

Jessica tapped on a holographic screen, pulling up an image of the Dimension Stone. "This... has the power to reshape realities. It's not a toy. Earth's governments and their rivals would wage wars over it."

Will nodded, making up his mind. "We tell them of our travels, the civilisations we've encountered, the lessons we've learned.

But the Stone and the device stay hidden, a secret shared only among us. Do you all agree?"

The rest of the crew nodded in agreement, understanding the gravity of the decision.

As the *Stardust II* began its descent, the familiar terrain of Earth came into view. Forests, oceans, cities— it was a nostalgic and heartening sight. The landing gear deployed with a soft thud, and the ship touched down smoothly, the advanced systems making it appear effortless.

As the hatch slid open with a hiss, sunlight streamed into the dimly lit cabin. The crew squinted, adjusting to the bright light, a symbol of the new reality they were about to face. Outside, a flurry of activity awaited them; ground crews hustled about, and an assembly of military officials, led by a stern-looking General Mitchell, prepared to greet them.

The General's presence was commanding as he stepped forward. "Captain Chambers," he began, extending a firm hand, his voice reflecting a mix of official duty and genuine curiosity. "It's an honour. The world thought you were lost. Your sudden reappearance has raised many questions."

Will took the General's hand firmly. "And we have many answers, General. Some of which may challenge what we know about our place in the universe."

The General nodded, a stern expression masking his intrigue. "Very well, Captain. We have a lot to discuss. Please, follow me."

Jessica took a deep breath, a mix of relief and apprehension filling her. "Back on Earth," she whispered to herself.

Sela linked arms with her, offering a supportive squeeze. "But maybe not the same Earth we left."

Jim, ever the pragmatist, sighed, "Let's just hope they have coffee. I'm still not fully awake."

As the crew started their journey towards the base's main building, they couldn't help but notice the subtle changes around them—the advanced technology, the new badges on uniforms, and unfamiliar faces.

But amidst all the chaos, the familiarity of home was a comforting constant.

PART SEVEN

Chapter Twenty-Two

In a high-security interrogation chamber, the atmosphere was thick with unspoken tension. General Mitchell stood like a statue, his imposing figure casting a long shadow across the cold metallic floor. His eyes, sharp and discerning, scanned the faces of the crew before settling with piercing intensity on Prince Richard. Tucked away in the room's shadowy corner, Captain Dani Alvers maintained a ghost-like presence. Her silhouette barely disturbed the dim light, yet her watchful eyes missed nothing. The insignia of her rank, along with the muted scars of service on her uniform, narrated silent tales of covert operations and hard-won battles. The subtle gleam of her dark hair, pulled back in a strict military bun, highlighted the resolute set of her jaw and the keen focus of her gaze.

General Mitchell broke the silence, his voice echoing slightly in the sparse room. "Captain Chambers, I need to fully understand this. You replaced this man with our Richard Coburg, expecting him to hold back an entire dimension from invading others?" The incredulity in his voice was evident, reflecting the high stakes involved.

Will, standing firm under the general's gaze, responded with a confidence that belied the gravity of their situation. "Yes, General. It was our only option. Our Richard agreed. He's brave and resourceful. He'll manage."

At this, Prince Richard let out a chilling chuckle, the sound reverberating off the steel walls, sending a shiver through the room. "Brave? Perhaps. But the moment my people realise the switch, he's as good as dead."

Jessica's expression remained stoic, though her eyes narrowed slightly in response to Prince Richard's words. "We've considered that. Our Richard has been briefed and equipped. He knows what he's doing."

"Equipped with what?" General Mitchell pressed, his eyes narrowing in concern. "You're playing with fire, Major. You've entangled us in an inter-dimensional cold war."

Jim, who had been quietly observing from the side, stepped forward, his voice steady but firm. "We had no choice, General. It's better to have a fight on our terms than be taken by surprise."

General Mitchell sighed deeply, the lines on his face deepening as he contemplated the implications of their actions. "Alright, we'll debrief thoroughly. Prince Richard will be taken to a black ops prison on this base."

The captive Prince's appearance remained unflappable, his eyes flickering with a trace of amusement as if enjoying the unfolding drama.

Days turned into weeks as the debriefing continued. The team worked tirelessly, sharing information, helping the military prepare defences, and keeping tabs on Prince Richard.

Will could feel a nagging doubt growing within him. Prince Richard was too calm, too complacent. He seemed to be playing a game they couldn't understand.

During one of their strategy sessions, Jessica voiced what they were all thinking. "He's plotting something. I can feel it. He's not just a captive; he's a master tactician."

Dani, who had been quietly observing from the back, nodded slightly at Jessica's words, her expression unreadable.

They talked to General Mitchell, and he agreed they could interrogate him personally, hoping their familiarity might lead to something.

Sela's tech had revealed no concealed devices, no hidden messages. Prince Richard was a closed book.

Yet, as they faced him across the cold steel table, Dani lingered near the doorway, watching. His smug expression unnerved them. "You think you're winning, don't you?" he taunted. "You believe you have the upper hand."

"We do," Will replied, his voice firm. "We've neutralised your threat."

Prince Richard's laughter filled the room. "You've merely delayed it."

As the days went by, his conversations with Will became more philosophical, probing the nature of power, duty, and morality. Will found himself drawn into debates that seemed to dance around hidden truths. Dani, under the guise of her official duties, occasionally passed by, her ears catching snippets of these conversations, a subtle reminder of her silent, watchful role.

One day, Prince Richard looked deep into Will's eyes. "You think you've saved your world, Captain. But you've merely invited chaos. I'm not the only one in the Empire with ambitions. And tell me, how much of your adventures, your decade away, do you think your government has disclosed to the world?"

Will stiffened, the question cutting deeper than expected. "What do you mean?"

With a cold smile, Prince Richard leaned closer. "You'll see, Captain. You'll see. Wouldn't it be ironic if you found yourself as much a prisoner of secrets as I am of these walls?"

Then, with seemingly casual cruelty, he added, "How is the family, by the way? Prepared for your triumphant return, or are they still mourning the heroes lost a decade ago?"

Will left the room, his thoughts clouded by what Prince Richard had said. As he returned to the common area that had become their makeshift home since their return, the weight of the conversation hung heavy on him.

In a quiet corner of their shared living space, he noticed Sela, absorbed in the glow of her tablet. The light illuminated her face, casting shadows that seemed to echo the turmoil within her. Her expression was one of deep contemplation, a stark reminder of how the journey had personally affected each of them.

Approaching quietly, Will observed her for a moment before speaking. "Sela, how are you holding up?"

Startled slightly, Sela looked up from her screen. "Oh, Will... it's a lot to process. You know, growing up in Cambodia, my grandparents were devout Hindus. They filled my childhood with tales of gods and deities, stories of Vishnu and Shiva, of creation and destruction. Those stories were just myths to me— until now."

Will nodded, understanding the magnitude of her revelation. "Meeting Ganesha, seeing what you've seen... I can't even begin to imagine how that must shake your beliefs."

Sela sighed, her eyes returning to the screen but her mind clearly elsewhere. "It's not just a shaking—it's a complete upheaval. I've seen proof that the gods of my childhood aren't just characters in tales. They are real, and they have a role in the cosmos. It's overwhelming to reconcile that with everything I thought I knew."

Will sat down beside her, offering a supportive presence. "It's a profound change to go through. But remember, you're not alone in this. We've all had our worlds turned upside down in one way or another."

Sela managed a small smile, grateful for the solidarity. "Thanks, Will. It helps to know we're in this together."

She sighed, her fingers pausing on the keyboard. "My grandparents believed so deeply. They would be in awe of what I've experienced. But it's not just awe I feel. It's confusion, fear, and a desperate need to make sense of it all. I mean, the stories of the Mahabharata and the Ramayana, the teachings of the Bhagavad Gita—they were always just part of our culture, not reality."

Jessica and Jim joined them, having overheard the conversation. Jessica sat down next to Sela, offering a sympathetic smile.

"You know, Sela, it's okay to feel overwhelmed. We've all been through something extraordinary. It's natural to seek understanding and clarity."

Jim added, "Remember, Sela, Hinduism teaches that the universe is vast and cyclical. The stories your grandparents told you about the gods and their avatars—they were always meant to be lessons in understanding the nature of existence, karma, and dharma. Maybe there's something in those teachings that can help us now."

Sela nodded, appreciating their support. "Thank you, all of you. I just... I need to know why. Why us? Why now? And what does it all mean? The concept of Maya, the illusion of the world, and the idea of Lila, the divine play of the gods—it all feels so real now."

Jessica squeezed her hand gently. "We'll find those answers, Sela. Together, we'll make sense of this. I promise."

Sela's eyes brightened a little as she returned to her laptop, delving deeper into the scriptures and philosophies she had grown up with. She searched for the meaning behind their experiences, looking up texts on Shiva's Tandava, the dance of creation and destruction, and Vishnu's ten avatars, each coming to Earth in times of crisis. She read about Ganesha's wisdom and the importance of removing obstacles, hoping to find parallels to their journey.

Over the next few days, she also explored the Vedas, the ancient sacred texts that formed the foundation of Hindu thought. The Rigveda, with its hymns and praises to the gods; the Yajurveda, with its rituals and ceremonies; the Samaveda, with its chants and melodies; and the Atharvaveda, with its spells and incantations. Each text offered insights into the divine forces she had encountered and the spiritual principles that might guide her understanding.

With renewed determination, Sela continued her research, diving deeper into the vast and intricate world of her heritage, hoping to find the understanding and acceptance Ganesha had spoken of. The journey ahead was uncertain, but with her friends by her side, it was achievable.

However, as the days passed, restlessness began to seep into the crew. They had all been wrestling with their own demons and revelations, each finding different paths to reconcile their past with their present. Yet, despite these personal battles, an overarching unease about their situation at the military base grew steadily.

Watching his crew sink deeper into depression, gripped by the bleak monotony of their seemingly endless captivity, Will felt a surge of resolve. It was clear that something drastic had to be done. With a firm set to his jaw, he decided it was time to confront General Mitchell and demand their release.

The stark fluorescent lights of the military base hummed softly overhead, a relentless reminder of their confinement. Will walked briskly down the corridors, each step propelled by a mix of duty and mounting frustration. Although they had successfully completed their mission, they remained trapped within the base's imposing concrete walls—a situation that grated on him more with each passing day.

Arriving at the doors to General Mitchell's office, Will pushed them open. The heavy steel doors swung shut behind him with a resounding thud, the sound reverberating through the expansive, sparsely decorated room. His footsteps, though quiet, echoed across the space, instantly drawing the General's focused attention. "Sir," Will began, his voice measured but underlined with a hint of urgency. "We've exhausted our lines of questioning with the prisoner.
General Mitchell looked up, his steely blue eyes locking onto Will's. "And?"

"We've extracted everything we possibly can, sir," Will continued, the weight of his duty pressing down on him. "Every technique, every question. We've turned every stone."

The general, leaning heavily on the table, exhaled slowly, processing the gravity of the situation. "Where is he now?"

"In the underground black ops site, sir," Will replied. "Securely held. Maximum security. No one in or out without clearance."

The general nodded slowly, taking in the information. "Any possibility of a leak? We can't afford any breaches."

Will shook his head firmly. "None, sir. The site is off the grid. Your best men are on it. The prisoner is in solitary. No contact, no communication."

General Mitchell tapped a pen against the table in thought. "Very well. Keep him there for now. We'll decide the next course of action soon."

"Yes, sir," Will affirmed strongly to the General. "My crew and I have fulfilled our duties and now wish to return to our homes."

The General reclined slightly in his chair, giving Will a contemplative look. "Of course, Captain, but as I've explained previously, you've all been registered dead for ten years. It takes considerable paperwork to reverse that," he responded, his voice soft yet carrying a weighty undertone. "Just a few more days. You must understand that when the world believed you and your crew died stopping that comet, there were parades and a hero's funeral for you all. It's a sensitive situation. Revealing your survival now... the world may not be ready for that kind of upheaval."

After the meeting with Will and the subsequent dismissal of the officers, General Mitchell remained seated, his gaze fixed on the door through which Captain Dani Alvers would soon enter. The soft hum of the base's air conditioning filled the brief silence, a stark contrast to the weight of decisions made within these walls.

The door opened quietly, and Captain Alvers stepped in, her posture straight, betraying nothing of the hours she spent in the shadows. She moved with a confidence that was as much a part of her uniform as the insignia on her shoulder.

"Captain Alvers," General Mitchell acknowledged, his voice carrying a mix of anticipation and weariness. "Report."

Dani approached the table, stopping at a respectful distance. "Sir, the team is showing signs of strain under the prolonged pressure. Their loyalty to the mission is intact, but cracks are beginning to show in their resolve. Doubts about the handling and containment of Prince Richard are growing."

She paused, ensuring she had the General's full attention. "Prince Richard remains a figure of concern. His interactions with Captain Chambers and the others are calculated. He's not just biding his time; he's actively sowing seeds of doubt, trying to manipulate their perceptions of the mission and each other."

General Mitchell leaned forward, interlocking his fingers. "And your assessment of Captain Chambers?"

"Dedicated, but increasingly sceptical of the isolation protocol we've imposed on him and his team. He's beginning to question not just our tactics but our motives. The more he interacts with Prince Richard, the more he seems to entertain the prince's insinuations about the wider implications of their mission."

Mitchell's eyes narrowed slightly. "Do you believe he poses a risk to the operation?"

"Not immediately, sir, but the potential is there. Will's loyalty is to his team and their safety. If he perceives that working within our directives compromises that, he may take... unilateral actions."

"And what of your own interactions with them? Have you managed to maintain your cover?"

Dani's expression remained neutral. "Yes, sir. My presence is accepted, if not entirely understood. They see me as an ally, albeit a mysterious one. I've managed to keep my true objectives obscured, focusing on the role of a military liaison."

The General nodded slowly, processing the information. "Keep a close watch on Will and Prince Richard. The balance of power is delicate, and we cannot afford any disruptions. If Will acts out of turn, we need to be ready to intervene."

"Understood, sir. I'll ensure we're prepared for any contingencies."

Dani paused, her expression resolute. "There's a significant issue with the *Stardust II*, sir. Despite our best efforts, the technology on board remains largely inaccessible. Our engineering team is struggling to decode the core systems," she explained, her voice a mix of frustration and resolve. She took a breath before adding, "There's a further complication: the ship's biometric access is locked, and only Prince Richard can alter it. Moreover, the ship automatically shuts down completely unless one of the original crew members is present."

General Mitchell's expression darkened; his concern evident as he massaged his temple thoughtfully. "This significantly complicates our situation," he admitted, his tone firm. "We will never allow Prince Richard anywhere near the *Stardust II*. We need to devise another method to circumvent these security protocols. Keep pushing for a breakthrough—it's vital that we master this technology. Our strategic goals depend on it, and ensuring the continuous presence of an original crew member is not a long-term solution."

As Dani turned to leave, General Mitchell spoke once more. "Captain, your work is invaluable. The security of our operation depends on the intelligence you gather. Stay vigilant."

"I will, sir." With a crisp salute, Dani exited the room, her steps echoing lightly as she returned to the shadows from which she so effectively observed and influenced the unfolding drama.

The General's assurances had provided little comfort and later that evening, in the dimly lit mess hall, Will, Jim, Jessica, and Sela gathered around a metal table for their customary dinner debrief.

Sela's usually calm expression displayed a hint of frustration as she spoke, "Every time we ask about our departure, it's the same story: 'Just a few more days.' It's been weeks now."

Will took a deep breath, replaying his conversation with the General. "He promised it would be just a few more."

Jessica's expression turned cynical. "It's like they're keeping us here on purpose."

Jim frowned in thought. "Remember Ganesha's warning before we returned home? I'm starting to understand what he was warning us about."

Will's face darkened, remembering another interaction. "And then there's what Prince Richard mentioned."

Jessica immediately rolled her eyes, her disdain for the prince evident. "That snake? Everything out of his mouth is a lie, meant to play with our minds."

Will nodded, acknowledging Jessica's concerns, but added, "While I don't trust him at all, he did bring up an unsettling point. He questioned the transparency of our government and whether our adventures, our findings, are being shared with the world or kept hidden for some ulterior motive."

Chapter Twenty-Three

Later that night, in the confines of their secure compound, the crew's sleep was invaded by a shared yet personal vision of Ganesha, the elephant god. Each dream was a mosaic of their innermost fears and aspirations intertwined with the god's wisdom.

In the stillness of the night, Will found himself in the grasp of a dream that transcended time and culture. It was a scene that juxtaposed the grandeur of ancient India with the heroic narrative of Alexander the Great, yet with a distinct twist: the Hindu god Ganesha, known for his wisdom and benevolence, was a silent observer to the unfolding events.

In this dream, the world was a canvas painted with the vibrant colours of history and mythology. At the centre stood Alexander the Great, his figure emanating the aura of a conqueror. Clad in Macedonian armour, his gaze was fixed on the distant horizon, a symbol of his unquenchable thirst for new conquests and adventures.

Hovering above this scene, blending seamlessly into the fabric of the dream, was Ganesha. Majestic with his elephant head and multiple arms, he was adorned in splendid attire that glittered under the dream's ethereal light. Unlike the usual depictions of Ganesha actively participating in the world's affairs, in Will's dream, the deity was a mere observer, a silent witness to the historical tapestry unfolding below.

This dreamscape was a curious blend of Greek and Indian elements. Greek columns and architecture stood alongside Hindu symbols and motifs, creating a harmonious fusion of two distinct cultures. The skies above were a canvas where mythological figures from both traditions coexisted, yet under the watchful eyes of Ganesha.

As Alexander strategized his next moves, consulting with his generals and poring over maps, Ganesha's presence loomed large, yet unobtrusive. The deity's eyes, wise and knowing, followed Alexander's every move, yet he remained aloof, a divine observer to the mortal endeavours below.

This juxtaposition of the active and the passive, the mortal and the divine, lent the dream a surreal quality. It was as if Ganesha's presence was a reminder of a higher wisdom, an acknowledgment that every ambition and conquest, no matter how grand, was but a fleeting moment in the grand tapestry of the universe.

As dawn crept in, the dream began to dissolve. Ganesha, the observer, faded into the morning light, his image lingering in Will's awakening mind. The silent deity had left no words, no direct messages, yet his presence in the dream was a profound statement in itself.

Jessica's vision was a bustling marketplace of ancient Egypt, alive with colours and sounds. Among the crowd, Ganesha appeared as a wise trader. "Beware those who deal in shadows," he warned, his eyes reflecting the bustling life around them.

In the realms of slumber, Jessica's mind wandered into a dreamscape where history and mythology intertwined in a captivating narrative. Her dream cast Alexander the Great not as a conqueror but as a curious traveller in the bustling marketplace of ancient Alexandria.

The dream unfolded in the vibrant streets of Alexandria, a city renowned for its cultural and intellectual richness. Alexander, devoid of his usual armour and regalia, strolled through the marketplace incognito, his eyes wide with the wonder of a traveller exploring new worlds. The sounds of the marketplace filled the air—traders calling out their wares, the clatter of pottery, the rich aroma of spices and herbs wafting through the air.

In this lively scene, one merchant stood out. He was a stout man with a kind face, his appearance calm and welcoming. This was Ganesha, masterfully disguised in the garb of an Alexandrian merchant. His stall was adorned with an array of exotic goods, from intricate textiles to rare spices, each item holding stories of distant lands.

Alexander, drawn by the stall's allure, approached the disguised Ganesha. The conversation that ensued was light and filled with wisdom, though Alexander was unaware of the merchant's true identity. Ganesha, as the merchant, spoke in parables and riddles, offering insights into life, leadership, and the pursuit of knowledge. Each word was a subtle nudge guiding Alexander towards a deeper understanding of his own ambitions and desires.

The marketplace around them was a melting pot of cultures and ideas, a fitting backdrop for this unusual encounter. Scholars debated in the corners while travellers from far-off lands exchanged stories, and the air buzzed with the energy of a world converging at a single point.

In the dream, the disguised Ganesha subtly steered the conversation towards topics of destiny, leadership, and the impact of one's actions on the world. Alexander, ever the keen mind, engaged eagerly, his thoughts provoked by the merchant's wise words. Yet, the true identity of the merchant remained a secret, adding a layer of intrigue to their exchange.

As the dream neared its end, Alexander left the stall, his mind enriched by the encounter. Ganesha, still in his disguise, watched the great king walk away, a knowing smile on his lips.

The marketplace continued its bustling rhythm, oblivious to the extraordinary meeting that had just taken place.

Jessica awoke from her dream with a sense of awe. The imagery of Alexander in a marketplace, engaging with a disguised Ganesha, lingered in her mind as she drifted back to sleep.

In his dream, Jim found himself in a modern-day international conference, a gathering of the world's leading historians, archaeologists, and engineers. The air was thick with anticipation and a hint of underlying tension. The reason for this assembly was groundbreaking: a series of recent archaeological discoveries had unearthed unknown technological advancements from the time of Alexander the Great.

The conference room was abuzz with activity. Screens displayed intricate diagrams and 3D models of ancient machinery and devices, far ahead of their time, attributed to the era of Alexander. These findings challenged the current understanding of historical technological progression and hinted at a lost chapter of innovation during Alexander's reign.

Jim, in his element, was deeply involved in discussions about the engineering aspects of these discoveries. There were debates about the possible uses of these ancient machines, their design principles, and how they might have been centuries ahead of their time. The atmosphere was a blend of excitement and scepticism, as each revelation seemed to unravel more mysteries than it solved.

However, the dream took a turn as the focus shifted from the marvel of discovery to the implications it had on current world tensions. Different nations vied for access to these technologies, seeing them as potential keys to modern-day advancements or as tools of power. The conference became a diplomatic battleground, with Jim and his peers caught in the midst of it.

Amidst this turmoil, Jim envisioned a series of hypothetical scenarios playing out on the global stage. In one, the rediscovered technologies led to a new era of collaboration and scientific advancement. In another, they became the catalyst for conflict as nations struggled for control over this newfound knowledge.

The dream wove these scenarios with a sense of urgency and a call for responsible stewardship of historical knowledge. It reflected Jim's own beliefs about the power of technology and the importance of using it wisely for the benefit of humanity.

As the dream faded and Jim awoke, he was left with a lingering sense of responsibility. The dream, though fictional, echoed his real-world concerns about how technology that is discovered rather than developed can impact the present and future. It reinforced his conviction that as a chief engineer, his role was not just to understand and innovate technology, but also to ensure its ethical and beneficial application in the world.

In Sela's dream, she embarked on a journey back to a place she had visited before: the Catholic mission near Libya, nestled in a landscape where the sands of the desert met the whispers of history.

The dream began with Sela traversing a vast expanse of desert. The sun hung high in the sky, casting a warm, golden hue over the endless sands. The air was filled with the scent of dry earth and the distant sound of wind chimes from the mission. As she walked, memories of her previous visit to this remote sanctuary flooded back, each step rekindling the sense of peace and purpose she had felt there.

Finally, the mission came into view. It was an imposing structure, built with sandstone blocks and crowned with a number of spires that gleamed in the sunlight. The mission was an oasis of tranquillity in the harsh desert environment, its walls offering shelter and its chapel a place for contemplation and prayer.

In her dream, Sela was greeted warmly by the mission's inhabitants – a small group of devoted nuns and priests who had dedicated their lives to serving the local community. Their faces were familiar and kind, and their welcome was a soothing balm to the weariness of her journey.

Sela spent her time at the mission engaging in various activities. She helped in the small garden where vegetables were grown for the mission's kitchen, joined in the daily prayer services in the chapel, and sat in on educational sessions the mission offered to local children. Each action was imbued with a sense of purpose and community.

As the day turned to evening, Sela found herself on the rooftop of the mission, gazing at the vast desert stretching out to the horizon. The sunset painted the sky in vibrant shades of orange and red, and at that moment, there was an overwhelming sense of connection – to the land, to the mission, and to the greater journey of life.

As Sela's dream continued, it took an unexpected turn. After spending time in the mission, engaged in various activities and feeling a deep connection with the people there, she decided to take a short walk into the surrounding desert. The landscape was serene, with the endless sands stretching under a vast sky, offering a sense of tranquillity and timelessness.

Upon returning from her walk, Sela was met with a sight that filled her with an eerie sense of solitude. The mission, which had just moments ago been a hub of activity and warmth, now stood abandoned. The doors that were once open and welcoming were shut, the windows empty, and the gentle buzz of life that had filled its walls was now replaced by silence.

Confusion and a sense of loss washed over Sela as she wandered through the deserted mission. The garden, where she had helped tend vegetables, was overgrown and untended. The chapel, which had resonated with prayers and songs, was empty, with dust settling on the pews and altar. The classrooms, once filled with the laughter and chatter of children, were now just hollow rooms.

The dream's atmosphere shifted, reflecting a poignant blend of nostalgia and melancholy. Sela felt a profound sense of abandonment, not just of the place but of the memories and connections she had formed there. The mission, once a symbol of community and hope in the harsh landscape, now stood as a testament to impermanence.

As she explored the empty mission, Sela grappled with feelings of confusion and sadness. The abandonment of such a place of refuge and service seemed inexplicable. Yet, in the dream's silence, she found a deeper understanding. The mission, though now empty, still held the echoes of the good done there, the lives touched, and the moments of peace and purpose shared.

The dream ended with Sela standing alone in the mission's chapel, the light of the setting sun casting long shadows across the room.

The soft light of dawn crept through the windows of the secure compound, gently stirring the crew from their deep, vision-filled slumber. As the sun's rays painted the room in hues of gold and amber, a profound silence hung in the air, a stark contrast to the vivid dreams that had just relinquished their grip on the crew's minds.

Will was the first to wake. He lay still for a moment, his mind teetering on the edge of his dream. In the dim light of dawn, he could still see the faint outline of Ganesha, the elephant-headed deity, silently observing Alexander the Great. He sat up, rubbing his eyes, the weight of the dream's message still heavy on his heart.

Next to awaken was Jessica. She stirred, her eyes fluttering open as the echoes of the bustling marketplace of Alexandria still rang in her ears. The vividness of the dream clung to her, a reminder of the hidden depths and truths that lie beneath the surface of every encounter. She rose from her bed, a sense of awe and introspection etched on her face.

Jim's awakening was more abrupt. His mind was still entangled in the complexities of his dream. He lay in bed for a few more moments, trying to piece together the significance of the dream, before finally swinging his legs over the side of the bed.

The last to awaken was Sela. She opened her eyes slowly, the sense of loss from her dream lingering, mixing with the cool morning air of her room. There was a profound sadness in her gaze but also a glimmer of understanding about the impermanence of life and the enduring impact of experiences.

As they gathered in the common area, a silence enveloped the crew. Each was wrapped in the remnants of their dreams, the images and messages still vivid in their minds. They sat around the table, cups of coffee in hand, the morning light spilling across the room, casting long shadows on the walls.

Will broke the silence. "I had a dream last night," he began, his voice tinged with a mix of wonder and solemnity. "It was about Alexander the Great and Ganesha. Ganesha was just... observing. It felt significant, like a reminder of something greater than us."

Jessica nodded, her eyes reflecting her own encounter with the deity. "Ganesha visited me too, in a marketplace in Alexandria. He was a merchant, sharing wisdom with Alexander. It was as if he was guiding us to look beyond what we see."

Jim leaned forward. "My dream was different, more modern. It was about the discovery of ancient technologies that could change the world. But it wasn't peaceful; it was a warning about the responsibility that comes with such knowledge."

Sela's voice was soft but clear. "In my dream, I returned to the Catholic mission, a place of peace. But it was abandoned, a shell of what it once was. It felt like a lesson in the impermanence of things and the lasting impact of our actions."

As they gathered around the dimly lit room, a sense of unity filled the air. Despite the differing narratives, a unifying thread had emerged—each dream had been a journey, a lesson, and seemingly a preparation for something greater. The recurring presence of Ganesha, appearing in various forms and contexts, suggested a guiding force leading them toward a deeper understanding and purpose.

Will leaned forward, his voice steady with newfound resolve. "It seems we were all visited by the same vision, albeit in different forms. Perhaps it's a sign, a direction for our next mission."

Jessica nodded, her expression thoughtful as she pieced together the implications. "The heart of these dreams," she added, "seems to be pointing us towards Egypt. There's something there, something we need to discover or understand."

Sela, who had been quietly listening, chimed in, her voice firm. "And my dream, although it did not involve Ganesha, points us to a familiar location. I think we need to be there."

Jim nodded in agreement as he connected the dots. "It's more than just a coincidence. These dreams are a call to action. There's a piece of the puzzle waiting for us in Egypt, and I'm guessing it's related to Alexander the Great's tomb."

Sela looked at each of her crewmates, a sense of camaraderie and shared destiny building among them. "Our dreams, though personal, seem to be pieces of a larger picture. The tomb might hold the key to understanding not just these visions but perhaps something crucial for our world."

Chapter Twenty-Four

As dawn broke, the *Stardust II*'s crew assembled in the faintly lit common room. Their shared dreams, each acting as a mysterious clue, collectively guided them to a singular place: the abandoned Catholic mission in Egypt. This location would serve as their base for planning the excavation of Alexander the Great's tomb.

Sela, with her characteristic calm, had already set up a secure computer feed. The soft hum of the equipment provided a subtle soundtrack to their intense discussion. Standing at the head of the table, Will broke the focused silence.

"First things first," he said, his voice steady, "we need to confirm the current status of the Catholic mission compound." He paused, casting a glance at the digital map on the screen. "Marie suggested that in her time, it was deserted until the tomb was discovered, so it's possible that it is also abandoned here in our world, which could work in our favour."

"And then," Jessica added, her tone underscored with urgency, "we need to make our escape."

"How do we shake off the General's pet pit-bull?" Jim's question broke the heavy silence, his voice laced with a mix of annoyance and concern.

Will, leaning against the cold metal table, gave a slight nod of acknowledgment. "Ah, you've noticed too," he said, his gaze meeting each of his crew members in turn.

"She's always snooping around," Jessica chimed in, her expression hardening at the thought. "I'm sure she's reporting everything we do and say back to the General."

Will's response was measured, his mind already racing through scenarios. "Then we play the game until we make our move. We'll need to be careful, feed misinformation, and keep our true intentions hidden."

As the planning progressed, Jim brought up crucial points: "These fancy tablet phones should be useful, but we may need some cash. Local currency will keep us under the radar in Egypt," he added, scanning the room for approval.

Will, quick to recognise an opportunity, suggested a plan that would blend perfectly with their covert operations. "There's a weekly poker game hosted by some of the other military personnel stationed here. It's friendly but competitive, and there's serious money on the table."

Sela chimed in with enthusiasm. "That's perfect. I've played a lot of poker during downtime at excavations, and if we can keep a cool head, we could walk away with enough to cover our needs in Egypt."

"Yeah, she's a bit of a shark," Jim added with a chuckle, speaking from experience. "I've seen her in action; the other players might as well just hand over their money."

"What's the buy-in?" Sela asked, her mind already strategizing.

"Four hundred," Will replied

"And how much have we got?" Sela inquired, already knowing the answer.

"Nothing," Will said flatly.

"Leave it to me," Sela continued confidently. "I'm sure I can persuade some of the soldiers to stake me."

The plan was set into motion. That night, Sela and Jim, under the guise of seeking some downtime, joined the poker game. The room buzzed with the quiet clink of chips and low murmurs of conversation.

Sela played with a calculated precision, her face an unreadable mask. As the hours ticked by, her pile of chips steadily grew. Jim, supporting her, occasionally bluffed and conversed with the others, helping to keep the atmosphere light and distracting from Sela's growing stack.

By the end of the night, they had achieved their goal. Sela pulled off a final spectacular hand, flopping a full house against a rivered Ace high flush. The other players applauded her skill and luck, jokingly lamenting their losses.

After reimbursing the soldiers that had staked her, Sela and Jim returned to their quarters, a significant amount of cash now at their disposal for the mission. This successful night at the poker table had not only boosted their funds but also their spirits, as they had managed to secure what they needed without raising any suspicions.

The planning took another three days, with each member of the crew playing their part to perfection. They went about their duties, dropping harmless bits of false information and engaging in deliberately misleading conversations whenever Dani was within earshot. All the while, the actual plan was communicated in hushed tones, through encrypted messages that Sela had set up, ensuring their escape plot remained a ghost in the system.

On the eve of their departure, Will had one last meeting with the General, Dani, lurking in the shadows as always. Will spoke of routine checks and mundane logistical requests, a performance worthy of the stage to keep their plans under wraps.

Later that evening, Will surveyed his crew in the dimly lit room, urgency etching his voice. "Team, the window's now. The shift change at the base gives us our best shot. Jim, I need those cameras blind. Sela, lead us through maintenance. Jess, keep our backs safe."

Jim, fingers flying over his tablet, confirmed, "Camera feeds are looped. We're practically ghosts."

"Got a path plotted through less patrolled zones. It'll be tight," Sela added, her eyes locked on her digital map.

They slipped out like shadows, a unit bound by a singular mission. The base hummed around them, oblivious to the spectres in its midst. Every corner they turned, every door they slipped through, was a testament to their meticulous planning and Sela's intimate knowledge of the layout. In the dimly lit corridors of the sprawling military complex, the crew cautiously made their way toward their objective. They were shadows among shadows, their movements calculated and silent.

As they neared a particularly critical junction, Jessica, who had taken the lead, suddenly raised her hand, signalling the group to stop. Her eyes, sharp and focused, scanned the corridor ahead. The soft murmur of voices grew louder, indicating the approach of two guards.

Hidden in the recesses of the hallway, the crew was just out of sight, their presence a secret kept by the shadows. The guards, clad in the standard uniform of the base's security personnel, walked past, engrossed in a low conversation about the mundane details of their shift. Their laughter echoed briefly in the sterile corridor, a sound starkly out of place in the tension-filled atmosphere.

Jessica, her hand still raised, watched them intently, waiting for the moment they would be far enough away. As the guards' footsteps and voices faded, disappearing around a distant corner, Jessica turned back to her companions, her face set in a determined expression. "All clear," she whispered, her voice barely above a breath.

With a quick, practised gesture, she signalled for the group to continue.

Sela confidently guided them. "That way." She pointed, guiding them through less monitored paths she remembered.

The base's layout was complex, but their plan was solid. The hangar loomed ahead, their ship a silent promise of escape and the next chapter of their journey.

Will signalled a brief halt. "Status, Jim?"

"Security's in the dark. But opening the hangar's going to raise some eyebrows. It won't be silent," Jim warned.

"No choice. Fast and silent as we can manage. Ready up," Will responded, his resolve mirrored in his team's nods.

Sela approached the hangar door, her toolkit at the ready. The door groaned open, the sound stark in the silent tension.

Their ship stood across the vast space, a beacon of hope. They sprinted across the hangar, the echo of their footsteps a defiant drumbeat against the quiet of the base.

As they neared their ship, the biometric locks, recognising their familiar signatures, swiftly disengaged. The hatch hissed open, welcoming them back.

Boarding their spacecraft, Will cast a final glance back at the military complex that had been their world for too long. "Egypt, here we come," he declared, a mix of regret and determination in his voice.

Inside, the crew sprang into action with practised ease. Jessica powered up the engines, the ship humming to life under her touch. Jim monitored their systems, ensuring everything was set for a stealthy exit. "We're clear. No alarms detected," he announced.

Will, standing by the hatch until the last moment, finally sealed it, confirming their readiness. "How's everyone doing?" he asked, joining the others in the cockpit.

As the engines roared to full power, the *Stardust II* began its ascent. Jessica maneuvered them expertly off the ground. "A bit too close for comfort, but we're good," she said, feeling the ship lift gently.

"Path's clear to Egypt. We're maintaining a speed equivalent to that of a standard aircraft to avoid being perceived as hostile," Sela confirmed, her eyes locked on the navigation console.

"Wait," Jessica said abruptly, turning to face Will. "Let's not head straight to Egypt. I'll take us straight up into space first— we need to add to the confusion."

Will raised an eyebrow but quickly grasped her plan. "Good thinking. Adjusting our trajectory for a vertical ascent. It'll look like we're sticking to our bogus moon mission."

Jim, from his seat behind them, leaned forward, a sly grin spreading across his face. "That should throw off anyone monitoring us. By the time they realise we've changed course, we'll be long gone."

Jessica's fingers danced over the controls. "Course adjusted. Ascending now."

As the ship surged upward, Jim kept a close eye on the instruments. "No alerts from ground control.

"Perfect," Will said, glancing out the viewport at the darkening sky. "Once we're beyond their radar, we'll set a direct course for Egypt."

Jessica nodded, her eyes reflecting the stars now coming into view. "This should buy us the time we need."

Jim exhaled slowly, tension easing from his shoulders. "Let's hope Egypt is ready when we arrive. We won't have the element of surprise for long.".

A short time later, Jessica's gaze lingered on the cockpit screen, her expression a tapestry of disbelief and wonder. "This is weird," she whispered, her voice barely above a hush, lost in the enormity of what she was seeing.

From across the cockpit, Will's attention shifted from the map he was analysing. "What's going on?" he inquired, his tone laced with a mix of concern and intrigue.

With a sigh that blended frustration with astonishment, Jessica swivelled in her chair to face him. "It's the computer system. It's completely open. All of Ganesha's security protocols and the blocks he set up are gone. We've been granted unrestricted access to everything."

Without missing a beat, Will seized the moment. "Computer, activate the cloak," he commanded, his voice carrying the weight of their precarious situation.

"Cloak activated," the computer responded promptly.

Will approached, his eyes narrowing as he peered at the screen over Jessica's shoulder. A subtle smile emerged, a sign of dawning realisation and confidence. "Now, set that course for Egypt," he instructed, his voice steady and resolute.

"This just strengthens my belief that we're headed in the right direction," he continued, an undercurrent of excitement threading through his words. "Ganesha had his reasons for locking us out, but this... it's as if it's a sign. A confirmation that we're meant to embark on this journey."

****

Meanwhile, back at the base, the atmosphere in General Mitchell's office was charged with tension. Captain Dani Alvers stood before him, the weight of failure pressing down on her shoulders. The general, a figure of authority and expectation, fixed her with a gaze that demanded answers.

"Explain." General Mitchell's voice was a controlled calm, belying the storm of frustration brewing beneath the surface.

Dani inhaled deeply, her mind racing to assemble the facts into a coherent report. "Sir, the crew of the *Stardust II* utilised an unforeseen method in their escape. It appears they exploited vulnerabilities in our surveillance and security systems that were not previously identified. Despite continuous monitoring, they managed to enact a plan that left no trace until it was too late."

She paused, aware that her next words would do little to temper the General's growing displeasure. "By the time we noticed the anomaly, they had already initiated their escape sequence. They then activated some sort of radar-masking device on the ship, rendering them invisible to our radar systems."

General Mitchell's expression hardened. "And you believe they're heading to the moon?" he asked, his tone sceptical.

"Yes, sir. It's the most logical destination based on the intel we collected and the initial course they were on before they vanished. Given their recent actions and the cryptic clues they've been chasing, it aligns with what we suspect to be their next move," Dani explained, her tone firm, despite the uncertainty of the situation.

The general leaned back in his chair, processing the information. The silence that followed was heavy, filled with unspoken recriminations and the weight of decisions to come.

"And is the prisoner still secure?" His voice cut through the quiet, direct and expectant.

"Yes, sir. Prince Richard remains confined within his cell, under constant watch," came the assured response.

"Very well," he finally said, his voice betraying none of his thoughts. "Initiate a covert surveillance operation on lunar activities. Use our satellites and come up with a story to inform our allies. I want to know the moment they reappear. As for the security breach—" He paused, his eyes locking onto Dani's— "ensure it's sealed. I won't tolerate another oversight."

Dani nodded, her response a mix of determination and acknowledgment of the gravity of her task. "Understood, sir. I'll take immediate action."

As she turned to leave, the challenge of redeeming herself in the general's eyes weighed heavily on her. The *Stardust II*'s crew had proven to be more resourceful than anticipated, but Dani was resolved not to underestimate them again. The game of cat and mouse had escalated, and she was determined to close the net before they could achieve their mysterious objective on the moon.

Chapter Twenty-Five

Back on the *Stardust II*, hours passed in a seamless flight, the spacecraft slicing through the atmosphere with ease. Eventually, they descended, coming to rest beside the old, deserted Catholic mission, a relic standing solitary amid the wilderness.

"It looks identical to the one on the other Earth," said Sela.

Will, standing beside her, nodded in agreement. "Just not as lived in," he added, his gaze lingering on the weathered walls of the mission, a stark contrast to their memories of a bustling community in a parallel world.

He turned to Jessica, who was skilfully manoeuvring the spacecraft. "Put it back where we used to park it," he instructed, pointing towards a dilapidated side building that once served as a makeshift hangar. "We'll convene in the War Room we used before."

The *Stardust II* glided towards the designated spot, its engines humming softly. As they landed, the cloak deactivated, revealing the ship's sleek exterior to the empty surroundings. The quiet of the abandoned mission enveloped them.

Stepping out, the foursome made their way towards the mission. The air was heavy with the scent of dust and old memories. The War Room, their makeshift command centre, awaited them.

In the dim, pre-dawn light, the crew huddled in the War Room around a sprawl of maps and texts they had managed to secure from the base. The air was thick with anticipation as they prepared for a mission that could redefine history.

Will, his finger tracing a labyrinthine path on a map, spoke with a blend of solemnity and excitement. "We kept this a secret for a reason, but the time has come to uncover the truths buried beneath these ancient sands," he declared.

Jessica meticulously arranged a set of sophisticated excavation tools. "Speed and stealth are crucial," she cautioned, her eyes scanning over the equipment. "This region isn't just isolated; it's steeped in political complexities."

Jim, focused on the satellite imagery displayed on his tablet, nodded in agreement. "The landscape is treacherous, but I've mapped out the most efficient approach. Our main issue is exposure. If we fly there and cloak our ship, we'll be vulnerable since the cloak only covers the ship. But now that we have full access to our systems, I found that the cloak is portable—we can disconnect it and it should cover the tomb and maybe a vehicle like a van or small truck."

"So, you're suggesting we leave our ship here at the mission and drive to the tomb site?" Will asked, seeking clarification.

"Exactly," Jim confirmed. "The ship should be safe here, thanks to the biometric locks—no one but us four can enter. Plus, we can launch one of our three survey drones to keep an eye out for anyone snooping around."

Jessica furrowed her brow, considering their options. "So, how do we get a van?"

Jim shrugged, a wry smile playing on his lips. "Well, we have that cash we won at the poker table."

"That won't be enough. How much have we got?" Will's pragmatic tone cut through the room.

"$1800," Jim replied, his expression grimacing slightly.

Sela laughed dryly, shaking her head as she thought about the cutting-edge equipment and sleek interfaces of their ship. "Look at us," she began, her voice tinged with irony, "travelling through space in the most powerful vessel in the world, equipped with technology that can travel through dimensions, and here we are, with only $1800 to our names."

Will's eyes narrowed in thought. "Our only option then is to steal one. There's a city called Mersa Matruh about 600 kilometres away. It has around 300,000 people, so it should have what we need."

"Won't we stick out?" Jessica voiced her concern, her arms crossed.

Will nodded thoughtfully. "It is a bit of a tourist city. People go there to travel to the oasis nearby, and it does have some interesting ruins from Ramesses II's time. So, we won't look completely out of place."

Sela summed up the plan with a determined nod. "Okay, so we fly to this city, steal a van, and then drive back without getting caught."

"That's the idea," said Will, his tone firm, as the team swiftly prepared for the mission. In no time, they were ready to embark.

Soon after, the *Stardust II* hovered silently above Mersa Matruh, its advanced cloaking device perfectly masking its presence. Jessica deftly manoeuvred the ship through the evening skies. The city sprawled below them, a mix of ancient architecture and modern advancements. Despite the predominance of electric vehicles in 2045, this remote part of Egypt still clung to the past, with petrol vans dotting the streets—a fortunate detail for the mission at hand.

"Focus on the older sections of the city," Jessica directed, scanning the layout below. "Petrol vans should be more common there, and they're easier for us to manage given the security tech in newer models."

From his station, Jim adjusted the ship's optical sensors, enhancing the resolution to pick out potential targets. "We need something inconspicuous, something that blends in but is old enough to hotwire," he muttered as his fingers danced across the controls.

As the ship drifted silently over the city, the crew's tension grew. Each member was acutely aware of the stakes. Suddenly, Jim's screen flashed as he zoomed in on a promising lead. "There." He pointed to a small, secluded driveway tucked behind a row of modest houses sheltered under the sprawling branches of vibrant bougainvillea. An ordinary, slightly weathered van sat quietly—just what they needed.

"Good eye, Jim," Will commented, peering over to view the screen. "Jessica, can you get us closer for a visual confirmation?"

With a nod, Jessica adjusted their altitude slightly, bringing them into a lower hover that offered a clearer view without compromising their cloak. The van was indeed an older model, likely running on petrol, and it looked perfectly ordinary—ideal for their needs.

"Let's prepare for touchdown," Will decided, turning to the rest of the crew. "We'll park a few blocks away, wait for night, and approach on foot. We need to keep this quick and quiet."

Will peered more closely at the imagery, his brow furrowed. "Looks like that van's been well used, probably essential for the family's livelihood or daily tasks," he mused aloud, a hint of concern in his voice. "Taking it... it's just a simple borrowing for us. For them, it could mean a lot more."

Jessica, noticing the shift in Will's tone, added, "We'll make it right, somehow."

Jessica guided the *Stardust II* to a discreet landing in an empty lot veiled by the remnants of an abandoned warehouse. The ship touched down with a soft whirr, the cloak still engaged and shielding them from any prying eyes.

As they disembarked, the cool night air hit their faces, a reminder of the world outside their high-tech bubble. The team moved with practised stealth towards the van.

Reaching the vehicle, Jim crouched by the driver's side, his toolkit spread out before him. "Okay, here goes nothing," he murmured, a determined glint in his eyes. Skilfully manoeuvring a piece of wire, he cracked the lock with a soft click and slid into the driver's seat. The initial attempt to hotwire the van was met with frustration—no sparks, no engine hum.

Sela, peering through the window and after Jim's fifth attempt, finally lost her patience. "Move over, Jim. Let me try." Without waiting for his response, she squeezed into the cramped space beside him.

"You know how to hotwire a car?" Jessica asked, a mix of amusement and disbelief in her tone

"Picked it up one summer back home in Cambodia," Sela responded with a smirk, her hands expertly manipulating the wires beneath the dashboard. "Had a bit of a wild streak. Hung out with a motorcycle gang, influenced by a very persuasive aunt. It's a long story."

With a victorious click, the engine roared to life under Sela's skilled touch. "And... we have ignition," she announced, her pride evident in her voice.

As they piled into the van, Will glanced back at the modest house, a knot of guilt tightening in his chest. Despite the necessity of their mission, he couldn't shake the feeling of wrongdoing. Quietly, he slipped off his watch—an Omega Speedmaster Professional issued to all astronauts after their first mission in space. Placing it in the house's mailbox as a token of apology, Will hoped this valuable piece of his history might somehow compensate for their desperate actions.

As Will returned to the van, his expression clouded with doubt, Jessica placed a reassuring hand on his shoulder. "You've done the right thing, Will. It's a tough call, but that watch... it's a meaningful gesture. It won't fix everything, but it means they won't be financially impacted."

"Alright everyone, buckle up," Sela commanded from the driver's seat, her voice tinged with excitement as she flashed a mischievous grin. "Time to see if my driving is as good as my hotwiring skills."

They quickly returned to the *Stardust II* to drop off Jessica, who would tail them from the skies and provide backup in case of emergencies. With a serious nod, Jessica settled into the cockpit, preparing to monitor their journey closely. Exchanging reassuring glances, Sela pressed down on the accelerator, propelling the van forward with a determined roar.

As they left the confines of the city, the road ahead was anything but forgiving. The van jostled and bounced over a series of potholes and navigated through sharp turns, challenging even Sela's skilled driving. Despite the rough ride, Sela's stories of her daring youthful escapades in Cambodia brought bursts of laughter from the crew, lightening the mood and momentarily easing the tension that hung in the air.

They continued their journey, leaving the bustling outskirts of Mersa Matruh behind. Sela expertly steered the van onto lesser-known back roads, weaving through the landscape to avoid any unwanted attention. The early excitement of their daring escape gradually morphed into high-stakes tension as they focused intently on executing their plan flawlessly.

As the van rumbled forward, a new issue emerged—the fuel gauge began its steady descent towards emptiness, casting a shadow of urgency over their adventure. Sela's eyes flicked to the dashboard, her brow furrowing at the sight of the blinking fuel light.

"Uh, guys, we're running low on petrol," she announced, her voice tight with concern as she pointed out the indicator. The rest of the crew leaned forward, peering at the gauge as the reality of their oversight settled in.

"We need to stop for petrol soon, or we're not going to make it back," Jim noted, his voice calm yet firm as he scanned their route options on his tablet. He pointed to a map display, highlighting a small icon. "There's a station coming up, the Kasr Petrol Station. It's small, but it should be low-key enough for us to refuel without drawing attention."

As Sela navigated the winding roads, the atmosphere in the van grew increasingly tense. Each kilometre they drove, the fuel gauge nudged closer to empty, amplifying the urgency of their situation. The crew sat in silence, their eyes occasionally flicking to the dashboard, as they passed sparse landscapes and occasional signs indicating their approach to the station.

Finally, the faded sign of the Kasr Petrol Station appeared ahead. Sela eased the van off the main road, and as they pulled into the station, it was quiet, with just a few locals milling about. The station, a convenient hybrid, offered both electric charging and petrol, alongside a modestly sized supermarket. Will took a deep breath as he stepped out to handle the refuelling, his mind focused on the importance of blending in.

"Sela, can you stock up on supplies? We'll need enough to last at least a week," he instructed, his voice low to avoid drawing attention.

Utilising a substantial portion of their US dollars, Will approached the attendant in a casual manner. "We'll take some petrol and need to pick up groceries, too," he murmured, passing over the cash. The transaction unfolded without a hitch; the attendant accepted the foreign currency with a nod, evidently used to the occasional tourist navigating this less-travelled path.

Just as Will began to ease his guard, the shrill peep of a police siren pierced the air briefly in the distance. In an instant, tension gripped him and Sela. Will shot a quick glance over his shoulder, spotting a police car meandering along the main road near the gas station. Though the car didn't stop, that fleeting moment stretched out, heavy with anxiety. They both held their breath, silently praying they wouldn't draw any unwanted attention.

With the police car disappearing down the road, the tension broke, and they allowed themselves a sigh of relief. Once the tank was full and the groceries loaded, they quickly got back into the van.

Jim, feeling the need to cut through the lingering tension, chuckled and threw out a line from an old classic movie. "It's 60 miles to the Catholic mission, we have a full tank of gas, it's dark, and we aren't wearing sunglasses," he quipped with a grin.

His laughter was met with mixed reactions. Will snorted in amusement, recognising the reference immediately. Jessica, connected remotely and watching over their progress, smiled faintly from the tablet's screen, appreciating the attempt to lighten the mood.

However, Sela looked around, puzzled. "What's that supposed to mean?" she asked, genuinely confused. Her expression only made Jim laugh harder.

"It's from an old movie—*The Blues Brothers*," he explained between chuckles. "They say something like that before a big mission of their own. Just trying to lighten things up."

Understanding dawned on Sela, and she rolled her eyes, though a small smile tugged at her lips. "You and your old movies," she teased, shaking her head as she started the engine and pulled away from the station.

The ride back to the mission was anything but smooth, filled with bumpy roads and sharp turns. However, the mood had lightened considerably. Sela's driving, confident and a bit reckless, brought occasional laughter amidst their anxiety, especially as she navigated the winding roads like a seasoned rally driver.

Chapter Twenty-Six

Returning to the abandoned Catholic mission, the crew felt a mix of exhilaration and the weight of responsibility. As they gathered in the old chapel, the light filtering through the stained glass cast colourful patterns on their faces and the ancient stone floor. Plans were quickly drawn up, and with everyone eager to tackle the next phase of their mission, Jessica raised a valid concern. "How long do you anticipate this taking? Remember, Lord Carnarvon spent over a decade on Tutankhamun's tomb."

Jim adjusted his glasses, his eyes never leaving the tablet. "True, but he was searching blindly. They only needed three days to uncover the tomb after finding the first step. That was in 1922, with primitive tools. We have precision equipment and exact coordinates, thanks to the data from the other dimension."

Sela, her gaze fixed on the distant horizon, interjected thoughtfully, "Our expedition is more than a physical endeavour. We're about to traverse the annals of time to reveal a narrative lost for over two thousand years."

The reality of their undertaking dawned on them as they approached their destination. It was a venture into the unknown, a site untouched by the hands of contemporary archaeologists. Under the shelter of the desert night, guided only by the celestial lights above, they drove their newly acquired vehicle to where the tomb awaited.

As they arrived, the crew felt a rush of exhilaration mixed with the weight of responsibility. They were on the cusp of a discovery that could rewrite history, standing at the threshold of a tomb that had eluded detection for eons.

"First things first," Jim announced as he swung open the van's back doors, revealing the portable cloaking device neatly stored next to a drone identical to the one currently monitoring the Catholic mission. The device was compact yet sophisticated—a testament to the advanced technology aboard the *Stardust II*. He carefully set it up on a makeshift stand they had prepared earlier.

"This drone will monitor the tomb area. We can control both drones from this panel," he added, pointing towards a sleek keyboard integrated into the control device.

"How long can the drone stay airborne?" Jessica inquired, peering at the setup with interest.

"Well, that's an intriguing aspect of this tech," Jim explained, his fingers deftly navigating the keyboard. "These drones are powered by the *Stardust II*'s nuclear reactor. However, the real genius behind this technology is Nikola Tesla. In the alternate timeline we visited, where the World Wars never occurred, Tesla never moved to the United States. Instead, he stayed in Europe and dove deeper into his research, becoming the eminent scientist everyone anticipated. He pushed the boundaries of energy transmission."

Jim paused, making sure his team grasped the significance. "Tesla perfected his theory of broadcast power there—wirelessly transmitting energy over vast distances. It revolutionised everything from transportation to how they powered devices like these drones. They can remain operational indefinitely as long as they are within range of the *Stardust II*, which, fortunately, they are."

As he resumed typing, Jim continued, "And it's not just about keeping the drones flying. This technology also powers our cloaking device, eliminating the need for an enormous external power supply." He tapped a few more keys, and the device hummed softly to life, its surface shimmering as it began to emit a faint, pulsating light.

"This setting here—" He pointed to a digital display that now lit up—"ensures air can flow through the cloak. Using Tesla's principles, we've created a series of micro-filters and environmental adjusters that keep the interior atmosphere stable without compromising our cover."

With a final tap, the cloak activated fully. The van, along with the surrounding area, blurred and then seemed to dissolve into the surroundings, perfectly camouflaged by the device's advanced light-bending technology. From the outside, it would be nearly impossible to detect their presence.

"We won't suffocate," Jim assured the team, noting a few looks of concern about the cloaking's effect. "The system is designed to balance oxygen levels and manage CO_2 emissions internally. Plus, it's equipped with sensors to alert us if the air quality drops below a certain threshold."

Satisfied with his work, Jim stepped back, admiring the invisible shield that now enveloped them. "We can move freely without worrying about being seen or, more importantly, running out of air."

"Good work, Jim," Will said, nodding in approval as he glanced around at the barren terrain. "Right, let's get on with it." He then turned to Sela with a puzzled look. "But looking at this desolate landscape, why would they bury Alexander here?"

Sela smiled, understanding the shift from technical marvels to historical mysteries was just as important. "Time for a history lesson," she began, her tone both apologetic and eager, aware of the lengthy tale she was about to unfold.

"Good idea," Jessica chimed in, settling down next to the equipment. "Tell us everything."

Sela cleared her throat before beginning. "Alexander the Great died in 323 BCE in Babylon, and after his death, his body became the subject of a significant power struggle among his generals. Initially, it was intended for his body to be taken back to Macedonia, his ancestral homeland. However, Ptolemy I Soter, one of Alexander's generals and the founder of the Ptolemaic Kingdom in Egypt, intercepted the funeral procession and brought Alexander's body to Egypt instead.

"Alexander was initially entombed in a provisional tomb in Memphis, Egypt's ancient capital. Later, his body was moved to Alexandria, a city he founded during his lifetime, which had become the cultural and political centre of the Hellenistic world. In Alexandria, Alexander was laid to rest in a mausoleum, which became known as the Soma or the 'Body' in Greek, becoming a site of great significance and reverence.

"We now know from the other world's history that after an earthquake in 300BCE, his followers, who still revered him as a god, moved his body to the Siwa Oasis. Alexander's original trip to the Siwa Oasis in 331 BCE is one of the most fabled episodes in his illustrious career of conquests and explorations. The oasis was renowned in the ancient world for its Oracle of Ammon. This oracle was considered by many in the ancient Mediterranean world to be as significant as the famous Oracle of Delphi in Greece.

"Following his conquest of Egypt and the founding of the city of Alexandria in the same year, Alexander embarked on the journey to Siwa Oasis to consult the oracle. The trip was arduous, fraught with the challenges posed by the harsh desert environment, including extreme temperatures and difficulty in navigating the vast, waterless expanse. Yet, Alexander was motivated by a desire that went beyond mere curiosity; he sought validation and divine endorsement of his kingship.

"Upon reaching the oasis," she continued, "Alexander is said to have consulted the Oracle of Ammon in private. While the exact details of what transpired are shrouded in mystery and steeped in legend, it is widely believed that the Oracle confirmed him as the son of Zeus-Ammon, effectively granting him divine status and legitimising his rule over Egypt. This acknowledgment not only solidified his position as a ruler in the eyes of his subjects but also aligned with his personal belief in his divine parentage and destiny to rule the world.

"The visit to this place stands as a testament to Alexander's deep-seated belief in his divine mission and his willingness to undertake significant risks to affirm his status as a ruler chosen by the gods, so it makes sense that his followers would bury him there."

"Great history lesson," Jim responded with enthusiasm. "Now, let's roll up our sleeves and get to work."

"We must proceed with proper care," Sela insisted, her voice carrying the weight of experience. "In Cambodia, it was us against the jungle, battling centuries of overgrowth and mud to reveal the temple beneath. Here, our adversary is the desert sand, concealing layers upon layers of history," she shared, drawing a parallel to underscore the gravity of their current endeavour. With that wisdom guiding them, the team meticulously laid out a grid across the excavation site, segmenting it into carefully planned sections. This systematic approach was not just about organising their work; it was a testament to their respect for the past, ensuring that the uncovering of each historical layer was approached with the reverence it deserved.

Jessica, equipped with her tablet and note-taking tools, meticulously recorded the grid setup and initial conditions of the site. Her notes and photographs would later prove invaluable in piecing together the chronology of the excavation.

The crew began the painstaking task of uncovering the tomb's entrance using brushes, trowels, and small picks. Jim's gadgets—ground-penetrating radar and 3D imaging tools—helped identify the outline of the structure beneath the sand, guiding their efforts.

As they removed layers of sand, the entrance slowly revealed itself. It was adorned with intricate carvings and faded inscriptions, hinting at the grandeur and historical significance of what lay within. The crew worked in shifts, ensuring that the excavation progressed steadily while preventing any potential damage due to fatigue or haste.

During the excavation, several small artifacts emerged from the sands. These included coins bearing Alexander's image, fragments of pottery, and small statuettes. Each find was carefully cleaned, catalogued, and stored by Jessica, who treated them with as much reverence as the tomb itself.

As they neared the entrance, the site's structural integrity became a concern. Sela, drawing again on her expertise from back in Cambodia, directed the team in reinforcing parts of the uncovered structure, ensuring that their activities didn't lead to any collapse or damage.

Finally, after six days of exhausting work, the entrance was fully exposed. Sealed for centuries, the door stood before them, an ancient barrier guarding its secrets. The crew paused in reverence before this historical threshold, aware they were about to enter a realm untouched since antiquity.

The actual opening of the tomb's entrance was a momentous event. Sela, with the help of Jim's equipment, carefully analysed the door mechanism, ensuring that their method of opening it would preserve its integrity.

As the door slowly gave way, the crew was hit by a wave of cool, stale air – a breath from the past, carrying with it the dust and echoes of a time long gone. They stood at the doorway, peering into the darkness, on the brink of making history.

The air inside the tomb was cool and heavy with history. Their lights pierced the darkness, revealing a passage lined with inscriptions and reliefs, narrating Alexander's journey from Macedonia to the heart of Egypt.

Will led the way, his torch casting shadows on the walls. "This is more than a tomb. It's a chronicle of a journey that changed the world," he whispered.

After thoroughly documenting the central chamber and its treasures, the crew moved deeper into the tomb. They encountered several smaller chambers off the main corridor, each revealing different aspects of Alexander's empire. One chamber was filled with military paraphernalia, including armour and weapons, while another contained a collection of diplomatic gifts from various regions of his empire, showcasing the vast reach and influence of his rule.

In one of the chambers, the crew found a library of sorts, containing scrolls and texts in ancient Greek, some of which were remarkably well-preserved. These texts appeared to be historical records, philosophical treatises, and perhaps even personal writings from Alexander himself. Jessica and Sela, overwhelmed by the historical significance, carefully catalogued each item, knowing that these texts could rewrite portions of ancient history.

The corridor led to a large central chamber. The air was warmer here, and the sense of stepping into a different world was notable. The chamber was circular, with a domed ceiling from which hung remnants of what might have been textiles or banners.

In the centre of the chamber stood a magnificent sarcophagus, intricately carved from stone and adorned with gold and precious gems. Surrounding the sarcophagus were various artifacts—ceremonial weapons, scrolls in ancient Greek, and items that might have been Alexander's personal belongings.

Jessica was in her element, documenting every detail. Her tablet clicked repeatedly, capturing the grandeur of the sarcophagus, the artistry of the artifacts, and the ancient inscriptions on the walls.

Jim, meanwhile, used his portable scanning equipment to create a 3D map of the chamber. This would allow them to study the tomb in detail later and preserve its layout for posterity.

The sarcophagus, positioned as the chamber's focal point, captivated everyone with its elaborate carvings—a blend of Greek and Egyptian motifs reflecting Alexander's vast empire. Sela, with an expert's eye, traced the delicate lines of each symbol, her admiration for the craftsmanship palpable.

As the team prepared to unveil the secrets held within, the air grew dense with anticipation. Gathering around the ancient relic, they positioned themselves carefully, each member placing their hands on the cool stone lid. Will nodded to Jim and Jessica, signalling the concerted effort to begin.

With a collective inhale, they pushed against the weight of history. The sarcophagus lid, unyielding at first, began to grind slowly open, the sound echoing ominously through the chamber. Stone scraped against stone, each movement punctuated by the crunch of debris falling from the crevices. It was as if the tomb itself was protesting the intrusion, exhaling dust that had lain undisturbed for millennia.

The gap widened enough to allow the ancient air to escape, merging with the modern atmosphere. They resumed their efforts, pushing the lid further, revealing the darkness within inch by painstaking inch.

To their profound astonishment, instead of the expected relics or inscriptions, they found Alexander the Great himself lying in eternal repose. His body was impeccably preserved, adorned in regal attire that time had scarcely touched, starkly contradicting their prior knowledge. Will, his voice a whisper laden with disbelief, captured the group's shock, said, "This isn't possible... Marie told us his tomb was empty in the other reality. The computer confirmed it—there was no body, just his belongings and texts."

This revelation deepened the mystery, casting a new light on their understanding of history and dimensional variations. As they absorbed this unexpected discovery, Jessica, her professional detachment forgotten, stepped closer to the sarcophagus. Then, her eyes caught sight of something even more extraordinary.

"What's that?" she murmured, her voice echoing softly in the sacred silence of the tomb, pointing to a singular object resting on Alexander's chest—a device, its design starkly modern against the ancient textiles.

Sela, usually composed, was visibly shaken by awe and excitement. "Oh my god, is that what I think it is?" The atmosphere thickened with the implications of their discovery.

Jim, with respect bordering on reverence, gently lifted the device from its resting place atop the ancient ruler. It was nearly identical to the one Ganesha had shown them, linked to dimensional travel.

"Do you think Alexander explored the Dimension Corridor?" Jessica's question lingered in the air, mingling with the dust motes dancing in the shafts of light.

"Or maybe he was not from our dimension," Will added, filled with wonder. The suggestion, once unthinkable, now seemed not only possible but probable in the face of such incontrovertible evidence.

The presence of Alexander's body when none was expected, alongside a device clearly linked to the mysteries of dimensional travel, reshaped their understanding of history. It suggested that the legends surrounding Alexander the Great might only scratch the surface of his true journey.

Jim handed the object to Will, who carefully secured it in his bag, now the guardian of a link to history's deepest mysteries. "We should keep exploring," Will murmured, his voice reverberating softly in the cryptic stillness of the tomb, urging them onward into the unknown.

As they ventured deeper into the ancient edifice, a curious draft, fresher than the stale air of the tomb, caught their attention. Following the source, they arrived at a section of the wall where the air seemed to seep through. Jim examined the surface closely, his fingers tracing over the stone until they caught on a subtle indentation. With a firm push, a low rumble filled the air, and a hidden door cracked open slightly but stubbornly refused to open fully.

Peering through the narrow gap, the beam of a flashlight revealed a passageway beyond, its walls unadorned, a stark contrast to the decorated chambers they had previously traversed. The corridor promised further mysteries, yet the immovable door blocked their path.

"We need more leverage," Jim concluded, his voice echoing off the unyielding stone. "Or some tools to help pry it open fully."

The group reluctantly retreated from the door to regroup and plan. As they ascended back to the main chamber, the urgency to explore what lay beyond that door grew. They discussed their next steps, deciding to return to the van to retrieve tools that could aid in their efforts to force the door open.

As they made their way back, the symbols that faintly glowed on the walls of the corridor seemed to beckon them, hinting at secrets just beyond reach. The weight of history pressed down upon them, a tangible presence urging them to return.

With renewed determination, Will spoke up as they gathered their tools, "Whatever is hidden beyond that door has waited centuries to be discovered. We're not turning back now."

Equipped with crowbars, ropes, and a hydraulic jack, the team returned to the site of the stubborn door. The cryptic stillness of the tomb now seemed charged with their anticipation. Each member took their position, tools in hand, ready to tackle the unyielding stone door.

Will positioned the jack at the base, giving a nod to Jim, who began pumping the lever. The door creaked ominously, the sound echoing through the silent corridors, a testament to the centuries it had remained sealed. Gradually, the gap widened, stone grinding against stone, until there was just enough space for them to squeeze through one at a time.

One by one, they entered the newly revealed passageway. The walls were blank, devoid of the embellishments that characterised the rest of the tomb. Here, the air was warmer, and the bare stone was intermittently marked with the same faintly glowing symbols they had noticed earlier. These symbols now seemed to guide them deeper into the heart of the earth, casting ghostly lights that flickered with each step they took.

Their path ended abruptly at a door, smaller yet echoing the imposing design of those they had encountered within the Dimension Corridor. Above the door loomed a statue of a giant snake similar to the five-headed snakes they had encountered before, its presence both majestic and foreboding. At the heart of the door, a recess awaited, perfectly shaped to accept the device they had been entrusted by Ganesha and its twin they had found with Alexander.

As Will fitted the device into the recess, a resonant click echoed through the cavernous chamber, bridging centuries in a single heartbeat. Dust motes danced in the air, disturbed after eons of stillness as the eyes of the snake head opened slowly, glowing with an ethereal, piercing light that filled the chamber. Silence enveloped them, thick and expectant. Then, as if from the very depths of the earth itself, a voice resonated within their minds, a whisper yet unmistakably clear:

"Destination?"

Epilogue

In the depths of an underground black ops facility, the corridor pulsated with the electronic hum of state-of-the-art security systems. Imprisoned within a cell forged from an unbreakable polymer, Prince Richard stood by a modest washbasin. The reflection staring back at him from a polished metal mirror was one of steely determination.

"Just one tooth," Richard murmured to himself. "That's all it takes."

His fingers deftly explored his mouth, searching for that one special tooth – recently designed as a last resort for situations precisely like this. After a brief moment, he located it.

He procured a string from his prison uniform and wrapped it around the tooth with practiced ease. Whispering a silent oath, he said, "Time for freedom."

With a swift, forceful tug, he wrenched the tooth free. The pain was immediate and sharp, but the prince's expression remained unfazed. Instead, a triumphant smile spread across his face as he held up the tooth, examining the tiny, essential piece of the Dimension Stone concealed within.

"It's heavier than I thought," he said to himself.

From outside the cell, a guard's inquisitive eyes peered through the observation window, catching the man in his peculiar act. "What are you up to, Prince?"

Feigning intense pain, Richard replied, "I've accidentally pulled out a tooth. It felt loose, and I didn't think it would come out. I might need a dentist."

Through the intercom, the guard's voice was tinged with concern. "Stay put. We're bringing in medical assistance."

Shortly after, a medic, flanked by heavily armed guards, approached. The door to Richard's cell creaked open, and weapons were unwaveringly trained on the prince. "Let's see the damage," the medic demanded.

Richard obligingly showed the gap where his tooth once resided. The medic frowned. "An X-ray is necessary to ensure no fragments remain."

With a glint of mischief in his eyes, Richard retorted, "I insist on an X-ray. After all, I wouldn't want complications later on, would I?"

The medic nodded. "Very well, Prince. We'll escort you to the medical wing in 15 minutes."

With a barely contained smirk, Richard reclined on his bunk. "Good," he murmured, the wheels of his plan now firmly in motion. "I can wait."

As he lay back, a chuckle escaped his lips. "And to think," he mused, "my father said my fascination with dentistry would never lead to anything."

THE END

The story continues in

The Dimension Rift

Book 2 of the Dimension Wars Saga

Unlock the past. Explore new worlds. Face the unknown.

After uncovering Alexander the Great's long-lost tomb, the crew of *Stardust II* starts to decipher the secrets of the Dimension Doors—ancient gateways that connect numerous worlds. Embarking on a thrilling expedition, they journey through multiple dimensions, each presenting new challenges and unforeseen dangers.

But their discoveries come with dire consequences. Mysterious rifts begin to appear, destabilising the very fabric of reality.

As chaos spreads across the various worlds, the crew must rally old friends and forge new alliances to confront unimaginable threats. Their quest will test the limits of their courage and challenge everything they thought they knew about the universe.

Brace yourself for an epic saga where the relics of ancient history ignite a cataclysmic interdimensional war.

Now available on Amazon

www.ingramcontent.com/pod-product-compliance
Lightning Source LLC
Chambersburg PA
CBHW061939170626
46813CB00006B/2462